Praise for Charlie Cochrane's
All Lessons Learned

"If you've never read Cochrane's books before, what are you waiting for? She is a wonderful author, such a talent. Smart humor, fully-fleshed characters, tight plots and great dialog all make for winners in my book."

~ *Reviews by Jessewave*

"This last book shows us that Cochrane is more than capable of stepping well outside the cozy mystery and dealing with the most disturbing of subjects, war, shellshock, duty and death—and of doing it every bit as well as writers such as Pat Barker or Susan Field. Bring hankies with you when you read it, but read it. It will touch you in many good ways."

~ *Speak Its Name*

"Charlie Cochrane knows how to add twists to the story that will leave you floored by the events. I truly didn't see some of them unfold until the signs were hard to ignore, thanks to her ability to build upon each with a mastery of a mason."

~ *Literary Nymphs*

"Charlie Cochrane has really outdone herself with this story. She has written a fantastic, truly heartwrenching tale about loss and survival."

~ *The Romance Studio*

Look for these titles by
Charlie Cochrane

Now Available:

Cambridge Fellows Mysteries
Lessons in Love
Lessons in Desire
Lessons in Discovery
Lessons in Power
Lessons in Temptation
Lessons in Seduction
Lessons in Trust
All Lessons Learned

All Lessons Learned

Charlie Cochrane

Samhain Publishing, Ltd.
11821 Mason Montgomery Road, 4B
Cincinnati, OH 45249
www.samhainpublishing.com

All Lessons Learned
Copyright © 2012 by Charlie Cochrane
Print ISBN: 978-1-60928-399-5
Digital ISBN: 978-1-60928-354-4

Editing by Tera Kleinfelter
Cover by Scott Carpenter

This book is a work of fiction. The names, characters, places, and incidents are products of the writer's imagination or have been used fictitiously and are not to be construed as real. Any resemblance to persons, living or dead, actual events, locale or organizations is entirely coincidental.

All Rights Are Reserved. No part of this book may be used or reproduced in any manner whatsoever without written permission, except in the case of brief quotations embodied in critical articles and reviews.

First Samhain Publishing, Ltd. electronic publication: February 2011
First Samhain Publishing, Ltd. print publication: January 2012

Dedication

This is for Ted and Jack. All the "Ted and Jacks".

Big thanks go to Cathy, who makes sure her biologist mother doesn't get the history bits wrong. And to Alex Broughton, who wrote Jonty's sonnets.

The twelfth day of the eleventh month, 1918

Orlando Coppersmith stood outside the prisoner of war camp and listened, almost unbelieving. No distant guns. No shouts or cries. No whinnying of frightened horses. Somewhere a bird was singing—two birds—and a distant dog barked. It felt unreal, as if this were a dream and the memory of the last few years the reality to which they would wake.

"I can't wait to get home." The tall lieutenant at Orlando's side sounded like one of his mathematics students at the end of term.

"Really?" A grizzled captain rubbed his moustache with the back of his hand. "Maybe home won't be what we thought it was going to be, every time we dreamed of it."

"Isn't that a bit much?" The lieutenant spoke as if the captain had committed treason. "Anyone would think you preferred it out here."

Orlando leaned against what had once been the post for a field gate, a single stump which had survived against all the odds, much as these three had. "It depends what you have to return to." He was amazed at how nervous his voice sounded— as nervous as any new recruit had been, those young lads full of the belief that they were going to win the war almost single handedly. That seemed a lifetime of disillusion ago. He took off his cap, pushing it back into some sort of respectable shape, although he wasn't sure anyone gave a toss about uniform at the moment. "The world's changed these last few years, like a pocket turned out of your trousers and everything you'd stored there shaken away."

The three of them turned towards the west, like a church congregation making ready to speak the creed yet facing the wrong way. *I believe in...*

Orlando wasn't sure what he believed in any more.

Chapter One

Cambridge, April 1919

Matthew Ainslie put the finishing touches to his black tie—immaculately fastened as always—and slid his dinner jacket on. *Tuxedo*, he could imagine the voice of his American business partner Rex Prefontaine saying, *It's a tux.* For Matthew it would always be a dinner jacket and he wouldn't be adopting Americanisms just yet, thank you. Especially with dinner at High Table of a Cambridge college in prospect.

He checked again in the mirror to ensure that he passed muster and was pleased with what he saw. *You've aged well, Matty.* He was now in his mid-forties but retained an almost entirely black mop of curls, smoothed down with brilliantine to a slick elegance. A twinkle in his eye belied middle age; there was life in the old dog yet. Leaving his room, descending the stairs, striding out through the doors of the University Arms Hotel. It was a routine he'd gone through often before. The first time he'd visited St. Bride's had been in 1907, the guest of two of the liveliest fellows ever to have graced the University. Well, to be exact, one extremely lively one and another who was being dragged from his shell like an intractable winkle being attacked by an extremely sharp pin.

He thought fondly of Jonty Stewart—the pin—and Orlando Coppersmith—the stubborn gastropod—as he made his way up

King's Parade. How many times over the years had he been their guest, or the guest of the Stewart family? Nothing had prepared him for those experiences; nothing could prepare anybody for close acquaintance with the chatelaine of the Stewart estate.

Happy days. He could say that of almost all the occasions he'd been with Jonty and Orlando, with the exception of the first few days of their acquaintance when Matthew had blotted his copy book. And the time spent clearing an ex-lover of murder. Happy and adventurous days, when the world was more innocent and the great grey and black cloud of war hadn't enveloped them. The war they said would end all conflicts.

Only time would tell if that were true, that never again would Europe march into battle, but plenty of lives had been invested in trying to test the supposition, young men laid to rest among the poppies and mud. A generation blighted as surely as if the horsemen of the apocalypse had passed through. Maybe they had.

Matthew had taken a commission but had been kept well behind the lines, employed in a tactical capacity at headquarters, owing to his excellent understanding of maps and topography. He'd seen very little danger or fighting, unlike his two special friends who'd been stationed in the thick of it. Both had gone over the top, and only one had returned. Some corner of a foreign field held Jonty Stewart's bones and Matthew only hoped it was already growing over with flowers, the burgeoning grass being grazed by sheep and the whole area surrounded by birdsong.

A tall, elegant figure paced the first court of St. Bride's College—Orlando Coppersmith doing what he always did when awaiting Matthew's arrival. The rest would follow the usual routine too; Matthew being led to Orlando's study for a dry sherry, the only personal guest who'd graced it in a long time. Groups of students still came for a tutorial, the new Master might attend on college business, but no one else was to be allowed there now, except those who still kept the memory of Jonty Stewart safe. St. Bride's may have kept a space permanently open for both Orlando and Jonty while they were away serving their country, but only one had returned to renew his employment.

It seemed like a whole generation had passed on, not just his lover. Even the college had lost its Master, Dr. Peters, as the result of a freak accident back in late 1916. He'd been to visit a sick student, one who'd appeared to be at death's door, had slipped on black ice in the court outside the sick bay and hit his head on a step. It was the same step he'd trodden on a hundred or more times over the years, as student, fellow or Master. The corner had taken a revenge for all the occasions he'd trampled it, striking him at a weak point in his majestic skull and cracking it open like an egg shell. Two days later Peters was dead, while the student he'd visited had undergone a remarkable recovery, regaining consciousness to find the college in mourning.

The Master's formidable sister lived on, and Mrs. Sheridan alone of all females, except for college servants, was allowed past the door of Orlando's study. She was even invited to tea up at his home, Forsythia Cottage, when she was in special favour or when Orlando could stand the loneliness no longer. He felt that way now; Matthew's visit was a timely one.

In previous times he and Orlando might have gone up to Jonty's study pre- or post-dinner, but those rooms now had a new occupant, a new name on the board at the foot of the staircase. A name that acted like a slap to Orlando's face every time he saw it. He'd taken to walking the long way around the court, to avoid it catching his eye. Only the chair in the Senior Common Room, the one to Orlando's right, was kept as a living memorial to the man who'd gone. Left unoccupied, and likely to be so until Orlando followed his friend to the undiscovered country from whose bourne no traveller returns. No one would have dared to sit in the place that had been Dr. Stewart's.

"Dr. Coppersmith!" The characteristic shout came through the air, the man himself turning with a startled grin to greet his guest.

"Ainslie!" Orlando offered his hand to be shaken. For all that he had rules and regulations to ensure that no one stepped on the memory of his lover, he *was* glad to see his guest. "You look ridiculously well."

"I feel it. You look..." The gap was a fraction too long as Matthew clearly sought for the right words.

Orlando put him out of his uneasiness. "I look tired, or so my mirror tells me every morning and I see no reason to doubt it." It told him he looked sad too. Bereft of that which had been the focal point of his life for a dozen or so years.

"It's been a hard few years for us all." Matthew lowered his voice. "Especially for you."

Orlando nodded, trying to swallow down the treacherous lump which had leapt into his throat. "Your letter was very kind. He'd have appreciated it."

"I meant every word." They stood for a moment, shared grief—shared understanding of what Jonty had meant to Orlando—forming both bond and barrier between them. Neither of them needed to speak yet of their loss—it was written large in their eyes, their voices.

"Come on, there's time for a sherry before Hall. Tell me about these maps they had you working on."

The sherry was small, of excellent quality and very welcome. If Jonty had been there they would have ended up gossiping like old women, all three of them, sharing the most ridiculous tittle-tattle—especially that which came from across the Atlantic courtesy of Rex. That's what it had been like every visit pre-war, but those times seemed a hundred years ago now, another age, another world. These were quieter times and the talk couldn't yet touch on what really mattered.

"I couldn't believe it when Dr. Peters died. I thought he was indestructible." Matthew gazed into the fire, face unreadable. "If it hadn't been for the obituary in *The Times* I'd have thought it a mistake."

"I wasn't here at the time. I was coming to the end of my spell with the ministry. We both were." Still working with his beloved codes and ciphers and Jonty acting as liaison between the men overseeing decryption and the people in the Admiralty interpreting the information. Jonty had often said trying to understand the gobbledegook on the paper was easier than understanding the idiots who were making use of it.

"I was never surprised when they offered you that job. Always had you pegged as being picked out for a Room 40 boy."

"That was Mr. Stewart's doing, him and his web of contacts. And after the reputation we earned solving the Woodville Ward case our names were always going to be top of the pile. Still—" Orlando deftly changed the subject— "I wish I'd been here to say a proper goodbye to *him*. Dr. Peters." He remembered how he'd grieved when he heard the news. It had been like a portent, a presager of all three of the deaths of people whom he loved. Only Miss Peters—Mrs. Sheridan, (would he ever get used to calling her that, even after ten years?)—remained of the old guard, as sprightly as a woman half her age and still with an indomitable zest for life.

"What's the new man like, or is that an indelicate question?" Matthew clearly knew when he was being sent along a new course and didn't seek to steer the conversation back.

"You should ask Mrs. Sheridan." Orlando smiled. "If St. Bride's had really been the forward-thinking institution it pretended it had become as the Edwardian era passed into the new Georgian, it might have made a bolder choice. "I can't deny that I felt Maurice Panesar would have been an eminently suitable candidate for new head of the college, although Jo...other people disagreed, not just on the grounds of his heritage."

"Ah. Clinging to traditional views of Empire?"

"Empire." Orlando sniffed, a sound which had acquired a wealth of interpretations down the years. "They didn't want to rock the boat, at least not publicly. Someone circulated the rumour that Maurice's eccentricity had prevented his nomination, but anyone with an ounce of sense knows it's his colour which counted against him."

"Does he mind? I'd have been inclined to up sticks and go." Matthew had always been intolerant of prejudice, the judging of a man on anything but his intrinsic worth.

"He's a pragmatist, he understands the way of things." A fond laugh bubbled up, memories of scrapes and adventures down the years, he, Jonty and Maurice Panesar with his mad schemes. "And he'll welcome not having extra demands on his time. He must have eleven odd different mechanical-physical projects to occupy him and his students. It's a wonder he's not blown the whole of Cambridge to kingdom come."

"So they settled for an Apostles' college man instead, rather than a homegrown one? I bet that went down like a lead weight."

"Best thing they could have done, if it couldn't be Dr.

Panesar." Orlando spoke with authority, as if explaining a theorem to one of the dunderheads. Dr. Sheridan himself, with his love for both mammal-like reptiles and his wife Ariadne, a late blossoming love affair. "He's been catapulted through the Cambridge ranks and he's taking to it like a duck to water."

"And would any man bet against his wife being a major force behind his success?" Matthew had met her several times and been impressed. "She'll be revelling in being chatelaine of St. Bride's lodge again, with all these young students to fret and fuss over. Still keeping up her feud with the college nurse?"

Orlando shook his head. "A truce had been set up in 1914, but battle lines were redrawn as soon as the Armistice was signed." Odd how he could joke about the war, be so flippant about the event which had destroyed his happiness. Maybe by keeping up the jokes he could keep his mind off the emptiness. "I'm glad to see her back. And her husband's quiet and competent like his predecessor, a steady hand to guide us through the next few years. It won't be easy." Many of the inhabitants of the Senior Common Room feared some sort of a backlash as a difficult decade passed into a bright new one. How could there not be, with the flower of a generation trampled in the mud? "There was a distinct sense of relief involved at his appointment."

"Relief? Because it wasn't Dr. Panesar?" Matthew's heckles were rising again.

"No, no." Orlando pulled himself up from his chair, stretching and straightening his jacket. He reached for the gowns which hung on the door, took the longer one and slipped it over his shoulders. "There'd been a constant rumour in the weeks after Dr. Peters's death that Dr. Owens was in the running." Owens. Ex St. Bride's man, traitor to his college and all-round swine.

Matthew's eyebrows couldn't have shot up further if he'd deliberately tried. "No wonder people were pleased. Even Kaiser Bill would have been preferable to him."

High Table was excellent as always and coffee back in the SCR was almost as good as the stuff Matthew had tasted in Boston with Rex. "I didn't think you could get coffee like this in England. Camp Coffee seems to be the standard fayre and that's hardly worth the effort of putting in the hot water."

"Might as well drink diluted shoe polish," Orlando agreed, with a smile. "The world's changing, Mr. Ainslie, and I'm not sure I like the way it's turning out." Outside the security of his study they were back to surnames, just as it had always been his custom with Jonty. They wouldn't change things, especially now the driving force for change had gone. "Goodnight, Dr. Panesar." Orlando waved a greeting as the man in question departed, grinning madly as he dragged a poor unsuspecting guest off to the labs to show him his latest heap of metal masquerading as a technological breakthrough.

"He was on good form tonight. Certainly lights this place up." Matthew tipped his head towards the other occupants of the SCR, only half a dozen remaining now and three of those apparently asleep.

"Aye, Panesar keeps this college alive at times. All the rest seem to have descended into semi-torpor." Just so must life in St. Bride's have been prior to 1905.

The comparative solitude gave the opportunity to speak more openly than usual in this room. "Why did you sign up for the army? You were doing such a worthwhile job already in Room 40."

"Worthwhile? I suppose it must have been. It was certainly

safe, if you're really asking why anyone should turn up a cushy number in search of a surefire way of getting himself killed." Orlando couldn't hide the bitterness in his voice.

"I'm not asking that. It just occurred to me that your brain was maybe more usefully employed doing things that only men of your intelligence could do."

"As opposed to being cannon-fodder like any other man with two arms and two legs and who cares how much brain?" Orlando frowned, passing his hand over his face. "I'm sorry, that was uncalled for. Your argument's a fair one and I had it put to me on more than one occasion. How best to serve my country and all that." He closed his eyes, rubbing his forehead as if soothing away the years. "Too many of them had died, Mr. Ainslie. My students. Did you know the Stewarts turned the Manor into a sort of hospital-cum-convalescent home? Opened the doors to a stream of soldiers—not just officers, other ranks as well—who needed some peace and quiet and care. My Italian sort-of-cousin took charge of the medical side and Mrs. Stewart was quartermistress."

"Ah, the Italian connection." Matthew grinned. "I saw the Baron Artigiano del Rame in *The Times* recently, taking over as chairman of Mrs. Stewart's charity for—what did she call them? Unfortunate Girls."

"That's the one." Orlando couldn't hide his pride in the family he'd never known he had, not until he was a grown man. "They've become quite pally, the houses of Coppersmith—Italian version—and Stewart. There'll be an intermarriage with one of the latest batch of offspring, no doubt. One of Paolo's girls and young George Broad is where the smart money lies." Shame the really great love match between the two families could never have been officially recognised.

"Do you see a lot of them?"

"Not as much as I should, I suppose. I like them, don't get me wrong, and they've welcomed me beyond all I could have hoped for, but it's not like it was with the Stewarts." Once experienced, nothing could compare to that family's love and generosity.

"The hospital at the Manor..." Matthew brought the conversation back before the silence became awkward.

"Of course. I went down and visited one of my ex-students there." Orlando shuddered in remembrance. "Physically it looked as if nothing had touched him and his mathematical capabilities were all still there, better than most of my dunderheads. But something had snapped inside him."

Matthew nodded. "Never to be put together, no matter what any of the king's horses or men could do?"

"It was that visit which made up my mind for me. How could I sit in a safe little room playing with letters and numbers when young men I'd had in my study, trying to understand vectors, were being sacrificed? Little more than boys, who'd not seen anything of life, some of them."

"So young." Matthew shook his head, staring into his coffee cup. So many fresh faced lads he'd seen, passing through on their way to the front, enthusiastic and emboldened. He'd seen a few of them passing back—broken shells, bare remnants of humanity.

"So many." The silence of the SCR was broken only by a murmuring from the other end of the room, one whispered conversation and the droning of gentle snores. "We had to go. We couldn't not go, in all conscience."

"At least you didn't have to lie about your ages."

"We'd have only had to if we'd been quick off the mark. By 1916, they weren't so choosy."

"I wish they'd been more scrupulous. Dear God, some of

the lads I saw looked no more than schoolboys." Such meticulous and painstaking checking there'd been at some of the recruitment centres, such desperation to get bodies into the system. *Seventeen, did you say? Go out and come back in and then answer the question again, there's a good man.* Babes in arms, literally.

"There were times I didn't think there'd be one of us left standing."

"I still can't believe I'll never see Mrs. Stewart again. Oh, I'm sorry." Matthew worried whether he'd overstepped the line, if the pain of bereavement was still too close for anything more than formal expressions of condolence. Orlando's face suggested too much hurt still lingered.

"No, please talk about them. So few people do talk of the dead." Orlando managed an unexpected smile. "A world without Mrs. Stewart's kind heart seems a much colder place. She meant a great deal to me."

"I saw the obituaries in the papers, although they didn't do either of their subjects justice." Matthew drew out his wallet. "I kept the clippings, just in case you wanted them and hadn't been able to get hold of the newspapers. I'll understand if you would find them too painful."

Orlando put out his hand, which was shaking slightly. "I'd appreciate them very much, thank you." He took the little pieces of paper without reading them, putting them in his notebook for later scrutiny. Perhaps.

"It was the flu, they said, that took both of them. Or complications following it." Matthew slipped his wallet back into his inside pocket, the action giving him time to choose his words. "The newspapers weren't very clear."

"Lavinia said they'd made a bit of a mess of things, one of the so-called correspondents getting all the details wrong. There was quite a stir, I believe, among the family." Orlando studied his hands. "I wish I'd been here to help, to clear up the mess. I felt so bloody helpless, miles from anyone."

The uncharacteristic swearing—especially in the SCR—the equally uncharacteristic baring of the Coppersmith soul, took Matthew aback. Still, it was understandable. *He* had Rex to tell his troubles to, if the occasion arose, but Orlando hadn't a confidante in all the world, except for him.

"The news shook me up pretty badly. God knows, I saw enough death out there, but that..." he ran his hands through his hair, "...that was almost the last straw. Something snapped inside me."

Matthew held his tongue. There'd been at least one occasion in the past when things had snapped, when things had overwhelmed Orlando to the extent he'd upped sticks and left, leaving Jonty and his family bereft and desperate to find their prodigal.

"I volunteered for a mission from which I didn't expect to return." Orlando raised his hand to prevent any interruption. "I was an idiot, I know. And apparently *they* didn't expect me to return, either. Missing, presumed dead, that's what everyone was told."

"Couldn't you get word back?"

"I did as soon as I could. Trouble is I was out for the count for a fortnight. I woke up in a German hospital and couldn't even remember who I was for the first few days. Lost a lot of blood, with it." Orlando passed his hand over his eyes, in remembrance of the previous time he'd lost his memory. Some mysterious part of his brain seemed inclined to shut down when it decided he needed protecting. "It seemed to take forever to get word back that I was still alive. It must have been the October of last year."

Matthew waited as Orlando gathered himself again. He knew what it was like to lose someone you loved to a violent death, but for loss to have piled upon loss... No wonder something "had snapped". Maybe it could never be repaired.

"I'm sorry, I sound like some snivelling child."

"That's fine, old man. God knows it doesn't bother me." Matthew reached into his pocket again. It was time for decisive action. "This may not be the opportune moment, but I've got something here—I'd be grateful if you could cast your eye, and your mind, over it." He produced an envelope, which he put in Orlando's shaking hand.

The effect was better than he'd hoped, his friend showing an instant, if slightly grave interest in the letter the envelope held. "It's from Collingwood." The genuine note of curiosity in Orlando's voice was a good sign. "Isn't he retired by now?"

"Do solicitors ever retire? He keeps his hand in, for favoured clients. He remembered the time you helped us and he wanted to turn to you again." Matthew was heartened by the glint in his friend's eye, one he hadn't seen there for a long time. "If you're still willing to take a commission."

"Willing?" Orlando turned the letter in his hands, as if he was trying to remember what a commission might entail, why it was being brought to him. He smiled, suddenly and unexpectedly. "Of course I will. It'll give me something to live for, Mr. Ainslie. I thought I would never have that feeling again."

Chapter Two

The evening had ended fairly solemnly, only a glimmer of hope among the sadness, but the next day dawned bright and an unfamiliar optimism hung in the air as Orlando pedalled down to the University Arms for lunch. Maybe it was a false hope, manufactured out of a simple letter, but it gave him a purpose again, even if a temporary one. How hard had it been for some of the old soldiers to adjust to their old lives back in Blighty? Nobody really *knew* unless they'd been out there, heard it, smelt it. Even men who had the luxury of a family to embrace them again had struggled.

St. Bride's was a safe haven, but it had lost its lustre and somehow the thought of spending day in day out educating dunderheads or indulging in abstruse research no longer held the appeal it once had. Nothing could ever be as fulfilling, now. Still, a mystery to solve would be nice, even if Orlando knew very little about the case at present; Collingwood's note hadn't been very forthcoming. He would need to telephone the man and arrange to meet his client, but not before seeing Matthew off. One task at a time.

The dining room at the hotel wasn't that busy, but the discussions over the meal kept to the general again. Matthew's publishing business, Orlando's interrupted research—now picked up once more—and the prospects for the rest of the

All Lessons Learned

rugby season. Only over coffee, in an almost deserted lounge, could they relax and speak more freely.

"Do you have any idea what this commission is that Collingwood wants me to take?" Orlando sipped his coffee, although the standard wasn't what he expected from a top-notch hotel. His housekeeper had spoiled him in that regard, Mrs. Ward still producing a stunning pot of coffee and dazzling cakes, even if she now had to have her eldest granddaughter help her with some of the heavier tasks.

"No idea. All I know is that it's very delicate and concerns something which happened *out there*." Matthew didn't need to be any more specific. "That's why he contacted me first. To see if it would be insensitive to get in touch with you. He'd read about Jo...about *him* in the newspapers."

"Jonty? That's his name, Mr. Ainslie, but you've not used it even the once since we met yesterday. Jonty Stewart of the East Surreys. He may be dead, but the memory of him isn't. Please do us both the honour of keeping that alive, at least." Orlando had been surprised at the level of anger in his own voice. Neither of them could keep avoiding clearing the air or Jonty's death would always hang like a curtain between them, casting an even greater shadow than it already did, darker and more menacing for being unspoken.

"I never intended..." Matthew stopped, clearly unsure of what to say next.

Orlando started to speak, then bit his tongue. The clock on the mantelpiece rang the hour, two bold strokes like a warning bell or the death knell for some poor infant. A reminder of time passing, of mortality. Then, from the window, came the voice of a child at play, urging its father to run faster so their kite might ascend more quickly. Life going on, even if it seemed to pass Orlando by. And in his brain, Jonty's voice was saying, *give him a chance, old man, don't be so harsh.*

Auditory hallucinations the doctor had called it when Orlando's father had heard voices. The advice was simple; *Ignore it and it's sure to pass.* When Orlando had first returned to England and asked why he could hear his loved ones so clearly in his mind, the explanation had been much the same. *A trick of the psyche brought on by a combination of grief and some lingering shell shock. Ignore them.* The strategy had always worked in the past; now he only listened if the voices spoke good sense.

"No, Matthew—I should be the one making the apology." Orlando used the Christian name deliberately, indicating the depth of his contrition. "What would Jonty say to see us like this? He'd be giving me a tongue lashing for discourtesy."

"And he'd be calling me an idiot for pussy footing about so much." Matthew smiled, looking more at ease now. "Tell me, if you will, what happened to him?" He gently edged his words into the conversation, clearly aware of how much the answer was going to cost his host.

"I wish I knew." Orlando passed one hand over his eyes, the other gripping his cup unsteadily.

"Easy there." Matthew took the coffee cup away before its contents were let loose on the floor. "Let's leave this subject for today shall we? Tell me the details on another occasion, just leave it as *some corner of a foreign field* for now."

Some corner of a foreign field. Yes, but which one? On the way home from the prisoner of war camp, Orlando had passed near the site in France where Jonty died. He'd diverted, made the pilgrimage—at the cost of much personal anguish— endeavouring to locate the particular foxhole but failing. He couldn't face going back for another attempt. He feared that the area would quickly become a Mecca for visitors; some genuine like him, looking for a loved one's last resting place, others who were just there to gawp and picnic on the ground where precious blood had been spilled. There'd been one or two people "sightseeing" there already. There was a grave here in England, of course, holding Jonty's bodily remains, but that wasn't the same.

"No, I have to tell you now. I must." Orlando leaned forward, hands steepled together as if he were about to expound on a tricky bit of calculus. "It happened in Cambrai, you know. Maybe I shouldn't make such a fuss about it. Jonty was just one of thousands, tens of thousands, wasn't he? I never ever worked out how many got lost in the mud of the Somme."

"Maybe only God kept a true count of all that went on."

"And our Lavinia." Orlando smiled at the efficiency with which Jonty's sister had kept the lines of communication open in all directions—maybe they should have put her in charge of communication out in France. She'd have been a damned sight more competent at it than the actual incumbents.

"Does she blame you? For dragging Jonty out to France?"

"It was our joint decision, you know that. Still, I wish to God I'd chosen another course." Orlando sighed then carried on, wearily. "He was burned. Jonty was burned. A freak accident with a leaking can of petrol and someone's discarded cigarette butt, I wouldn't be surprised, although the official word was that either the puddle of fuel or the can itself had been hit during an intense burst of shelling." He snorted his opinion of that story. "Whatever it was, it made a hell of a conflagration. He lit the night."

"Steady, old man." Matthew leaned over to take hold of his friend's trembling arm.

"I'm sorry. Stupid of me. I just feel so angry about him not even getting a hero's death. He'd gone out to check why there was a reek of petrol coming from one of the foxholes, found a pair of blokes sitting there and one of them smoking like an idiot. It's a wonder the three of them didn't go up like a Roman candle."

"Did the other two survive?" Matthew took a cigarette of his own from the elegant case Rex had given him when they'd first become lovers. He offered Orlando one, purely for form's sake, and seemed amazed when it was accepted. "I didn't think you indulged."

"I never used to. Had the odd one out in the prisoner of war camp and then carried on when things...when things got a bit much." He accepted a light awkwardly, inhaling only a little of the smoke. The small amount of nicotine was enough to calm him and, more importantly, he had something to do with his trembling, treacherous hands. "One of the men got back, or so the story said. I had it fourth hand and pretty muddled up. Jonty had sent him back to get some sort of help and while he was gone the whole lot went up. The third man..." Orlando shrugged. "I did hear that someone saw him running away while Jonty was left in the foxhole, but whether that was a case of Chinese whispers, who knows? It was all a bloody mess out there."

"They could identify him?"

Orlando nodded, then took another drag on his cigarette. "He had his disc with him. With what remained of him. They never told Lavinia the exact details but I'm not sure there was a lot of him left to bury. His platoon couldn't even get out to his body until two days later, what with coming under bombardment and being picked off by snipers if they even stuck a finger out." Thin tendrils of smoke seeped out with his breath. "What they did find was badly burned, all except his jacket which he'd taken off—I suppose he didn't want it getting petrol all over it. They found that folded up neatly a few yards away and for some reason the flames had barely touched it. The silly idiot never folded up anything neatly in his life and that was the day he had to decide to do it."

"He was buried out there?"

"Sort of. They did give him a decent enough burial, or so Lavinia says, but I insisted he be brought back to England." Orlando stubbed the cigarette out, angrily. "I wanted him here, where I could keep an eye on him." The absurdity made them both laugh, even if it had a strange ring of truth. It was highly likely that Jonty was at that moment somewhere in the angelic realms causing chaos and Gabriel himself would have been grateful for someone keeping him in line. "He's buried in Sussex, in the churchyard by the Manor, near his parents." Orlando produced a photograph, slightly dog-eared from having been brought in and out of his pocket for consideration so often. A depiction of a neat, white marble headstone.

Jonathan "Jonty" Stewart

12th May 1876

8th October 1918

Deeply beloved

Very much missed

Greater love hath no man than he lay down his life for his friends

"It's a handsome stone." Matthew read the inscription again. "And an apt tribute. You chose it?"

"He always said he wanted a different Bible verse on his tombstone, the toad. Something from the Song of Songs, but I couldn't approve of it. This one is heart breaking enough. He'd have laid down his life for me without a thought. And I mine for him." Orlando carefully returned the picture to its rightful place near his heart and produced another. "I'm sorry I couldn't have you staying up at Forsythia Cottage. I have the decorators in, sprucing the old place up. Wanted you to see this."

Matthew took this second photograph with a surprised look. "Is this your garden?"

"Yes, a special part of it." While Jonty's name was on a memorial—more than one, at home and abroad—his special place of remembrance was in the sheltered garden of the house they had shared together. A small corner had been planted up with his beloved roses and a variety of plants that would make a glorious show for spring and autumn, Jonty's favourite seasons. Some sea shells, brought home from various holidays, clustered in a corner at the very edge of the plot, to bring back unmistakable memories of the first time they'd made love properly, in a hotel in the Channel Islands. "It'll be splendid once it's all matured."

"Have you done this all yourself since you've been back?" If Matthew had noticed the unmistakable ormer shells he was too polite to bring up the subject of Jersey.

"No, I employ a gardener for most of it, otherwise I'd get mud all over my students' work. Not that a bit of mud might not improve some of the answers they produce." Orlando was being more than frugal with the truth. Employ a gardener he did, a young lad who'd been badly scarred at the Somme and who seemed to find other employers more likely to be put off by his disagreeable appearance than impressed by his undoubted talents in the garden.

The memorial garden, Jonty's particular section, never saw another person's touch, only Orlando's. Not a weed appeared but it was hoed out—stones were picked up and discarded, slugs discouraged, cats positively shooed away. The blooms would be tended with infinite care as if they represented the body of his lover; white lilies for the tender skin, red roses for the blood that had been spilled in his country's name. Jonty would have been so very proud.

Matthew produced a broad smile, suddenly looking more like the young man they'd met back in St. Aubin. "He'd have liked this, your Jonty. Life affirming nature rather than a cold piece of marble."

"That's what I thought." Orlando looked carefully at the picture before he put it away to join the other one. There'd been times these last few weeks that he wasn't sure he'd see that garden to maturity. Jonty had gone where he couldn't and what was there left for him to do here? "He left me everything you know, in his will. I had no idea, until his solicitor told me, just how much it might represent, once it comes to it. The thing's not gone through probate yet. The Stewarts left me a legacy too—books from the library, a set of crystal glasses I'd always admired, a portrait of Jonty as a boy." Orlando suddenly stopped, aware both that he was rambling on and that Matthew looked uncomfortable. No, not uncomfortable—surprised at being made privy to such private matters. They'd never spoken so intimately before, not even with Jonty around to egg them on. "I'm sorry, I shouldn't burden you with my affairs."

"There's no need to apologise. Aren't we old friends enough to be able to listen to one another?" Still, neither man was happy with wearing his heart on his sleeve except with the one he loved most.

Orlando nodded, genuinely grateful for the consideration. He had no one else to talk to now and there'd been the need of it so sorely these last months. Funny how he'd been able to hold all his feelings in the first twenty-seven years of his life, dealing with them by denial and damming them up. Once Jonty had unleashed the waters, shown him that sharing emotions wasn't shameful or unmanly, there was to be no returning to the former state of affairs. He needed to let the hurt and confusion pour out and Matthew, poor soul, was going to have to mop it up.

"Did he make any strange bequests?" Matthew was speaking again, and Orlando had to focus his mind on the present. The lonely, achingly empty present. "I could imagine him willing huge sums on homes for crippled sailors or endowing scholarships for people with red hair."

Orlando smiled. "I was the major beneficiary named, but he did have his jokes, even at the end. He kept threatening to leave some money to a home for bewildered bookmakers, as he said he'd supported so many during his lifetime they'd miss him when he'd gone."

"I remember him telling Rex that and the idiot almost falling for it."

"He'd told his solicitor too and the man spent ten minutes preaching against it, convinced he'd persuaded him otherwise."

"So where did he leave the money?" Matthew waved away one of the waiters who'd come bearing more coffee.

"He'd made a generous contribution to Great Ormond Street hospital." Orlando summoned the waiter back and ordered brandies for them both. "But that's not the funny part. Do you know what the little bugger did? He left a specific bequest for a one-year zoology scholarship, looking into the mating habits of honey buzzards."

"Never!"

"It's the honest truth. He made such game of me about honey buzzards over the years. Every time he saw one—and there were a pair who seemed to appear over our cottage every summer—he would point them out. Say what handsome specimens they were." Orlando grinned and, to his relief, Matthew grinned too. It had been so very long ago, when Orlando had been immature and silly and hadn't read some obvious signs of attraction until too late. They were more mature now and the pain had receded far enough to let the laughter sweep in. The waiter returning with the brandies must have thought they'd been ordered for medicinal purposes, seeing the two men wheezing and gasping for breath like a pair of schoolboys.

"Only he could have got away with that. I hope you'll allow me to have a copy on the finished paper when it gets written?" Matthew wiped his eyes.

"Of course." Strange how they could still find things to laugh about, how old hurts which had once rankled so much had been put into their proper perspective. "When the money's all sorted I'm going to endow a chair in medieval literature—the Stewart Professorship. The holder will have to give an annual talk on Shakespeare's sonnets and present the Mathematics professor with a crate of claret every Christmas. I thought Jonty would have appreciated that."

"He'll be up there smiling down on us now—glass of champagne or nectar or whatever it is in his hand and a look on his face that would make the most respectable of angels seem like naughty schoolboys." They sat in companionable silence, all the awkwardness between them gone. The friendship had vaulted a great hurdle and survived.

"There are times I can almost believe it, Matthew." Orlando had never had anything like the deep faith Jonty had possessed, a closeness to God and delight in his creator that had permeated the man's very being. Orlando had asked him on particular occasions when Jonty had been in high-spirits just what had made him so happy and the answer had simply been *It's a lovely day and I'm thanking God for it. And for sending you to me.*

"He was always a good friend, to me and to Rex." The

brandy was working its magic and turning laughter into sentiment. Matthew was becoming maudlin and Orlando wasn't far behind.

"Are you off to America soon?" Time for Orlando to turn the subject to business, to things which couldn't dig a knife into his heart.

"I am indeed, tickets booked and new suit being stitched as we speak. I'll be there for much of the summer." Matthew seemed to consider his next words carefully, wary about opening the old wound. When he'd asked on his pre-war visits about future plans, Jonty had always blethered on enthusiastically about all the things that he and Orlando wanted to do. Many of the dreams had been realised, but not all. "Will you stay in Cambridge for your holidays?"

"No, not this year. I must go and see Lavinia and Ralph in London again. It's been far too long since we last met. I'll take the children to the zoo and the grown-ups out to the theatre and for supper—quite like old times." Orlando shrugged. "And Jonty always wanted to visit the Isle of Wight again—he'd been there, as a child, to meet the royal family you know."

"I had no idea of that. I mean, I knew Mr. Stewart was well in with the old king but not the rest of it."

"You wouldn't have known. Never one for boasting, our Jonty. I'll take myself there for a few days and visit some of the places he'd planned for us to walk. It seems right." Orlando's gaze shifted to the window, looking unseeing at the trees and skies, focussed only on an image of Jonty on a beach, running on the sand and into the waves. "France too. We never made it further along the coast than Deauville and he kept telling Miss...Mrs. Sheridan that one day he'd bring her home a case full of fossils. More than there are in the SCR."

Matthew smiled and rose, offering his hand for his host to

shake. "I hate to break the party up but I've a train to catch, so I'll have to get my bag and go. You'll come and have dinner in London when I get back from across the Atlantic?"

Orlando nodded, letting his guest depart with little more in the way of conversation. They'd mined that seam pretty well dry for the day. The cycle ride back to St. Bride's was quick and mercifully free of dunderheads dawdling in the road. He left his bicycle by the porters' lodge and went up to his rooms to finish marking some papers. Work before play; once he was done with these, he could tackle the more agreeable task of contacting Collingwood and finding out about this intriguing commission.

They'd not played at detectives since early 1914, when they'd got involved with a mysterious death at a nursing home just outside Bedford and uncovered a case of jealousy, betrayal and downright sadism at work. The matron had ended up being hanged and plenty of people had murmured the opinion that it had been a light sentence. The solution had been found by a mixture of Orlando's severe logic and Jonty's intuition, a perfect combination of qualities.

How would logic fare on its own? And was there going to be any real pleasure in solving a problem if there was no one to share the solution with you?

Chapter Three

Collingwood had always been a man of surprising action—Orlando had never quite got over his shock at finding out he kept a girlfriend who obliged him every Sunday afternoon—and his efforts were put into work as well as pleasure. Just three days after Matthew had departed, the porters told Orlando he had a visitor waiting at the lodge.

"Dr. Coppersmith?" The lady appeared to be slightly younger than Helena Stewart would have been had she survived. And she was certainly a lady—there was something about the cut of her purple tweed coat and skirt, the shape of her cheekbones and the air which hung about her which confirmed it. She seemed remarkably at ease within the male-dominated, cloistered environment of St. Bride's, even if her eyes looked troubled.

"At your service." Orlando bowed over the lady's hand. "Mrs. McNeil? And is Mr. Collingwood here too?" It was clear that he wasn't, unless he'd made himself small enough to have hidden under one of the porters' discarded bowler hats.

"No. It's not, I hasten to add, that I don't trust Mr. Collingwood, but this is something I must do entirely on my own. Is there somewhere I can consult you confidentially?" Mrs. McNeil's gloves were of the best kid leather—she'd taken them off to shake hands and now, instead of replacing them, she twisted the fine material in her grip.

Orlando swallowed hard. There was nowhere he could take her that would guarantee they'd be alone and not overheard. One of the local hotels wouldn't be suitable; they were always awash with people coming in and out, especially on a market day. Nor was there anywhere in St. Bride's. He even thought of the chapel but remembered it was choir practice soon. It would have to be his study, that sacred piece of ground where no intruding foot was allowed to tread. This commission had come as a lifeline, bringing a renewed purpose to Orlando's existence. Was it worth breaking a cardinal rule for?

He was rescued from making the decision by a tap on the shoulder from Mrs. Sheridan, who'd probably been hovering around trying not to intrude on the conversation while hearing every word. As usual, she'd seen the need to effect a rescue and had steamed in all guns blazing.

"Dr. Coppersmith." She turned to Mrs. McNeil, waiting for an introduction. After it had been made, she smiled brightly and held out as elegantly gloved a hand as the one she offered to shake. "Mrs. McNeil. I so rarely get the chance to welcome a sister in arms into this monstrous brotherhood of mathematicians and biologists. You'll forgive me if I can't stay but I'm en route to St. Thomas's, to see an unusual planarian worm, possibly a newly discovered species." She beamed again. "Such an unexpected pleasure it will be, although it means I can't offer you our hospitality. Dr. Coppersmith, would you be so kind as to show this lady to the lodge and ask Mr. Wilding to provide you with tea and a cake or two? In lieu of me being able to oblige?" She nodded, turned on her heels and departed before anyone dared to argue with the invitation.

"The lodge it is, then." Orlando ushered his guest towards the court. "That was a fortuitous meeting. There's no other place in the college so suited to important matters."

Mrs. McNeil nodded as they walked over the grass—fellows' privilege being made the most of. "I'm pleased to hear you refer to it as important. Mr. Collingwood said that you would be the proper person to consult and I rely on his judgment. I'm afraid..." she hesitated slightly, almost stumbling as they reached the gravel path again, "...that not everyone I know regards this matter in the same light as I do."

They reached the lodge in silence, Orlando bringing his guest in and making the necessary arrangements with Wilding, the butler. The chief manservant of the Master's lodge—a hallowed role passed down from bachelor uncle to nephew through countless generations—didn't even raise an eyebrow at the arrival of unexpected visitors, even in the absence of the normal occupants of the magnificent sitting room. Clearly he was used to Mrs. Sheridan's eccentricities, although that wasn't necessarily the only reason for the warm reception they'd received. Every member of the college staff was being particularly kind to Orlando at present.

Mrs. McNeil seemed pleased with the choice of venue, settling into one of the elegant chairs next to a little table where the refreshments would be close to hand. "Shall I begin, or wait for the tea and cakes?"

Tea and cakes. Time was when Orlando and Jonty had spent many happy hours over the teapot, at breakfast or in the afternoon or once in the middle of the night when a storm had brought down a tree outside their cottage and they'd been drafted in to help clear the road. He looked at Mrs. McNeil and realised he'd been lost longer in contemplation than he'd thought. "I'm sorry. I was woolgathering." Orlando swallowed hard again at the inadvertent use of one of Jonty's favourite phrases. "Begin whenever you wish. Wilding is remarkably discreet. You'd be surprised how many secrets will have been aired down the years in this lodge."

"I might well be, but I would prefer to wait until there is no risk of us being interrupted or overheard."

The pot of tea, when it came, didn't seem to have the immediate magic effect it had always had in Jonty's hands. Far from easing tension or loosening tongues it had seemed to inhibit Mrs. McNeil; or maybe it was the magnificence of the lodge overwhelming her. Orlando saw her often looking out into the court, upwards towards the windows of the inward facing rooms. Ah, that must be it. There had been some reference in Collingwood's letter to the fact that a young McNeil had been at Cambridge and then served abroad. It didn't take a long trail of logic to connect the view towards what might have been an undergraduate's room with a grieving mother. He returned to small talk again, letting his guest come round to things in her own good time. That's what Jonty would have done, if with more winsome aplomb.

"It's about my son, Daniel." Mrs. McNeil changed the subject quite abruptly, as startling as a rapid fire of bullets on a previously quiet day. "He was here, you know, taking History down at St. Francis's. He had a room overlooking the magnolia trees there—I'm sure you've seen them. Then he went to University College."

More echoes of Jonty. Like a ghost was walking over his grave—both their graves. Orlando nodded, unable to trust himself to speak.

"He was conducting research into the Napoleonic wars. We tried to dissuade him from signing up until he'd finished his studies but he wasn't to be argued with. I'd hoped the war would have been finished by then, if he'd waited, although it wouldn't have been. Even if he'd taken my advice it would have been no use." The end of the hail of words was as abrupt as the beginning had been.

"When did he enlist?"

"Nineteen fifteen. He waited until he'd done a year at University College and then..." Mrs. McNeil produced a little lace handkerchief, although she didn't hold it to her eyes, simply twisting it in her hands, instead. "He was out in Belgium, like so many of you were." She looked up. "Sorry, you must think me rude. Mr. Collingwood told me that you'd seen action. He'd had it from a Mr. MacBride who'd handled some of your family business, I believe?"

Orlando nodded. MacBride had been his grandmother's solicitor, what seemed another lifetime ago but what was really only just over ten years. Just over ten years, similar to the amount of time Jonty and he had been together, in England.

"These solicitors seem to gossip amongst themselves worse than a bunch of old women at the parish pump." Mrs. McNeil almost managed a smile. "That's one of the reasons I wanted to consult you, because I was sure you'd understand. So many old buffers have no idea what it must have been like for you lads. I've heard such nonsense spouted..." She stopped abruptly again. "I'm sorry. I don't need to tell you any of this. You must know full well for yourself. Daniel was with the Lancashire Fusiliers and he was a good soldier. He'd have made a wonderful career for himself, perhaps, under less...unforgiving conditions." She took a deep breath, clearly composing herself. "He went missing, last September. And I want to know what happened to him."

St. Bride's bells struck the hour, quickly echoed by the chimes from *the college next door*, still the old enemy, their hostility not even laid aside during or after a time of national conflict. Orlando felt like it had taken an hour for him to be able to answer his guest. "Do you believe he was killed?"

Mrs. McNeil shook her head. "No. That's what the official

story was and such a thing would of course be entirely possible. A lot of young men went over the top that same day and not everyone who died had their body recovered. But, you see, I know who wrote the official story." She twisted her handkerchief again. "My cousin was Daniel's commanding officer—I'm not sure if that's a stroke of irony or some cruel twist of fate. He won't discuss what happened with me, even though I've almost pleaded on bended knees."

Orlando could believe it; the devotion in this lady's eyes at the mention of her son, her obvious pain at the loss of him and the lack of certainty at what had gone on were testimony to her doubts. The not knowing was the worst thing of all. Looking at Mrs. McNeil was like looking at himself in a glass and Orlando would have literally gone on his knees and begged if it had meant finding out what Jonty's last few hours had been like or locating the exact spot where he'd died.

He tried to concentrate on the matter in hand. "You believe your cousin covered over the true story. So that you wouldn't be hurt?"

"Andrew is a very clever man. When Daniel was first showing signs of illness, he tried to get him out of the front line—I know that because of what they both wrote in their letters. Little hints and clues which I could put together, two and two which definitely made five." Mrs. McNeil smiled, wanly. "Andrew would have moved heaven and earth to make things better, but he couldn't move my son, however much he tried. For all that Daniel hated it, he felt duty bound to stay at the front."

Duty. Orlando had heard that word too often in the years of hell, usually out of the mouths of those who'd never be more affected by the great guns than hearing them away in the distance on a quiet Surrey morning. An exaggerated sense of duty was what had sent him away from the safety of his codes and cryptograms, out of the little niche of secure usefulness he'd carved, out to where he and Jonty could make a practical difference to the war effort. What an idiot he'd been.

"Dr. Coppersmith, are you quite well?" Mrs. McNeil was speaking again, had clearly been speaking these last few minutes while Orlando was lost in reverie.

He thought about bluffing, making some story up as he'd done when they were interviewing suspects—back in the days when he and Jonty had played this game together. His heart no longer lay in such silliness. "I'm sorry. I was miles away, back across the channel, thinking about some of my comrades. The ones who never returned. Oh..." He rummaged in his pocket for a clean handkerchief. "I'm sorry, that was thoughtless."

"No. You were right to think of them. We must never forget." Mrs. McNeil took the handkerchief with gratitude, her own being so twisted and tattered as to be almost useless. "If I had a body to put in the ground, or at least some indication, some real indication, that Daniel died at the front and someone could show me the very spot, if I could eliminate all my doubts then at least I could begin to mourn properly. I'd know for sure, you see."

Orlando nodded. He saw, entirely, much more than the words could say. "Otherwise there's always the possibility, isn't there, the chance that he'll just appear..." No chance of that for Jonty, though, no matter how much Orlando hoped or deluded himself. He at least had the benefit of a body, no matter how battered, to put in the ground.

"That's it, entirely." Mrs. McNeil's eyes were abnormally bright, almost fey. "I keep thinking I see him, out of the corner of my eye. Or there'll be a man wearing the St. Francis's rowing blazer like the one he had, and I think 'how did he get his hands on that, from out of the wardrobe?'"

Or someone walks along in front of you with a familiar sort of gait. Orlando had experienced those sorts of moments himself, glimpses of a shock of blond hair or a particular type of spectacles. Like a slap in the face, or a stab to the heart, every one of them.

"I'm always watching, always praying or hoping." Mrs. McNeil continued, seemingly oblivious to whether or not her host was giving her his full attention. "I can't spend the rest of my life doing that, Dr. Coppersmith. I have to know, once and for all, and I believe you're the only man who can help me to find out."

Orlando thought carefully before he spoke again. "You will forgive me, I hope, if this question offends you, but we have to be candid with one another. What would you do if we discover that Daniel deserted?" He carefully avoided the words *that Daniel turned conchie.* Jonty had hated the term; God knew he understood mental anguish better than the average man, they both did.

Once they'd been catching a train together, not long before they'd first left Room 40 on their eventual way to France. They'd been sharing what might have been—what turned out to be in fact—a last weekend with the Stewarts. Both of them in uniform, uniforms which had seen no more action than a series of exercises at their training camp.

There'd been an ex-porter from St. Bride's on the station platform, on leave from the front, en route to see his young lady—and in his best suit. Some stupid chit of a woman, noting his age and his apparent lack of khaki, had given him a white feather. The man had held the thing dumbstruck while she smiled cruelly. Jonty had taken her arm, smiling himself, guiding her to a quiet corner where he could lay into her, with words as harsh as Orlando had ever heard him use on a woman. Did she not know that this man had lain awake in the trenches listening for the next wave of shells to come over while she lay in her bed—safe, warm and dry—with nothing more to worry about than whether her maid had laid out the correct costume for the morning? Could she find no better use for her time than annoying soldiers on leave? What purpose, what twisted god, did she serve? Orlando had almost had to drag him away, frightened he'd resort to violence. Decent, sensible Jonty, who wouldn't have hurt a fly.

Orlando returned to the present with a jolt, as Mrs. McNeil answered his question at last. "I would still love Daniel, even if he had disgraced himself and his family." She turned his handkerchief in her hands, bending it like a rope. "I will always love him. He is my son."

Nothing more needed to be said, except for the exchange of papers—as many details of Daniel McNeil's life as his mother could provide and which seemed relevant to the case—and some clarification of certain points. Orlando assured his guest that he would take the commission, not least because Jonty's voice was ringing in his ear now, charging him with taking up this lady's cause as clear as if he were in the room. Not that he shared this information with her, making do with saying, "It would be my pleasure to serve a fellow soldier's family."

He escorted her to the lodge and then returned to his set of rooms, sure it was the right thing to do, no matter what the outcome. He poured himself a small sherry and sat before the fire, in thought. In the past, he'd have fallen straight onto the papers, poring through them, making notes and formulating a plan of action. This time he wanted to gather himself before attempting it. He might even leave it until he'd returned home, plotting his campaign over a gloriously tasty but solitary meal at Forsythia Cottage.

He had to admit he was uncertain about the case, maybe even frightened. Frightened of failure, of letting this lady down, of losing his reputation as someone who could be relied on to find a solution where others had failed. Of failing Jonty. God knew he'd faced worse things over the past few years, but then all that had been at risk was his life—that seemed small beer compared to Jonty's memory. He heard the voice in his head once more. "This is the right thing to do." Yes, the right thing at the right time, and maybe part of the completion of this chapter of his life.

Orlando took a final tour around the garden before settling down in his study with the McNeil case. Spring was in full bloom, the late-flowering cherry a mass of sumptuous pink blossoms and the tulips still a riot of colour. The daffodils had gone, no longer standing proudly like trumpeters waiting to give the last post, but one or two late narcissi could still be found if you tried hard enough. He'd not yet got the bulbs planted in Jonty's patch—that was a job for later this year—but there were plenty of buds on the shrubs. It would be fine, given a bit of time.

Orlando started reading Mrs. McNeil's notes, a disconnected narrative of Daniel's service history, interspersed with recollections of how much her son had loved France as a child, but he was unable to concentrate on them. His eye kept straying to the little writing desk, the one which had been his grandmother's and which had been privy to all her secrets, given her habit of hiding important letters in a concealed drawer. Now it kept all the correspondence he'd had from Jonty when they'd been apart.

They'd always known, of course, from the moment that war was declared, that things had changed somehow, even if the early part of the war saw only their relocation to London. They'd lived with the Stewarts and life had been much the same as when they'd been in Cambridge, except for the lack of dunderheads. When they'd put their names down to fight, that change had become more marked, given the increased chance of one of them not returning. From that moment, even though they were still together in training, Jonty had written to him every week.

He opened the little desk and took out the precious contents.

What do they use to make these uniforms? Scouring pads?

Orlando had often tried to figure out how Jonty had managed to get away with some of the comments he'd smuggled past the censors. Some of the letters had evaded other eyes entirely, delivered by hand or left under pillows.

Do you remember how you said you'd have liked to serve under the old King George, fighting Napoleon on land or sea? We have a new King George now and you're to have your wish.

Their eventual parting had been so painful, preceded as it was by snatched nights of shared passion and tender longeurs—giving and receiving each other's bodies, lying in one another's arms without speaking, reacquainting themselves with every inch of each other, lest they be parted. Lest they might then forget. The last meeting, on a crowded railway station, had been almost wordless, from both necessity of discretion and aching in their hearts. They had shaken hands, exchanged notes and gone off into the smoky night. And each note had been almost identical.

I love you. Do not forget me. Love again if I don't return.

That note wasn't among the others. It was kept safe in Orlando's wallet, in the inner pocket of whichever jacket he was wearing, alongside some other notes Jonty had written when they'd first been courting.

All Lessons Learned

These wartime notes and letters had continued on active service, a weekly exchange of news and tittle-tattle, forceful opinion and deeply veiled words of affection. The letters had obviously stopped when Orlando had been captured, although he'd not guessed the real reason why. He hadn't been able to grieve at the time—he was an officer, he couldn't give in to emotions or self-indulgence. Nor could he expect anyone really to understand what the loss of this "friend" had meant to him. He'd always imagined, before they set off across the Channel, that he'd have the Stewarts' shoulders to cry on but even that had been denied him.

All he'd got was a letter, one that Jonty had left with Lavinia, *just in case.* He took it, last and most precious of all, from its wooden coffin.

Don't weep overmuch. Remember me with fondness but allow yourself to let me go. Orlando remembered the first time he'd read it—in little snippets, phrase by phrase, racked with anguish at every word. *Don't just return to your old ways. Keep up the bridge with Matheson—assuming he survives—and have Matthew to High Table ditto. Find someone else to love. You've learned what it is now to share your life, don't snatch it back and hoard it again. I wrote you this sonnet. Don't laugh at my efforts.*

I'll live on in you, though time transform
My face into a faded print and dust embrace
the relics of our love. May there be born
in you nothing but joy, I would your face
wear no long-time mourning. True, awhile
the agonies of loss, the memory pain
brings, will cut you through. But then, dear friend, smile
at solved equation, number off the gain
we had between us. Even there in seventh hell

47

> *of mud-drenched, bloody waste, to think of you*
> *is still to sing of beauty, heart as well*
> *as body's grace; and mind which much can do*
> *to shape a different world. Let this not be*
> *our end: with you, love is infinity.*

Orlando wished, not for the first time, that he'd died back in the trenches—it would have been fairer, easier, more fit. To face the rest of his life without the one thing that made everything worthwhile was far too cruel a fate. He'd tried hard since to do what Jonty wanted, keeping up his contacts with his Italian relatives and his colleagues at other colleges who, like him, had been through the fire and survived. But another person to share his life he could not oblige with. There was only ever room for one man in his heart and the gap he'd left wasn't shaped to fit anyone else.

Chapter Four

France, April 1919

Cabourg looked particularly lovely, the piercing blue of the sky mirrored in both the sea and a shimmering mist that lay over the waters. Monsieur Cesario had been there as a child and had longed to return; if only he'd done it sooner, in happier days when it might have really meant something. His family had always loved France, especially his mother, and if Cesario's visit was tinged with guilt, that emotion only slightly detracted from the wonder of it. The town was as handsome as he remembered it, the beach as golden, even if it had become more fashionable than he recalled. Maybe it had always been so and eight-year-old boys didn't notice whether a place was popular with high society. In those days all he'd cared for was bathing and catching fish in his net, or day trips to Villers-sur-Mer where he could fill his pockets with fossils.

He'd worn shorts and sandals back then, never dreaming that one day he'd be putteed and uniformed, picking the lice out of his seams like he'd picked the winkles from the pools. Fresh faced and full of hope, not bearded and resigned to fate. Those were happier days, perhaps—certainly happier than now, although he'd known wonderful times in between. More innocent days, definitely. Perhaps he would find happiness again one day, although the possibility seemed very remote.

"Bonjour, Monsieur." A deep, friendly voice sounded at his side, unusually deep for a man who was still relatively young. Lamboley could barely be more than thirty, perhaps less, if the years had been as rough to him as they'd been to many a man of a similar age.

"Bonjour, Monsieur Lamboley." Cesario raised his hat and smiled. He continued in French, even though the language still didn't come quite trippingly to his tongue. "It's a fine day, for the time of year."

"It is. One of the best we've seen the last few springs. Still, everything seems brighter this spring." Lamboley was tall and sleek, like an elegant cypress slightly bending into the wind.

"Aye, that's true. No one would ask to see the last few years return. I pray God I will not see their like again in my lifetime." Cesario shivered, turning to the sea to hide the pain he was sure suffused his face. "I think the hotel did us proud at breakfast."

"They did indeed." Lamboley moved to stand next to his acquaintance, the pair of them looking out as the mist slowly burned off for the morning. "I believe it is impossible to excel the food and drink of Normandy. I missed it greatly."

They'd met the previous night, arriving at the Hotel Casino almost simultaneously and finding they were at adjacent tables for dinner. They'd spoken briefly, confessed they were both in Cabourg on holiday, a holiday which might be extended if the situation proved favourable. They shared memories of the town, past and happy times spent there, arranging to meet for a walk the next morning, both being without a travelling companion. The war they'd hardly touched on, but it came into the conversation now, naturally. No matter how much people wanted to forget the horrors, it had been such a huge part of their lives—particularly those who'd seen action—that it wasn't as easy to lay down the war as laying down their arms had been. Some old soldiers even yearned, in their heart of hearts, for the comradeship and sense of belonging they'd had in the trenches, having returned home to families who could not or would not understand.

"I assume you saw action, Monsieur? There's something about those who fought which doesn't go away easily." Cesario had another fight now, with a tongue which resented the awkward words. How difficult not to simply revert to his usual idiom, but that was part of the decision he'd made, the irrevocable break from home.

Lamboley nodded. "I did. More than enough for any man's lifetime." He indicated that they should walk along the promenade, by the casino and along the front. Maybe in search of some pension or café where they could take a coffee, or into the countryside to drink in the smell of spring. Either would be pleasant on a day like this.

"Army or navy?"

"Neither," Lamboley said, laughing. Cesario got the impression laughing wasn't the sort of thing he did that often. "I'd had experience of aviation research here, before the war. I decided I'd cross the Channel and make myself available to anyone who wanted me. Your Royal Flying Corps let me help push their fledglings from the nest."

"You didn't stay with them, though? After they'd metamorphosed from ugly ducklings into the elegant swans of the Royal Air Force?" Cesario undid the buttons of his greatcoat; the temperature was creeping up and soon he'd regret having worn it.

"As I said, I'd seen enough action to last a lifetime. I know the world is supposedly at peace but I'm not so naïve as to think it will stay that way. In pockets at least."

51

"And you wouldn't want to find yourself in one of those pockets?" Strange how easy it was to talk to this seemingly reserved man, much easier than it had been to talk to anyone else these last few months. But then, Cesario hadn't really stayed anywhere long enough to build up a rapport with someone, to reach the point where he could unburden himself of the feelings lodging in his heart and mind. Maybe he'd never find that freedom again, although at least with Lamboley he'd progressed beyond pleasantries and platitudes.

"Would any of us? I can anticipate things moving fast, Monsieur, faster than any of us might expect. The future of war may lie in the air one day but I wouldn't wish to be part of it."

They stopped for a while, watching a pair of men mending a net, as men must have mended nets year in year out for hundreds, if not thousands, of years along this and other coasts. To see them huddled by their little wooden boats it was easy to have no faith in any man taking to the air like a bird.

"And you?" Lamboley resumed the conversation as they walked on, turning inland up a little lane. "The army wasn't an option for peacetime?"

How had this man come to the conclusion—the correct one—that Cesario had fought on land rather than been in the navy? "No. It would never have been, not even when I was a boy. Far too interested in my studies. It could only have been something on this scale which would have got me to stir my stumps. I'm sorry." Cesario saw the pained look in the other man's face, immediately regretting his choice of words.

"Please, forgive me my response. I had a friend, a good friend, who wasn't as lucky as I was. His plane went down and..." Lamboley gave an eloquent shrug, "...the word stumps makes me think of him. He has a wife and family to support and a farm to run. Not the easiest thing to do from a chair."

"No indeed." They looked out to sea, recalling the hale and hearty young men they'd known who now wore a sleeve pinned across their jacket or whose trouser legs hung loose and empty. Cesario remembered an old sea shanty, one he'd sung as a child. "My son John was tall and slim and he had a leg for every limb. But now he's got no legs at all, they were both shot away by a cannonball..." He shivered. "There is no need to apologise, as I was the one in error. Tell me what it's like to fly in an aeroplane."

"You've never been up in one?" The pained expression eased from Lamboley's face as he began to speak about something which was clearly dear to him. "The nearest thing to being a bird, I suppose." He continued enthusiastically as they carried on their walk, touching on such esoteric things as *take-off velocity, uplift*, so many words which Cesario had to ask to be explained. Lamboley didn't seem to mind his ignorance and Cesario welcomed the chance to think of something else, to turn his thoughts away from what had occupied them—occupied so many people's thoughts—these last few years.

"It all sounds too wonderful to be true." A small café beckoned them, tables neatly placed outside to capture the sun but keep away the prevailing wind. A pot of coffee seemed right, to be enjoyed along with this fledgling friendship. "I've driven a car, both pre-war and when I've had the chance since. I thought that was the height of mechanical ingenuity, the pinnacle of man's engineering achievements." He wouldn't mention that he'd heard tanks described in the same way.

"Then you must try an aeroplane and see that you were wrong!" A seagull swooped close, as if sent to illustrate the point. "Might I ask you a personal question?"

Cesario tried to respond lightly, as if it didn't matter one way or the other. "Of course. There is no guarantee I'll answer it."

"Naturally." Lamboley inclined his head, evidently aware of the sort of things old soldiers might be asked that they might not want to give an honest reply to. "I have made the assumption, and it could be the wrong one, that you're not from here. Not from Normandy nor from France herself. Am I correct?"

Cesario nodded, slowly, looking for the right words and not just because the language still didn't feel entirely natural on his tongue. "You are quite correct." He left it at that, gathering a range of replies together into his armoury.

"You speak our language very well, if with a little...stiffness? I am also making a guess that you are English, but that supposition comes more from the colour of your eyes and beard than from your accent, which is good."

Cesario wondered if he was being teased, patronised, but his new friend seemed in earnest. "That is an accurate assessment. I learned French at school and got to practice it when my family brought us here on holiday."

"And that's exactly how I learned English." Lamboley smiled and refilled their cups. "I never thought I would have made the use of it that I did."

"Nor I my French." Cesario cradled his cup, remembering the way the men in his platoon had stared, impressed—or rolled their eyes—when he'd addressed some of the locals wherever they happened to find themselves. He'd pretended not to notice their expressions, nor to hear the muttered remarks about French tarts. The tarts had never interested him, no matter how tempting his men, or fellow officers, had found their wares. He shuddered to think of what some of the men got up to, and who they'd done it with; prolonged absence from home seemed as effective as alcohol in increasing a woman's charms. He drove the memories from his mind. "Where did you holiday in

England?"

"Along the Devon coast—Dartmouth, Torbay, such places as might remind one of here." Lamboley waved his hand in a vaguely northerly direction. "But not just England, I loved Scotland too. We had such wonderful times in Edinburgh." His eyes danced with delight. "They say the link between my country and the Scots runs a long way back and very deep. When I was there I felt like I had found another home."

"Auld Reekie." It was nice to feel proper words on his tongue again, if only for a moment. "I have known happy times there too."

"Is that where you live?"

"No." A guardedness fell over Cesario's words. So much he'd revealed already, more perhaps than he'd wanted to, in word and inflection. He wasn't ready to delve much deeper at present. "Like you, we visited there."

Lamboley evidently knew when the shutters were being pulled down. He eased the topic onto Edinburgh itself and stories of Mary Queen of Scots, her French husband, the plots and intrigues of the Tudor court. Cesario began to relax again, enjoying the conversation although without ever letting his guard down entirely. Eventually the wind turned, buffeting their faces as it gained in strength and reminding them that late Spring still had a bite and wasn't going to cede her place to Summer quite yet.

Cesario was grateful for his overcoat as they strolled back to the hotel. He was tired, too tired to take up Lamboley's offer of lunch, pleading that he had a headache and needed to lie down with the curtains closed or else he'd never make it go away. His new friend had been gracious, saying that he would see him at dinner if he felt better.

"I have my watercolours with me and would like to take

advantage of the light, if it remains good this afternoon, to make a little picture of those boats we saw. I shall return there after lunch to make some sketches. Maybe you might feel up to looking at them this evening and choosing one of them for me to progress?" Lamboley smiled, his gentle, handsome face full of concern.

"If my wretched head is up to it and you can bear the assessment of a layman then I'd be most pleased to oblige, thank you." Cesario held out his hand to be shaken. "Good luck with your sketching." He cut the pleasantries as short as he could without being rude, walking unsteadily up the stairs and along to his room. If what he thought was going to happen really did come to pass, then he'd not be seeing any sketches for several days.

The bed was cool and slow to warm, even though Cesario had snuggled into it before the shivering started. It had been weeks since he'd had one of these attacks, the longest he'd gone without one since November and, in a moment of optimistic delusion, he'd hoped they were done with, at least for the time being. Would he hear the guns this time, or see the faces of the lads who'd served in his platoon? The faces themselves—no matter how distorted—were less frightening than the eyes, the vacant hopeless looks of the living much worse than the vacant lifeless eyes of the dead.

He should seek help, of course he should, although some of the stories he'd heard at second hand about the treatments for—what did they call it—neurasthenia, seemed worse than just putting up with visions for a few days. They went, eventually, and in a pseudonymous bed in a hotel or pension, he could pretend it was the flu and be cosseted without the need to produce his real name or a service history.

He shut his eyes, hugged himself tight, and tried to think of nothing.

Chapter Five

Saturday morning, only the day after meeting Mrs. McNeil, Orlando sprang into action. Escaping Cambridge, he'd taken a train to London, heading for an address which had been among the information she'd left him. It was easy enough to find—an elegant house, set in a small square near the Thames, close enough to hear the seagulls mewing above the water. Maybe a storm was brewing—that's what Grandmother Coppersmith had always said, that gulls possessed enough weather sense to come inland when there was trouble likely out at sea. There was certainly a tempest on its way for Andrew Wilson-Gore, Mrs. McNeil's cousin and possible defender of the family honour, a knight on a white charger of subterfuge and bearing the lance of economy with the truth.

This branch of the family clearly had both money and breeding and, if the location wasn't quite in the same bracket as the Stewarts' house had been, the quality of the surrounding streets was more than "fair-to-middling". Orlando took a turn around the square and along one of the neighbouring roads before he approached his destination. He tried to persuade himself that he was building up a feel for the area, seeking out little subtle, subjective clues to something or other, but in reality he was building up his nerves. Of course he'd done sleuthing on his own, before now; many times he and Jonty had shared the work on a case, dividing to conquer the solution.

But even apart they'd had the other in the background, somebody to lay the fruits of one's detective labours at the feet of, somebody to support and be encouraged by. Grief for a lover was lonely enough, but to have lost the one person you could really share your thoughts with was another level of heartbreak.

Orlando steeled himself, swallowing his self-doubt—or at least hiding it behind some sort of facade—and knocked on the door. The demeanour of the butler was encouraging, the decoration and furnishings of the hall seemed hopeful and the morning room Orlando was ushered into was light and cheerful. He hoped his host would be as pleasant.

The door sprang open and the man himself appeared, smiling and holding out his hand. "Dr. Coppersmith?" Andrew Wilson-Gore didn't look like a knight on a charger, nor anyone's commanding officer, but appearances were clearly deceptive; the first time the man spoke a calm authority exuded from him. For such men people had gone over the top to almost certain death, as they'd gone for and with Orlando. Wilson-Gore indicated a chair by the fireplace. "Please make yourself at home." Even this pleasantry sounded almost like an order.

Orlando settled into the chair, which was more comfortable than it looked. He fiddled with his papers to hide any lingering discomfort and to summon up the right way to begin his questioning. Why couldn't he stop thinking about what sort of small talk Jonty would have used? "Thank you. I appreciate your making time for me."

"I won't say that it's my pleasure, given the circumstances, although I'm happy to help you in any way I can. My cousin said you would be in touch so your telegram was no surprise. Poor Clemmie." Wilson-Gore rose, moving to the mantelpiece to pick up a photograph which he placed in his guest's hands. "Here we all are. You'll recognise Clemmie—Mrs. McNeil—of course, and that's her husband. My late wife, too, and our boys, all rubbing along together."

Orlando angled the photograph to appreciate it best. "They're fine-looking children." He didn't enquire further about them—all of them boys, all just the wrong age. It was wiser in cases like this to let people explain. If they had anything to explain.

"They were. My William still is." He indicated the youngest of the three boys. "He's back at Oxford now. Insisted on signing up, as they all did, although he didn't see much action. Thank God." He gently touched the glass over the face of another boy. "Thomas wasn't so lucky."

Orlando looked again at his host. Either the man was older than he appeared or he'd married early, very early, to have boys of this age. "They look so much like their mother." It seemed a bland remark, although it proved surprisingly fortuitous.

"Her image. They're not mine by birth, Dr. Coppersmith. Martitia married young and the boys came as soon as they decently might." Wilson-Gore's eyes twinkled with affection. "I'd known her husband since I was just a lad myself, our families being great friends, and it seemed natural for us to grow close when she was widowed. John was no age when he died, thrown from his horse when it stumbled at a fence. Instantaneous, my father said, and he saw it happen. I pray Thomas was as fortunate."

Orlando didn't need to answer. Old soldiers; they all knew how death had taken a long time to spread her wings on occasions, out in muddy holes or dank hospital wards. "Then this must be Daniel." Orlando pointed to the third lad in the picture. "You reported that he died in action but no body was ever identified or given burial. If I may be entirely blunt, Mrs. McNeil doubts the veracity of that report."

"Many men never received a Christian burial, Dr.

Coppersmith. You know that." Wilson-Gore answered the question with a steady gaze, just as he might have faced the enemy. Did this man bear the same mental scars as Orlando did, scars much worse than the marks his body wore?

"I know that indeed, from bitter experience. Sometimes there was so little left to bury..." Orlando stopped, aware that he was straying down paths he'd rather not tread. Where had Jonty's corporeal frame actually come to rest, the bits which had gone up into the air like an offering? In how many places had his ashes landed? Were any of them under a tree where birds could sing a eulogy and sweet blossoms fall and decorate the grave? "But there's more to this particular story, isn't there? Your cousin believes that your version of events is perhaps not the most accurate one." How else to say, "Are you lying to me as well as to her?"

Wilson-Gore steepled his fingers and held them to his determined chin. He thought carefully before responding. "I am relying on your judgment and candour, one officer speaking to another and expecting his trust. How much do you value the truth?"

Orlando weighed his response and opted for the side of truth itself. "If you had asked me that in 1914, I'd have said I prized it beyond all things." Beyond all I could mention here; not beyond *him*. "What I have seen since has made me reconsider. I value absolute accuracy in my work, of course, but when it comes to people, I've learned that some questions are best answered with a kind lie. When the wife of a soldier asks if her husband had a swift death, and a painless one, the reality might serve no purpose."

"Better to let the lie eat into the heart of the man who tells it, rather than break the heart of the hearer." Wilson-Gore nodded. "Clemmie says she wants to know everything..."

"And you have things to say that you believe she should never hear?"

"Not from me." Wilson-Gore studied his hands as a silence fell over the room, a silence that seemed to extend out into the streets, where suddenly neither child nor carriage could be heard. It was easy to imagine, on days like this, how the distant gunfire would have rumbled and be heard even here. "You will think me a coward, perhaps, or maybe too brave for my own good, clasping this thing to me when I could share it."

"I don't judge you at all, sir. God knows none of us should judge each other, after..." Orlando gestured vaguely in the direction of the continent. "Let me share this burden. You don't need to tell your cousin anything, nor even do you need to divulge all the details to me. Give me clues enough to go looking in the right places and let me do the rest."

Wilson-Gore paused, a light in his eyes suggesting he would be relieved to see part of the load eased. "And you wouldn't judge Daniel, even if you found he'd run away, deserting his duty in his country's hour of need?" The irony in his voice was plain; these were other people's words and opinions, not his own.

Jonty would have assured this man immediately and the very words he would have used seemed to ring in his lover's ears. If Orlando was a fraction slow in giving his own answer, it was because he wanted to savour that voice, even if only in his imagination. "My commission isn't to judge or to bring anyone to justice, if a long line of trail-following came to that. Mrs. McNeil wants to know where her boy is, whether in the earth of Belgium or hiding in some village in Switzerland. That's the problem I have to solve, and no other."

Wilson-Gore nodded, decisively, his mind clearly made up. "Then I will tell you all I know, such as it is."

The testimony didn't amount to much, not when it was written as notes in Orlando's notebook. He concentrated hard on getting the details correct, picking out the nuances of what was said as well as the words. Not just because it would help him with the case; he needed something to take his mind off the similarities to his own condition, off the circumstances in which Jonty had died.

Second lieutenant McNeil had been part of a big push, one intended to re-secure a significant piece of ground. He'd taken a group of men and pushed ahead, the vanguard of an attack which was supposed to be supported by a barrage of covering fire from the big guns behind the lines. None of the men had returned.

"They never recovered his body. One of his fellow officers saw him go down into a dugout with some of his men, out on a forward raid about a hundred yards ahead of where the main body of his company was stationed. And then all hell broke loose." Wilson-Gore took another swig of coffee from an unsteady cup held in shaking hands. "They managed to get up to the spot later the next day. None of them left alive. Two with broken necks, lying like rag dolls in the mud. Some of them in pieces..."

Both men sat quiet over their coffee for a moment, images—pictures long consigned to the back of their memories, never to be willingly disinterred—flickering through their minds. Wilson-Gore carried on, explaining how soldiers who'd been in a foxhole nearby gave conflicting accounts of what had happened although they'd all been sure of one thing—the British guns hadn't got the right range, or the orders given had caused an overshoot of the safe zone and Daniel and his men had come under fire from their own side. One of the old salts had said he'd seen Lieutenant McNeil stumble, surrounded by his men, before an enormous shell had struck. In the aftermath they hadn't even been able to establish the number of the dead, nor piece them together.

"And this was the testimony you relied on? There was no other evidence such as identity discs?" Orlando's head buzzed with discomfort, imagining Jonty spread in a hundred pieces and trampled into the mud under unknowing boots. Jonty's body lighting the night sky.

"By the time the confusion had cleared and we had time to go back, there was almost nothing to be found. Nothing you could necessarily recognise of him, nor of several others. A badge, a piece of uniform, someone managed to put together some gruesome jigsaws, but I'm not convinced the pieces ever fitted into the correct pictures." Wilson-Gore's hands began to tremble and he had to steady them on the arm of his chair. "We had one eyewitness report and that was good enough for me."

"No one else could corroborate this?" Orlando remembered men meeting their deaths and no one any the wiser about when and where it had happened.

"No." The older man's face creased in distress. "I had someone contradict it, though. Said he'd seen Daniel stumble, just before the shell came down, but that he'd not fallen with the others. He'd turned and gone off into a little copse, him and another man, before the strike hit home. Another blast took out a couple of trees, and apparently killed the other soldier, so it's possible Daniel also died there, if not out in the field." Wilson-Gore didn't sound convinced, but he hadn't at any point spoken with any real conviction about the incident.

"And it's equally possible he bided his time and made off in the confusion? Or waited until dark?" Orlando wouldn't use the word "desert". He'd heard too much rubbish spouted about men who'd lost their nerve, especially from people who'd been no nearer the front than the promenade at Dover.

"It is. The man who said he'd seen him go into the copse inferred that's what he thought, but nobody was prepared to believe him. Daniel had had him up on a charge before then and plenty of the men said it was just sour grapes. Nobody had a bad word to say for Lieutenant McNeil."

"And what do you believe? Not what was 'good enough for you'. What does your heart tell you?" The question had to be asked. It cut right to the root of the issue.

"I believe that it's all been an enormous waste of time and life, those four blighted years, but what else choice did we have? As men or as a nation?"

Orlando had no answer for the question. The same conundrum had bothered him frequently these last few months.

"Daniel didn't like being out there any more than any of us did. He performed his duty, but he was scared, always had been, and getting more so all the time. I met him, at a briefing, just a few days before he disappeared, and he was deeply troubled, I could see that. Anyone could see that." Wilson-Gore passed a trembling hand over his eyes. "He wouldn't be persuaded to seek help, though. And until it became an encumbrance to his leadership—and it never did—then he had to see his time out. It's ironic, he was due to get a rest in just a few weeks. His platoon was to secure the ground and then be relieved. Such a waste."

Orlando waited to speak his piece. There was no point in unsettling his host further and the man seemed near to tears or some other equally embarrassing manifestation of emotion. He'd just keep to the objective, the straightforward. "May I have the name of both men, if you have them? The one who saw him fall and the one who saw him run?"

"I can give you both names, they're etched deeply in my memory, but in the first case it will do you no good. He's gone to meet his maker." Wilson-Gore went over to his desk and produced a little folder, one which seemed to have been prepared ready for Orlando's visit. Among the contents was a newspaper clipping, a list of dead and wounded. "Here he is. Last October." Neither man commented on the date, the irony of having survived so long and missing a safe ending by weeks. "And here's the other one. Fred Giggs." He held out a letter, written in a firm hand, one which employed all capitals.

Orlando had seen the style of writing before, among some of his men. "You wouldn't have expected this?" It was an open invitation to Lieutenant McNeil's family to have a drink "on the house" any time they should be in the Bear and Ragged Staff on the Holloway Road.

"No." Wilson-Gore smiled. "I've never seen the like, nor have I taken up the invitation. Clemmie would be distraught if she were to know about it. I'm not sure I understand the man's motives."

"Quite." Orlando copied down the address, even though he'd committed it to memory. Belt and braces, Jonty used to call it, backing up things in case the old brain played tricks. "I won't mention it. But I might just take up the chance of visiting the place."

There was a small, elegant church at the end of the road leading from the square where Wilson-Gore lived, a church set in a square between tall, white fronted houses. It was a handsome little building surrounded by grass with an assortment of tombs and memorials, the sort of place Jonty would have dragged Orlando around, given half the chance. One ornate monument caught Orlando's eye—it featured a marble angel, a statue which almost glowed in the light. Jonty would have scoffed at such flamboyance, saying that all he wanted was a plain stone with his name, age and a simple verse, like his favourite collect, the second one from evensong.

They'd stood together once, on the way home from Room 40 duties, looking at a similar church—London was awash with little churches in little squares. Orlando could hear the conversation as if it were happening now. "If anything should happen, you're not to grieve too much." Jonty had kept his gaze fixed on the monuments, avoiding Orlando's eyes.

"How much is too much?" Orlando had reached over to caress—briefly, given that it was full daylight—the nape of Jonty's neck.

"Too much is when you forget to love again. Enough is when you can lay flowers on my grave—or cast them in the sea if she were ever to claim me—and say, 'There's this chap I rather like. He may not be you, Jonty, but he'll do'."

"You know..." Orlando had wanted to say, *You know I'll never love again, please don't demand it of me*, but he'd held his tongue. They'd had that conversation, or a variation of it, too often.

Now he looked vacantly at the little graveyard as if he'd never seen such a thing before, or if he had couldn't put a name or use to it. Was there a memorial to Daniel McNeil somewhere? A cenotaph to keep his memory alive while his corporeal form still walked the earth, skulking somewhere while his mother broke her heart? He slapped his hand along the railings, determined that he'd get to the bottom of this, not just for Mrs. McNeil, but for all the soldiers who hadn't run, who had stared at death and not blinked an eye.

He went off in search of a cab to take him to the Holloway Road and whatever waited at the Bear and Ragged Staff.

When Orlando reached the pub, he was in two minds whether to make use of the open invitation Wilson-Gore had received, pretending he was one of the family. It might prove useful, shedding some light on why such an offer had been made—was it a genuine gesture of friendship from one old soldier to another, now that ranks were meaningless, or was there some darker motive, the disdain of the regular Tommy for the family of a man he'd thought had run?

What would Jonty have done? Jonty, who wasn't averse to a bit of subterfuge when necessary. *There are times for legitimate deception and there are times for honesty.* The voice was clear and uncompromising. *This is the time for the latter.* Orlando nodded, as if answering that internal voice, and went through the door. The lounge bar was clean, neat and a cut above what he'd been expecting; shipshape and Bristol fashion, the sort of place you found at the seaside run by an old tar. Definitely not in keeping with this part of London. He bought himself a pint—an exceptionally good one, at that—and leaned on the bar.

"This is the best pint I've had since 1914, landlord. I wasn't sure they still made beer like this." Orlando fished in his pocket for some coppers. "Will you join me in one?"

"That's very kind of you, sir, but I hope you'll excuse me if I let the offer pass. It's a mite early in the day for me." Giggs resembled the sort of men who made good college porters; big and bluff. Orlando had seen plenty of soldiers like this man over the years too—competent, not a scrap of nonsense about them or to be tolerated by them. How could he have ended up on a charge? "I appreciate your kind words on the beer, though. Everyone else seems to think that nothing's like it was before the war." He wiped some glasses and put them into one of the serried ranks behind the counter.

"Would I be correct in saying that you're Mr. Giggs?" Orlando laid down his pint and took out his notepad.

"I am." Giggs eyed the notepad. "You wouldn't be from the Customs, would you?" It was said only half jokingly.

"God forbid." Orlando grinned. "I'm actually a fellow of St. Bride's, up in Cambridge, for my sins. I'm here on behalf of a friend of mine, whose son fought with you out in Belgium. She wants to find out more about his death."

"You're Dr. Coppersmith, aren't you?" Giggs beamed, slapping his tea towel on the counter. "Mary! Mary! Guess who we've got here."

A handsome woman, built on the lines of a tank, bustled into the bar but didn't seem impressed by what she saw leaning there. "Fred, the way you were shouting, I thought it was King George himself come to pay a call."

"It's almost as good. Dr. Coppersmith—you remember, we used to read about him in the newspapers, solving all those mysteries. My wife, Mary, loves a good mystery, sir."

The face of the lady in question suddenly turned from a scowl to a beaming smile. "Oh, sir, please excuse my manners. It's a pleasure to have you here. Would you be interested in a little luncheon? I've an excellent beef stew out the back and I'd be honoured to serve you it."

Orlando's stomach told his brain what the answer should be. "That would be most kind of you, madam." He watched her bustle off, dreading all the while what the next question might be.

It soon came. "Dr. Stewart not with you, sir?"

"I'm afraid Dr. Stewart didn't return from the front." It didn't become any easier to say, not even at the eighteenth or eightieth time. "And please dispense with the 'sir'. It's been Dr. Coppersmith since I returned home and I hope never have to take rank again."

Giggs nodded. "Please accept my condolences, Doctor. I

must have missed his obituary."

"I doubt you'd have seen it. It would have been while you were still abroad." Orlando's nostrils twitched as a sumptuous aroma drifted in from the kitchen. "As you'll have guessed, I'm involved in one of my 'cases'. I'm trying to clarify what happened to Lieutenant Daniel McNeil." Orlando didn't beat about the bush or try to pussy foot his way up to the point of his visit. One look at Fred Giggs showed taking a direct line was the correct approach.

"Are you really a friend of his family then, or is this what you'd call a professional commission?" Giggs had a broad northern accent—Lancashire rather than the other side of the Pennines—and it added to his air of forcefulness.

"I'm hardly Sherlock Holmes, Mr. Giggs." Orlando laughed, but it didn't feel comfortable to be interrogated so. "I'm acting on behalf of his mother as a favour to a friend of a friend. Although I have to assure you that, having met the lady, I'm convinced she only wants to know the truth."

"Aye. There's plenty of mothers want to know the truth about what happened to their lads and there's plenty who'd be better off with white lies." Giggs produced a cigarette case, offered one to Orlando, shrugged—not maliciously—when it was refused, then lit one up for himself. The arrival of a plate of beef stew, adorned with dumplings as light as a cloud, eased their passage round a potentially dangerous corner. "Mrs. McNeil will want to hear that he died in battle, her brave boy, but that's not the way of it. I saw him run off, Dr. Coppersmith. Off into the trees and leaving his men to be blown to smithereens." A thin stream of smoke left Gigg's nostrils, maybe an exhalation of a stream of contempt.

"And you couldn't have been mistaken?" Orlando wiped his mouth in between mouthfuls—the beef tasted as good as it smelt. "About the man's identity or his intent?"

"I wish I could have been mistaken, Doctor, but there's not a scrap of doubt in my mind. I've got very sharp eyes—have done since I was just a sprat of a boy." Giggs shook his head and tipped the ash from his cigarette as if to emphasise the point. "You can dress a man up in someone else's clothes, dye his hair or get him to put on an accent, but you can't change the way a man walks or the way he runs and that was Lieutenant McNeil running as sure as eggs is eggs."

"But his intent, Mr. Giggs? Is there any possibility that he was trying to lead his men out of harm's way? That he could have anticipated their being under fire and wanted to get them into the woods?"

"If he did, then he didn't succeed. Only the one man followed him." Giggs put out his cigarette with a decisiveness that seemed to say, "This is how it was. You have my word for it." Before Orlando could ask the awkward follow-up question he'd planned, the landlord spoke again. "And my answer isn't coloured by what happened out there, being put on a charge. Lieutenant McNeil was right to haul me over the coals—I got into a fight when I should have known better."

There was no point in following that up; Giggs had clearly said his piece and wasn't going to say much more. "And if I may clarify one last thing, please?" Orlando flipped over a page in his notebook, mainly for effect. "I believe the wood itself was struck in the bombardment. It is possible Lieutenant McNeil was killed there, as the soldier who went with him died? Have you anything you can tell me on that score?"

"Not much. Eoin O'Leary certainly met his maker that day—half his face taken off with shrapnel or something."

Orlando's ears pricked up. "Was the half the face that was left enough to definitely identify this O'Leary chap?" They'd come across mistaken identity before. Who was to say it wouldn't cross their—Orlando had to correct himself and think *his*—path again?

"Enough for me, and the rest of the lads who found him, to know." Giggs narrowed his eyes. "You were thinking that maybe it was McNeil who we found?"

"I have to eliminate all the possibilities." Orlando realised he was sounding too much like the dreaded Sherlock. "That sounds pompous, I'm sorry. I just wanted to get everything clear."

"That's all right, sir. You're just doing your job. No, O'Leary was dead and I was too busy with other things to see whether the Lieutenant ever left his shelter." Giggs screwed up his face in thought. "Poor O'Leary. He was frightened almost all the time, towards the end—it was a merciful release when the Jerries got him. Maybe that would be right and just for Lieutenant McNeil, as well, if he'd run and then the bombs had caught him anyway. He wasn't a bad officer, very honourable, and I'd have said very brave up until then. Maybe braver than most if he was scared all that time. Strange as it seems to be, I'd like to know he was killed outright there and then, rather than turn up in a few years' time and bring disgrace on all his family."

"Aye." Orlando finished the rest of his meal in silence, a party of men having come into the lounge bar and needing the landlord's attention. He was scooping up the last atom of dumpling when Mrs. Giggs appeared again, beaming at his empty plate. He had to refuse seconds but complimented her soundly on the excellence of her cooking.

"I heard you talking about the war with my Fred. You were over there yourself, I could tell that. You always know the ones who went." She fussed over plate, napkin and cutlery, giving the impression she had something to say but wasn't sure of how to impart it. "He won't like me saying this..." she lowered her voice, casting a quick glance at her husband although he was deep in conversation, "...but he doesn't have much time for cowards. He doesn't mind some of the conchies, the ones who drove the ambulances and did the sort of mucky jobs no one else was going to turn a hand to. Says a lot of them were braver than some officers he could name."

"The ones who got themselves nice cushy jobs at home or far behind the lines?" Orlando knew the type.

"That's them. And the ordinary lads, especially the young ones who thought they'd signed up for a bit of adventure—I could slap that Marie Lloyd with her songs about how much better the men looked in uniform—Fred could understand when they went a bit strange. Found themselves in hell, he said, when they thought they'd be in some boys' book of adventures. It was like when the ones who were happy to send the nippers to their deaths couldn't face standing alongside them. That's the sort of thing that gets him mad."

Orlando couldn't help wondering if McNeil would be one of those "ones" and whether that opinion had coloured Giggs's testimony. He thanked Mrs. Giggs, waved goodbye to the landlord and went out into the fresh air, trying to clear his mind.

If Giggs had been speaking the truth, if Daniel McNeil really had deserted, where had he gone after hiding in the wood? Had he slipped his way back through the British lines in the smoke and confusion—and he must have been damned lucky not to have been caught and shot—and then gone to ground somewhere? In which case how did Orlando have a snowball in hell's chance of finding him?

Chapter Six

The porters at St. Bride's were still being annoyingly deferential, as if an overabundance of politeness could in some way compensate for the lack of Jonty Stewart. Orlando was now having to bite his tongue every time he was plied with conspicuously good manners; the men obviously meant well but they were paving a neat road to making his life hell with their good intentions. Perhaps he should find some useful outlet for their good will.

"Tait."

"Yes, Dr. Coppersmith?" The newest and most obsequious porter almost sprang to attention. Belgium, and the time he'd spent there, was evidently still having its effect.

"Where can I find information on a soldier who was presumed dead in action and might not have been?" Orlando was amused to see Tait's jaw working up and down and the frightened look in his eye. The sudden recollection of lads who'd looked like that minutes before meeting their death brought him up with a round turn. "I'm sorry, I was voicing my thoughts aloud."

"Dr. Coppersmith?" The ever reliable Summerbee, the doyen of St. Bride's porters and the most experienced man still in the lodge, appeared from the inner office, looking calm and collected. "If I can be so bold as to intrude, sir, I could answer your question. Possibly."

"Intrude away, Summerbee." Orlando had always had a soft spot for this man, who'd turned a blind eye to the state he and Jonty had sometimes been in after a visit to the Bishop's Cope and a pint too many. "I've a puzzle to solve and very little idea of where to look for a solution."

"I know one of the porters down at Ascension." Funny how all other colleges were "down" from St. Bride's, even though it sat in one of the lowest lying parts of Cambridge. "They've a man there, a historian, who's studying the effects of the war on men's nerves. He's working with some doctor who specialises in mental...nervous cases." Summerbee quickly corrected himself. "Maybe he'd have some idea of what direction to send you in. If you don't mind working with a historian."

"It doesn't bother me, but don't let Mrs. Sheridan know." Orlando turned to Tait, who was looking terrified at this strange turn in the conversation. "Mrs. Sheridan doesn't approve of them, historians. You'll need to remember that if you want a long and happy career here."

Tait's Adam's apple did a curtsey as he swallowed hard. "I'll do that, sir."

"You wouldn't happen to know the name of this chap at Ascension, would you?"

"I don't remember offhand but I could nip down there during my break and find out from Johnson. If Mr. Clough allows it." Summerbee showed an appropriate deference as he spoke the name of the head porter, even if they were old allies. He'd been offered the job himself, Orlando and all the other fellows were well aware of that, but he'd refused it on the grounds that he wanted to carry on working with his mates. Even though Clough might bear the title, Summerbee was the spiritual head of the lodge.

"I'll ask him to let you have the time in lieu." Orlando put down his college post on the counter. "Better still, we'll ask him if you can accompany me there now. I'll collect these—" he indicated the little pile of letters and notes, "—when I return."

"I'll replace them in your pigeon hole, sir." Tait scuttled away, clearly pleased to be out from under Orlando's eagle eye.

Summerbee watched him, grinning all the while. "I can remember when I was as nervous as him. He'll be fine once we've built his confidence up. You'll have seen a few like him, out in France."

"I did." Lots of them. Some had found their feet, gained in confidence and skill. Some, too many, had only found a premature grave. "I'm glad those days are behind us. Please God we won't see their like again in our lifetime."

"Amen to that, sir. Shall we consult Mr. Clough?"

Ascension College wasn't as old as St. Bride's, although it regarded itself with self-importance—it had a Nobel prize winner in its ranks, even if he hadn't won his prize while in residence, and therefore could lord it over some of the other institutions. While it didn't quite rank in Bride's lore alongside the abominated *college next door*, it came a close second. Still, Orlando's welcome was warm enough, probably because he had Summerbee at his side. It reminded him of his old divisional sergeant, who'd watched Orlando's back and fended off any unwanted assaults—whether those came from enemy soldiers or tiresome English officers.

They were in luck; Johnson was in the lodge and delighted to help. It being Sunday, he assured his guests there were no dunderheads likely to be needing Dr. Beattie's attention during the afternoon, so they'd probably catch him putting his feet up in his study. But the historian wasn't in his rooms, so Johnson dragged the visitors off to the library where they ran their quarry to ground, the Bride's men having to wait outside like naughty schoolboys, clearly not to be trusted not to scribble on the books or do something equally bad.

"Dr. Coppersmith." Beattie held out his hand, a serious smile gracing his striking face—his extremely handsome face. The adjective springing to Orlando's mind came as a shock. He'd only ever thought of one person as extremely handsome.

He quickly regained his composure. "Ced. Dr. Beattie, thank you for taking the time to meet me. I'm sure you're busy."

"Never too busy to help out a fellow officer." He smiled, and the adjective "handsome" turned into the more appropriate "stunning".

Orlando swallowed hard, turning to Summerbee for some temporary distraction. "Thank you, both of you." He nodded to Johnson as well. "I'm sure my client will be extremely grateful."

"That's fine, sir." Johnson answered smartly for the both of them and looked perilously close to saluting. He ushered Summerbee away, with vague mutterings about a bottle or two of beer stowed away in the back of the lodge.

"Your client?" Beattie had clearly not been given all the information about Orlando's visit. He raised his hand. "No, don't tell me here. I'll have a pot of tea sent up to my rooms and we can talk everything over. I suspect there's more to this than just helping you with a piece of research."

"There is." Orlando's collar seemed to tighten, the temperature in the corridor unaccountably rising five degrees. "I'm sorry if you've been misled, but it's concerning an investigation I've been commissioned to take."

Beattie's face lit up. "Oh, of course. *Dr. Coppersmith.* I should have guessed this wouldn't just be university business." He led the way out into the court and over the grass. "The great and good of Ascension are terribly jealous, of course. They'd love to have their own Holmes and Watson here but Bride's has stolen a march on them."

"I'm sure it wasn't deliberate." They ascended a dark staircase, even more poorly lit than the ones at St. Bride's.

"Tell that to the Dean. He's convinced it was done out of spite. Bother." Beattie had his hand on the door knob when he drew it away as if stung. "I forgot to order the tea. Go in and make yourself at home while I nip down and get it organised."

"There's no need to..." Orlando's words followed his host down the stairs, unheard. He'd have to do as he was told, or how else explain why he was still lurking on the stairs when Beattie returned? The main room was airy and light, in total contrast to the stairway, and was both neat and orderly without losing the personal touch. Pictures graced the walls and mantelpiece, a fuzzy one of Beattie rowing stroke in a Christ Church boat next to a more formal composition, the man as a boy with what were clearly his parents and grandparents. There was a small photograph of an officer, as well—maybe he'd fought in the same regiment as Beattie had, or was an old school pal. He had a shy, gentle face and a neat little moustache; for some reason seeing him made Orlando unaccountably sad.

He took a seat next to a set of bookshelves and looked methodically at the titles, gradually realising how much he'd been at ease here when normally he'd have been tense and uncertain in a stranger's study, especially if the man himself wasn't present.

"Sorry about that."

Beattie's sudden reappearance made Orlando jump, he'd been so lost in some pleasant reverie. "Please, it wasn't a problem. Now I should answer your question." Orlando explained why Mrs. McNeil had consulted him and, broadly, the nature of his commission. "The word reaching St. Bride's via the porters' telegraph was that you had an interest in neurasthenia, which is why I'd like to consult you."

"This lad had the condition, did he?" Beattie took out a notepad and made a few notes as they spoke.

"I have no idea. Let me tell you what I've found out." Orlando gave a résumé of what he'd been told by Wilson-Gore and Giggs. "So I'm at a bit of a loss in terms of how to proceed. It's an awfully long shot, given how many men there were serving on the continent—it's not as if I expect you to have come across him in your research, but I'd be grateful to pick your brains."

"Pick away. Maybe it would benefit relations between Ascension and Bride's to see a little cross-college collaboration." Beattie smiled again.

A wave of red swept up Orlando's neck and cheeks, such as had often plagued him when he was first courting Jonty. What on earth was going on? Whatever it was, he mustn't smile back. "Aye, it might." He studied his notes. "McNeil was with the Lancashire Fusiliers. Have you come across them in your studies?"

Beattie scratched his head. "I may have done. I'd need to consult my records to be sure. I was with the Manchesters myself. How about you? I thought all the Bride's men ended up in Room 40?"

"I—we, Dr. Stewart and I—were there at the start of the war, then we signed up. He ended up with the East Surreys and I was with Queen Victoria's Rifles." Orlando turned back to his notes. "As I said, it's the Fusiliers which occupy us now. September 1918, that's when McNeil was reported killed."

Beattie shuddered. "So many men died that last year,

especially in the spring, before the tide turned again. To be driven backwards, to see all that ground which we'd earned at such a price going straight back to the Jerrys." He passed his hand over his eyes. "I'm sorry. I would say it was particularly poignant for our lads in the Manchesters but I won't claim anything for us over and above the others. We all felt it."

"Aye." Orlando remembered the madness of those days; 1918 had been the year from hell. He sat quietly while Beattie brought down a stack of box files, crammed full of notes but at least appearing to be in some sort of logical order. He also opened a small pair of boxes, filled with cards and clearly part of some neat and efficient cross referencing system. After checking something in both of them he began to rummage among the boxes.

"Ah, this might help..." Beattie produced a handful of papers just as there was a knock on the door and the tea and cakes made their welcome arrival in the room. He fussed over the pot, producing a cup of a brew that was almost—if not quite—as good as the one Bride's prided itself on. "There are some Fusiliers here, although I'm not sure I can guarantee it's the same battalion." He spread out the notes; one of the cases matched McNeil's battalion and the dates were sufficiently similar.

Orlando read the document, sipping his tea as he did so, although less from thirst than from trying to hide his discomfort. To read about another man's degradation into mental illness wasn't edifying, especially when he recalled his own father and the terrible black moods Mr. Coppersmith suffered. Orlando had never espoused the view that these men were somehow degenerate, whether they suffered in war or peacetime. Heaven alone knew he understood how men's own brains, their fears and imaginations, might prove to be the worst enemy they had to face.

In the case he was reading about, there was some mention of how appalling the conditions had been, how this officer's mind had been turned by spending two nights under bombardment listening to the pitiful cries of some of his men, a dozen of them dying slowly out in the mud and him not able to arrange any help. Might McNeil have known him? The dates made it at least possible that they'd served together—they might even have been in the same division.

"Now this *is* interesting." Beattie had been sifting through a pile of unfiled notes while Orlando read the case—by the spark in his eye, he'd found something of significance. "There's a McNeil mentioned here and the location is correct." He held out the closely written sheet, not scribed by *his* hand if the evidence of the other documents was anything to go by. "These are some case notes made by one of our research students, a chap who's interested in psychology. He visited St. Judith's hospital in London, to talk to some of the patients still there."

"Still there?" Would this war ever relinquish its effect on people's minds?

"Aye. Some men aren't ready to return to the life they knew. Perhaps they never will be. Some have gone back home and found either it or themselves sorely wanting. St. Judith's is a safe haven." Beattie looked over the notes with a rueful smile. "I think my young friend could do with a little instruction in keeping decent notes. No regiment listed, no dates of when the men were in action, no details other than a name and a date for the interview with the patient. And they call themselves research students." He shook his head at such sloppy scholarship. "But then, what can you expect from these people? This one took his degree at the college next to yours."

"Ah." No more needed to be said about academic falling short, not where *the college next door* was concerned. Orlando scanned the paper, quickly fixing his attention on the name

McNeil. *Lieutenant McNeil saw it happen, he did. He tried to stop it. He would have stopped it.* "Curious." He indicated the paragraph in question.

"Yes. It seems to be part of a stream of words, reported verbatim. Something similar occurs again, later."

Orlando continued to read, but the soldier—an officer's servant, called Wiggins—had changed tack, talking about keeping his officer's puttees clean and how it had been the hardest thing of all. When fighting the lice hadn't been the most challenging task, of course; the Germans seemed to come a poor third behind those two considerations. The rambling came back eventually to McNeil, although it didn't appear that he was the officer this man served directly. *Jones was lucky. He had a good man to attend to, in Lieutenant McNeil. He wouldn't have let it happen if he could. He tried but they wouldn't let him. On and on but it was no use. No use at all, you see.* The rambling turned to Wiggins's wounds; his leg had come a cropper and a bullet glancing along his head had made a depression in his skull, which he related with seeming relish. "Is there any more about McNeil?"

"I could only see the two references, but you might be more successful."

Orlando scanned the rest of the document, but the lieutenant's name didn't crop up again, nor anything which might have been an allusion to him. "No, there's no more. But this is a start, I suppose. Might I copy down the exact words?"

"Of course. I'll give you the student's name too, and you can ask him yourself."

"No." Orlando held up his pen in a gesture of refusal. "That won't be necessary. If I may, I'll make a note of the soldier's name and see if I would be allowed to talk to him directly. If not, I'll come back to you."

Beattie nodded. "Always go to the primary sources before the secondary ones. That's what I tell my students but they rarely listen." He stayed quiet while Orlando made his notes. "I saw the tribute to Dr. Stewart in the newspaper. It was last October, I believe?" Beattie proffered another cake, but Orlando's appetite failed him, no matter how attractive the pastries looked. The unexpected mention of his lover was enough to turn any man's stomach away from eating.

He slowly shut his notebook and put away his pen. "It was. He almost made it home, but not quite."

"There are plenty of good men didn't return, men for whom the end of the war came just a little too late. That October was as deadly as any month had been." Beattie cast a sideways glance, a wistful longing look at the officer's picture on his mantelpiece.

An old friend, then. Maybe more than a friend. Orlando kept his eyes fixed on his notes, not daring to catch Beattie's gaze, to risk feeling sorry for him, or some other strange and powerful emotion. He stood, abruptly. "Thank you. I can make a start now."

Beattie nodded. "Please feel free to return if there's anything further I can do. I'll tell Frogmore—my researcher—that he's been invaluable to you. The lad could do with some reassurance, even if he also needs a boot for his imprecision." He offered his hand to be shaken. Orlando eyed it warily, conscious that he must be looking an idiot for not simply obeying his reflexes and offering his own in return. After what must have seemed an age to his host, he shook hands and departed, highly aware of the feeling Beattie's fingers had made as they brushed his wrist, how strong his grip had been.

The walk back to Forsythia Cottage passed in a daze, thoughts scurrying around Orlando's brain like rats in a cage.

All Lessons Learned

The handshake—he'd try not to think of it again. And again. He was halfway back along the Madingley Road when he realised he'd left his post waiting at the Bride's porters' lodge. Well, it would have to wait until the Monday, now—he had other things to think about and not just the case of Daniel McNeil. Why on earth had he had to go and consult Beattie? Or, more to the point, why did Beattie have to have turned out to be so very attractive?

How could he go back to the cottage now and take a final look at Jonty's garden, as he did morning and evening, every day—how could he keep countenance with such a burden of guilt on his shoulders? Wasn't it bad enough that he'd survived while his lover hadn't? How could he betray him now by feeling attraction for another man—feel attraction for someone other than his Jonty for the first time in his life? He swept along the road in a cloud of anger leavened with despair, furious at his own weakness and frailty.

The last thing he did every night before retiring was to visit Jonty's study, a room which had been left—by instruction—just as it was when he'd last been in occupation. It was a command they'd laid on Mrs. Ward every time they'd left the cottage during the war years, even if it was just for the period they'd spent living and working in London. She was allowed to dust around things, or even under them, so long as she returned everything to exactly the place where it had originally stood. Orlando had only found out much later that Jonty had offered her the loan of a micrometer so that she could replace the Coppersmith oddments to within the nearest thirty-second of an inch.

How could he go and visit that study tonight and say good evening in his usual way? He determined to go home, have a cold shower and a pot of strong coffee and console himself with a nice book on Euclid before he'd even think about Daniel

McNeil. Or Beattie. The whole bloody thing was hopeless. *Find someone else to love?* He'd rather kill himself.

Chapter Seven

St. Judith's looked bleak and uninviting, especially in the fading light. Tall windows like blank eyes stared out at the road, eyes as blank as the ones Orlando was sure to see inside.

He should have waited until the next weekend, come in the bright and less depressing light of day, but he was driven now, driven to get closer to the solution of this mystery. And he'd have to be sharp about it, so he could get the train back to Cambridge and get his brain ready to tackle the dunderheads next day. Part of him kept asking why he had to be so precipitate—didn't he have all the time in the world to get to the bottom of this? If he ended up having to go wandering around France, wouldn't he have to wait until the summer?

And what bloody use would he be, anyway, trying to interview Wiggins if he couldn't even summon up the courage to get through the door? Orlando dithered by the hospital entrance, frightened that what he'd find inside would take his mind back to France, a place he wasn't ready to contemplate yet. Or perhaps frightened that what he found would set off a new train of thought which had dogged him these last few days, the uneasy sensation he kept putting to the back of his brain until he could think it through logically. If it was ignored for long enough it might go away.

But he'd made an appointment with the matron—and with

the doctor—to see Wiggins, and his innate courtesy and sense of fair play meant he couldn't leave them in the lurch. What would Jonty's mother have said about such discourtesy? She'd have had her almost-son-in-law's guts for garters just for contemplating such incivility. Orlando smiled, suddenly lighter in heart. He hadn't thought of Mrs. Stewart in that way since he'd heard of her death. Previous memories had been tinged with anguish, black clouds lodged in his consciousness. Such an unexpected gift, to be able to think of her with a wistful affection.

Eventually he summoned up enough courage to mount the steps, find the matron and plead his case. Miss Jacques wasn't quite what Orlando expected; her stern exterior wasn't matched by the twinkling glint in her eye. Funny how so many nurses seemed to be built on the scale of a battleship—Mrs. Hatfield at St. Bride's would have made three of the average nurse and that from her bosom alone—and this lady was no exception. She clearly ruled St. Judith's with an iron rod even if it was held in a warm velvet glove.

"Mr. Wiggins seems very popular with people from Cambridge." Matron led Orlando from her office, like a spaniel on a lead, along to the ward. "You'll be all doing research on him and his like, I suppose. To stop this happening the next time around."

"The next time?" Orlando passed a hand over his brow as they walked. "Please God we won't see the like."

Miss Jacques stopped momentarily and gave him an odd glance. The look seemed to say, "You may be very clever at Cambridge but you're not very *bright,* are you?" Her words merely said, "I agree with your intercession but perhaps it's slightly optimistic." They stopped at the ward door. "Please don't disturb Wiggins unduly. He's making progress—slowly, but it's still progress. I'd hate to see that jeopardised."

"I'll be gentle, I promise. It's not him I'm here about really and I wouldn't want you to think I've deluded you into believing that this is University business. I'm engaged in an enquiry for a client, concerning what happened to her son in France." Orlando tried to look contrite; he truly didn't want to appear a liar.

Miss Jacques suddenly laughed. "I'd already guessed that, young man. *Dr. Coppersmith.* Of course it has to be a case." She swung the door open, to find a calm and ordered ward. Perhaps it was always her way to stand by the door talking loudly so that the nurses and their less tidy patients would have time to make sure they weren't caught unduly unawares. "Dr. Coppersmith is here to see Mr. Wiggins, Nurse Barmby." She passed her guest into the care of a wiry, efficient-looking young lady. "See that he has all he needs but don't let him overtire the patient."

Before Orlando could make a proper expression of his gratitude or formulate the correct reply, Miss Jacques had turned on her heels and was off in search of her next task. "Miss Barmby?" He smiled in his most winning manner, was gratified to see the woman flush slightly and was quickly ushered to Wiggins's bedside. The man was sleeping, looking very young and vulnerable yet peaceful—giving rise in Orlando's mind to all manner of second thoughts. If this old soldier was finding some contentment in his sleep, why should *he* have any right to come along and shatter that peace with the sort of questions which would take him back to the source of his problems? "Perhaps I should wait awhile?"

"No. He'll enjoy talking to you. He likes visitors." It was as if the nurse was talking about an old man waiting in a nursing home, either for his grandchildren who never visited any more or death who would be paying a call all too soon. Wiggins appeared to be no more than thirty, if that. "Mr. Wiggins? You have someone to see you."

"Eh?" The patient's eyes shot open to reveal a piercing blue gaze. He seemed instantly awake, as Orlando had always heard old sailors were when the drums beat them to quarters in the middle of the night. Maybe some old soldiers had the same facility? "You must be the detective chappy." The accent wasn't what Orlando had expected—this was a well spoken man, whose innate breeding couldn't be hidden. What strange story lay behind Wiggins having ended up as an officer's servant?

"Not an official detective, Mr. Wiggins. Just helping out a friend of a friend." Orlando manoeuvred himself into the chair at the bedside. "You spoke recently to another friend of a friend, a Mr. Frogmore." Orlando stopped, bemused. When had Beattie gained the appellation *friend* in his mind? Perhaps it wasn't something he should consider too closely. "You were so kind as to tell him about Lieutenant McNeil. Daniel McNeil."

"Oh yes." Wiggins sat up in bed, arranging himself neatly on the pillows but clearly not neatly enough for Nurse Barmby's sharp eye. She twitched his sheet and blankets into order then, suddenly seeming to soften, offered them both a cup of tea. Wiggins's gaze followed her as she went off to the kitchen to produce the brew. The nurse was clearly an attractive woman, for those who liked such things. "He was a good man, a good officer."

Not just the man's class was a surprise; Wiggins seemed much more coherent and lucid than Orlando had expected. Perhaps this was a particularly good day to catch him. "He died in action, I believe?"

Wiggins shrugged. "So they say. He was a good man. He wouldn't have let it happen."

An echo of the words in Beattie's notes. "What wouldn't he have let happen?"

"Jones. If he could have done he'd have stopped it." Wiggins looked as if he was addressing a particularly dim seven-year-old. "No use, of course. They wouldn't change a damn thing no matter what he said. On and on and on."

Maybe this wasn't as lucid a day as Orlando had supposed; maybe there were no really lucid days for Wiggins any more. He just had to trust that the ramblings contained enough grains of truth. "I'm afraid I'm being rather obtuse about things, so you'll have to assist me with clarifying the facts. I've come across Jones's name before but I'm not aware of the whole story."

"Ah." Wiggins caught sight of Nurse Barmby returning—the pot must still have been pretty warm or the kettle almost on the boil—and gave his guest the sort of look which always meant *cave* at school. "Thank you, Nurse. Most kind." His manners clearly remained, or at least on Wiggins's better days. Once she was out of earshot, he continued. "Jones was McNeil's servant. They shot him. For desertion. Oh, steady on there."

"I'm sorry." Orlando steadied his shaking cup as it clattered in the saucer. Why was he so jumpy at the moment? "Jones deserted and was recaptured?"

"Indeed. Lieutenant McNeil tried to plead his case, arguing about all the pressure we were under. Poor Jones was barely more than a boy—we all suspected he'd lied about his age when he signed up. Such things he saw. Such things we all saw." Wiggins's eyes seemed focussed on events far away or long ago. "No use at all, you see."

"His arguments were no use?" Orlando kept his voice low and as reassuring as he could make it.

"Might as well have argued with the wind." Wiggins sipped his tea, back in the present. "It had to be done to discourage the rest from having the same idea or some such nonsense. Couldn't have us all casting aside our guns and going off."

"No." Orlando wasn't sure he could honestly comment. He wasn't sure how he felt about anything he'd seen or heard the last four years. "They shot this Jones lad?"

"Yes. He'd been taken off and court martialled, pretty perfunctorily I suspect, but we heard all about it when Lieutenant McNeil got back from trying to take his part." Wiggins drained his cup in a sudden movement, laying it on the bedside table with finality. "That was that."

"Had McNeil changed at all when he came back?"

"Gone potty, do you mean? I wouldn't put it in quite that way." Wiggins produced a lopsided, boyish smile.

"I wasn't aware I'd put it like anything." Orlando drew breath, surprised at how this conversation had progressed—certainly not as he'd anticipated it would. He'd expected to encounter what Frogmore had, a stream of words out of which he'd have to pick a rational trail. Instead he was part of a—mostly—coherent conversation but he wasn't sure how much of it was truth and how much fantasy. "I just wondered if he was different, perhaps more troubled."

Wiggins cocked his head to one side in a slightly exaggerated mime of thinking. It the same sort of gesture that Jonty had employed and cut his one-time lover to the quick. "Troubled? We were all troubled unless we were one of the lucky ones—already loopy. He couldn't stop it, you know, he tried but he couldn't. On and on and on he tried and on and on it went."

Orlando wasn't sure there was a lot else to be gained but he ploughed on. "Did you see what happened to Lieutenant McNeil? The day he was killed?"

"Oh, he wasn't killed." Wiggins's eyes were suddenly bright again, as if they only gained focus as he gained clarity. "No, no, you've been misled there."

Prickles of excitement nipped up Orlando's spine, as they

All Lessons Learned

always had when he and Jonty had been gaining ground in an investigation. Or when they'd been inching across the bedroom floor in each other's arms. "So what happened to him? I was told by his superior officer that he'd been killed in action—was he wrong?"

"Completely, old boy. I didn't see it myself but I was told." Wiggins nodded and fell silent.

"Told by Fred Giggs?" Orlando tried to nudge the patient into clarifying, if he could clarify, what he meant.

"Giggs?" Wiggins shook his head. "Not sure I know anyone called Fred Giggs. There was a lad at school called Billy Giggs, right little stinker he was. They caught him stealing apples and had him thrashed. Our house master was a good man. He tried to stop them but it was no use. The thrashing went on and on."

With a sinking heart, Orlando wondered how many other things in Wiggins's life had gone *on and on* despite someone *trying to stop them* and whether the whole story about McNeil and Jones was a variation on a recurrent and implausible theme. "So who told you about McNeil?" It had to be asked, even if he had little hope about getting a useful answer.

"Paddy Rice." Wiggins spoke with authority. "Little Paddy Rice from Dublin. He saw the whole thing, McNeil running out from the trees where he'd been hiding after his company came under fire. Turning tail like Jones had done. Perhaps he was trying to find Jones, but he was mistaken. It was too late by then as they'd already shot him." He nodded. "Unless he thought the other man *was* Jones, of course, and tried to get him away from the firing, but that's all speculation."

"Which other man?" Orlando could guess the answer.

"The man who went with McNeil, into the copse. Paddy Rice said he was called Eoin O'Leary. That's *E-O-I-N*, not *O-W-E-N*. They found him, later on, dead as a doornail." Wiggins shook his head. "The lieutenant couldn't stop that, either. O'Leary had been waving his gun around and making all sorts of threats. Anyway, Paddy Rice knew all about it and he told me."

So, even if he'd been dealing with O'Leary, McNeil wasn't killed when the wood was hit; all hope of a semi-honourable death seemed to have disappeared. "When was this?"

"When Lieutenant McNeil ran away from the front line." Wiggins looked disappointed at Orlando's evident mental sluggishness.

"No, I haven't made myself plain. When did Mr. Rice tell you?" If Paddy Rice was any more of a real person than Molly Malone, or whoever it was sold cockles and mussels in that song Jonty used to sing when in his cups.

"In the field hospital. We were both in with our feet. He'd lost one to a shell, quite gone." Wiggins indicated his own left leg. "Mine was just shattered a bit—still got it even though it's not much cop. Lieutenant McNeil..."

Luckily the story was interrupted by Nurse Barmby bustling over to say that an unexpected ward round seemed to be imminent and she'd have to break up their nice tête-à-tête. Orlando could hardly hide his relief, just in case he was about to find out that McNeil had tried to get the leg amputated *but they hadn't let him, so it had gone on and on*. He thanked both Wiggins and the nurse, then slipped out before matron could catch him. She'd had a peculiar look in her eye when they'd met and he wasn't going to risk finding out if it was either attraction or belligerence.

Orlando caught a cab straight outside the hospital—thank goodness they hadn't all changed into metal monsters yet, even if *he'd* swallowed his pride and learned to drive the ones which Jonty had bought. The latest in a line of several automobile monstrosities, each faster and more vile than all the rest, stood outside Forsythia cottage, infecting the place like a great wen or boil, and Orlando still wanted to kick it every time he passed. The sight of tanks had only confirmed him in his belief that if God had meant us to proceed in such a manner he'd never have given mankind anything so magnificent as a horse.

Paddy Rice was the next link in Orlando's chain. While the odds seemed to be stacking themselves in favour of McNeil having done a runner, one had to explore the possibility that he'd been initially trying to help another one of his men, as he'd tried to help Jones. Could O'Leary have taken fright and run into the woods and McNeil followed him? Or had McNeil drawn him away when he became a threat to his platoon—if the story of the gun waving could be verified. At least that would allow for an honourable initial motive and what happened next only Paddy Rice could clarify. Maybe he had something to add about the mysterious O'Leary, if only to make clear who led the way into the copse and who followed. And, if he confirmed that he'd seen McNeil leave the wood, maybe he could also supply the name of another observer along the trail. Would this be a case of tracking McNeil almost step by step, witness by witness along the way, if witnesses were still to be found?

As the train sped northwards out of smoky London into verdant Cambridgeshire, Orlando became more impatient. This couldn't wait until morning; he had Collingwood's number and would use it as soon as he was through his own front door. He could have found a telephone in London—that wasn't beyond the wit of any man, let alone *the* Dr. Coppersmith—but it wouldn't have felt right. A man rang from his own home or not at all.

He'd got his hand on the earpiece almost as soon as he'd got the door open, ignoring Mrs. Ward's offers of tea or coffee or a small sherry and a large cake. The delights of the table would have to wait, for once. It sounded as if he'd roused Collingwood out of his bed, but Orlando had no remorse—this business was on *his* behest, for goodness sake. He gave the name and as many details as he knew about Paddy Rice and asked to be contacted as soon as the solicitor had any information concerning the man's whereabouts or could confirm the story about Jones deserting and being shot.

One day later he was, if not pleased, then at least satisfied to be told McNeil *had* possessed a servant called Jones, and that the man had indeed deserted and been shot, despite his Lieutenant interceding on his behalf.

Two days later, Orlando's plans were in disarray—he couldn't interview Rice because the man was dead, his wound having turned gangrenous probably just days after he'd spoken to Wiggins. The trail of witnesses had fizzled out, so where next? Logically it was down to London to see Mrs. McNeil or back to Ascension to talk to Dr. Beattie. Neither seemed a particularly appealing prospect.

Chapter Eight

Cesario had almost begun to think of Cabourg as home, if he could ever think of anywhere with that degree of reassurance. He'd moved out of the hotel, for the first time in months finding the impersonality of such a place uncomfortable. He'd found a little pension with a nice landlady to fuss over him maternally and Lamboley had followed suit, pleading a lack of the necessary funds to continue too long with the high life. Whether that was the truth or a harmless necessary lie, who could tell, but Cesario was pleased to have his new friend close at hand, especially as the nightmares wouldn't go, even if the shakes had given him respite and he'd not had to take to his bed again.

Life had fallen into a gentle routine, Lamboley sketching and painting, selling the profits of his labours to a little gallery which specialised in providing such things for tourists. It was hardly the quality of art that would warrant exhibition at the Louvre, but it did well enough for the better end of the seaside trade. Cesario himself had no need to work—he'd managed to support himself well, if through labyrinthine channels— although he'd done a little tutoring of children along his travels, simply to stave off boredom. At Cabourg he'd easily found a wealthy family who were grateful to have someone to develop their sons' use of the English language and improve their appreciation of history.

As a means of existence went, it was more pleasant than the last few years had been, if it lacked the contentment he'd had before he'd enlisted. That was another world, now, far away and almost dream-like in its quality. And like a dream loses its lucidity in the act of waking, so those pre-enlistment years had lost their clarity and focus. The happiness he'd known had certainly become intangible; almost impossible to remember what it had actually been like, how sweet life had been.

He wasn't totally inured to the possibility of life being sweet again, of finding a companion to walk the days and years with, to share a bed with on warm summer evenings or dark and cold winter nights. Lamboley was an agreeable enough friend but, even though Cesario found him attractive, he wasn't sure there'd be any reciprocation of feelings. And yet, and yet...he was lonely, God knew he was lonely and any port might be the place to shelter from a storm of solitude.

He'd woken this morning full of something that might almost be hope, the bright sunshine lifting his spirits, and resolute that he'd have the matter clarified. For his own peace of mind, while the attraction was still controllable and could be moulded into a strong feeling of friendship if love wasn't an option.

They met over breakfast, eating almost in silence in the pension's little dining room, basking in the slanted rays of the morning sun, two strangers who'd found almost by chance a companionship and understanding. Cesario glanced sidelong at Lamboley, feeling a sudden pang of guilt at the pull on his heart—a pull he'd not felt in a long while. A small thread of magnetism drawing him closer and saying, "Why not? I have no ties now." The existence of some similar barrier to Lamboley's old life—to the lives they'd both left behind—was apparent not just in what they'd discussed but in what they'd always left unsaid since they'd met. Questions about family, loved ones,

All Lessons Learned

the bricks and mortar of ordinary conversation, had been noticeably ignored in favour of memories of the war or university days. Perhaps the time had come to rectify that.

Cesario suddenly shivered, not sure he really was ready to commit himself again, to be tied in bonds of love and risk having them rent apart and his heart with it. He'd always vowed that, if anything happened to his lover, then he would give his heart again; it had been fine as a concept, so easy to make promises to himself as he'd marched away—sheer bravado. He caught Lamboley smiling at him and returned the look, unsure. "I have been meaning to ask you something, but the time has never seemed right. Not to be so forward."

"You sound like my maiden aunt. What's brought on this burst of timidity?" Lamboley refilled his friend's cup, the pungent aroma of coffee hanging in the air between them.

"Nothing more than my English reserve. Because you haven't spoken of something, I've wondered whether it's appropriate even to broach the subject." Cesario laughed. "Now I sound like *my* maiden great-aunt. I wanted to ask if you had a young lady waiting for you, at home? I believe in England young men are in such short supply that the stallions all have their pick of the mares. Tattersalls and a buyers' market, if one can be so crude." He stopped, aware that his nerves were making his tongue run on ahead of both his brain and his discretion.

"There was a young lady." Lamboley replied naturally, clearly not offended at the personal nature of the enquiry even if his eyes registered that it caused him some pain. "She and her sister were both taken by pneumonia last year, following the influenza. Within hours of each other, I believe, although I didn't know until it was too late even to ask for compassionate leave, should it have been granted."

"I'm sorry." Not just for the loss; the answer had probably

nipped any of Cesario's hopes in the bud. Perhaps it was as well—maybe this wasn't really what he wanted and he'd have turned from it tomorrow, sickened at his own weakness at grabbing the first opportunity without due consideration. "It's hard enough to bear when you lose someone close and you're at hand. To have been so far away—it makes one feel helpless."

"There is nothing I could have done, near at hand or far off, to affect the outcome." Lamboley laid down his cup and peered through the window out into the garden. "But I could have been there to say goodbye."

"Aye." How many men had made similar remarks since 1914? How many more wives, mothers, daughters felt the same way—too far away to have made a difference, to have performed the offices they would have performed had death come quietly, decently, at home. "Will you take a walk in the garden before you start your work? It seems too fine a morning to waste."

They strolled past flower beds which were just beginning to hint at the summer glories to come, stopping to sit on a rustic wooden bench, the seat already warm from the sunshine.

"As you've asked me your question, allow me to ask you mine. How long will you stay here?" Lamboley produced his cigarette case, offering one to Cesario who graciously refused, producing a small cigar of his own. They lit them within cupped hands, a soft breeze having sprung up to caress the little patch of green.

"I have no idea. Until I know when to go." It sounded stupid, although it made entire sense to Cesario. He'd been drawn here, in search of something, and couldn't leave until he could be sure if he'd found it or not. For fleeting moments the last few days he'd been wondering whether the man he was sitting next to had been the end of his quest. Clearly not. "That probably makes no sense."

"No, I understand. For me it is the same. When I've found peace I can go home. Maybe I will find it in Cabourg or perhaps I'll have to travel further. God alone knows." Lamboley tapped the side of his head. "It's in here, of course, peace. Happiness or sadness, joy or despair, they aren't just about where a man is or what happens to him. He carries them around with him all the time."

"You're preaching to the converted there. It's something I've always believed, that we carry our own fortunes with us." He'd found that at the front, of course. The mud and death and misery couldn't penetrate past the walls of your working mind and into your consciousness—unless you let it do so. He'd controlled his feelings well in the trenches, even found moments of joy, like when his mother's letters had arrived and he'd pored over them, devouring every word like it was ambrosia. "If *I'm* to find peace, perhaps I'm looking in the wrong place. I should turn in, not out." Cesario took a long pull on his cigar.

"And is it peace you're looking for?"

"I wish to God I knew."

By evening the sun had disappeared and heavy clouds were scudding in from the sea on a fierce westerly wind. They'd arranged to eat at a restaurant, honouring Lamboley's sale of a half a dozen watercolours at an exorbitant price to a couple from Paris who'd been to Cabourg on honeymoon many years ago. Cesario was in a good mood too, having taught his three young charges to recite—perfectly if a little perfidiously—the St. Crispin's day speech from Henry V. If there was any argument from their parents he'd pass it off as an appropriate introduction to one of the most glorious exponents of the English language—surely no one could argue with him teaching

Shakespeare so long as it wasn't anything bawdy?

They scurried along from the pension, umbrellas in hand but hoping not to use them in such blustery conditions, rushing through the door of the restaurant just as the first fat drops of rain began to fall. They found a table and ordered a carafe of wine to fortify themselves. The sky darkened as suddenly as if its light had been extinguished with a snuffer and the candles on the table fought bravely to provide a cheery illumination. They chose seafood—whatever the best catch had been today—and raised a glass in anticipation of the delights to come. They'd eaten here before and the mussels had been astounding.

Cesario didn't want to deal with pleasantries and chit-chat. Maybe the feeling of being in a safe haven as a storm worked up steam outside helped to focus his mood and give him the courage to talk about private matters again. "We spoke this morning about only returning home when the time is right. What if it never is?"

Lamboley shrugged. "Then I stay here or move on again. I think if I learned anything these last few years it's not to plan too much for tomorrow." He sipped his wine, keeping his gaze fixed on the rain lashing the pavement. "Do you think it possible you might not ever return home?"

It was Cesario's turn to shrug—the gesture had become more expressively Gallic as the months of his self-imposed exile moved on. He deflected the question. "I've never really established where home is, for you. Not all accents sound the same to John Bull's cauliflower ear, and I can tell you're no Norman." Cesario knew what kept *him* here, but in Lamboley's case was it grief for his girlfriend, wanderlust or some other equally strong force separating him from the world he'd once known and keeping him from the peace he sought?

"I was born not far from Toulouse. Sometimes this coast feels as foreign a place as England did." Lamboley smiled and raised his cup. "Except at least they can make good coffee here—morning, noon and night. That skill doesn't seem to have crossed the Channel."

"You can find a decent brew in certain pockets but they're few and far between." He couldn't pussy foot around like this forever—Cesario had come here to get away from stress, to ease the tensions of the burdens borne. "But even the promise of good coffee, or a great steaming pot of tea, couldn't get me back there. There's nothing at home for me, any more. No," Cesario corrected himself, "not quite. I should say that what, or who, is there might not welcome me. Not now."

"I'm sorry." Lamboley spoke as if he meant every word, that he wasn't spouting the platitudes any stranger might produce. "The old soldier returning home isn't always greeted with flowers and kisses. The lady who said she would always wait has lost patience and has another man's ring on her finger or his babe in her arms."

Cesario nodded. Best to let his friend think that might be the root of the issue; it would save future questioning. "Sometimes one has worse things to face than another man's gun."

Lamboley's long, expressive hands produced an eloquent gesture of letting something precious go. "I understand, truly. Sometimes it is worse to be faced with having to explain, to grieve all over again when one has played one's grief out already. Letters aren't quite as painful as conversations."

"That's just it." Cesario turned to the window, looking out at the lowering clouds which had hastened the sunset and brought the tempest. God help all sailors out this night. God help all old soldiers while He was about it. "I don't think I've even written home since..." He tried to remember the last time he'd put pen to paper. He was sitting on top of a broken gun carriage, somewhere outside...somewhere. Funny how he could recall the scene so clearly, the smell of smoke and horse dung in the air, his company resting in a nearby field. And him—trying to make his words sound brave and cheerful when he was already crumbling inside. "Not since last September." He said no more.

"It seems so long since I walked under the trees with a pretty girl." Lamboley sighed, flexing his long fingers where a prolonged bout of sketching had tired them. He wasn't wrong in thinking the loss of a loved one lay at the bottom of Cesario's problems, even if he'd assumed—as most men might—the wrong sex. "Those days with Bernadette seem like a dream. Or a passage I read in a book."

"Or something which happened to someone else." Cesario's happy times certainly seemed like another lifetime—or another person's lifetime—ago. "Some days I believe it might never happen again. Not to me, at least. Will you find another pretty girl to press hands with under the cypresses?"

Lamboley turned to the window again. Lightning was rending the sky, far out at sea and maybe as far as the coast of England. "Who knows? I'm not a monk and no matter how much my heart aches for Bernadette now, I can't envisage committing myself to a life entirely without certain pleasures. I denied myself during the war, which is more than some men did. Then I had reason to do so. Now..." He shrugged again.

"Aye." They were still relatively young, the pair of them. Certainly too young to make such rash promises. So what was left for them if they didn't give their hearts? Some fumbling with a willing and agreeable party, someone equally adrift and bereft? A night of something that pretended to be happiness, followed by awkward silences over the breakfast table? Or something less socially awkward, a matter of monetary exchange, buying and selling a service rather than pretending it was anything more? It would be simple and uncomplicated but Cesario's heart wasn't in that as yet, either—he'd never been inclined to pay for pleasures in the past. "A man's a man for all that."

Lamboley turned to face his friend, a serious look in his eyes, much more grave than when he spoke of fighting. Perhaps love was more important than war, after all. "There is a lovely girl here, I see her every morning as I go out to make the most of the light. She is staying in a little villa, with her mother, I believe…" Lamboley waxed lyrical about her beauty, her exquisite dark eyes and hair, the pallor of her smooth skin, but Cesario only listened with half an ear. He didn't want to hear the virtues of any girl espoused—he had no fundamental interest except as it concerned the happiness of a friend. Girls were nice but he preferred a harsher skin and a deeper voice. Dark eyes and hair he could appreciate, though—he'd always preferred his men along those lines.

"Have you spoken to her?" It seemed easiest and safest to ask the simple questions which oiled the wheels of conversation. Who, what, where, when? He could half take in the replies and let his mind drift back to his own affairs. He'd not been tempted in the front line—he wouldn't have been, his lover was still alive then and his eye wasn't ready to rove. Of course there'd been handsome faces to admire, as a woman who was watching her weight might admire a cream cake in the patisserie window; she wouldn't necessarily buy it nor eat it and he hadn't been inclined to indulge, either.

"We pass the time of day. Once she seemed upset but she didn't say why and I couldn't ask her. Madame DesRues was more forthcoming."

"That wouldn't surprise me." Their landlady served what

must have been the best omelettes in the whole of Normandy, if not France, and her skill with the frying pan was matched by her ability to know the goings-on of every family in the town.

"Mademoiselle Celeste had a brother. He was shot for cowardice in 1917. The family told everyone that he died of wounds."

"Good God. I..." Cesario stopped and leaned back, allowing the waiter to lay the steaming plates before them. The food looked good but suddenly his appetite was found wanting. "I'm so sorry for her, for them. Clearly they didn't tell that story to Madame DesRues."

"I think she has some sort of espionage network." Lamboley scooped up a forkful of peas. "It's something I find hard to swallow. How men could fail to do their duty while others risked their lives."

Cesario bit his tongue, the words resonating for a number of reasons. He'd encountered this attitude before, usually among men he didn't respect, and it hurt to hear it coming from the mouth of someone he'd built up affection for. When he did speak, his voice was quiet and as piercing as an assassin's knife. "No one can see the workings of another man's heart or live in another man's mind. I've never sought to judge them, the deserters and the objectors."

"I..." Lamboley began to speak, stopped himself then laid down his fork. "I'm sorry, this clearly touches on your experience. You knew someone in the same case as Mademoiselle Celeste's brother?"

Cesario nodded; he pushed his plate away, barely touched. "One of the men in my platoon. He was at the very end of what he could take—a good man, a good soldier up until that point. He didn't deserve the death he found but I couldn't save him."

Lamboley's voice was soft, consoling. "Is it at all possible that the example made of him stopped others going the same way?"

"Eh?" Cesario ran his hand through his hair. He'd found grey threads there today, the first he'd ever encountered; another souvenir of the war, like the scar on his cheek. "Ah yes, the taking of a life to discourage the rest. Maybe it worked. Or else why didn't more men of good conscience and sound mind stand up and say, 'enough is enough'?"

"Even I might not have blamed them for that last spring, when the Germans ran us backwards." Lamboley pushed his plate away too, earning them a hurried visit from the waiter. *Was the fish not to their liking? Shall I speak to the chef?* They reassured him that the fault lay with themselves and not the food. Perhaps if he came back later they might like to try a dessert. Once he was safely out of earshot, Lamboley resumed. "Maybe it took more courage to run and try to speak out than to stay and just accept. Not long ago I saw an ex-soldier, I believe he may have been British, on his knees in the church at Trouville, breaking his heart because he'd not been able to save his men."

"None of us managed to save all our men." Cesario shivered. "Plenty of us bear that burden."

"He seemed less concerned about all than about one or two in particular. I wasn't eavesdropping on private grief, believe me. He spoke loudly enough for anyone to hear." Lamboley refilled their glasses; at least they could appreciate the last of the wine. "I came away—and I left as soon as I decently could— with the impression that he'd seen two of his men shot, for cowardice or desertion or something similar. And that he felt it had been his hand on the trigger."

"Extraordinary." The evening had been pleasantly mild but something—the rain or the turn of conversation—had made it feel cold now. "Did you try to get help for him?" It wasn't the thought at the top of Cesario's mind, but it served as a conversational place saver.

"I suppose I could have done—some people might say I had a duty to—but I didn't. Who would I have taken him to, anyway? He wasn't French and I wasn't going to pack him onto a ferry and send him across the Channel." Lamboley shrugged and Cesario was, for the first time, pleased that their relationship had stayed on a purely friendly footing. That shrug could become distinctly annoying with time. "Perhaps France and Belgium are full of men weeping over their guilt in church pews. Or maybe hiding on farms, the ones who saw their chance and slipped away—although I find it hard to believe that they escaped the net."

"I know of at least one man who may have walked away and wasn't caught." The words were painful to speak, like acid in Cesario's mouth; he'd not confessed this to anyone.

"He was lucky, then."

"The devil's luck or God's angels guiding him? Who knows?" Cesario caressed his glass, choosing his words carefully. "It was a moment of chaos—there were plenty of them—and it was assumed he was killed."

"And you know he wasn't?" If Lamboley thought Cesario might be referring to himself he gave no indication. Let the man think what he wished—Cesario wasn't ready to expose all his soul just yet.

"Certain sure." He took a drink of wine and laid down the glass with care. "And I knew others so close to the brink that the slightest breath might have toppled them. I should have reported them to my lieutenant colonel—I probably betrayed my duty as an officer, but I couldn't betray my duty as a man. Not at the time."

"How many of us ever balanced those two sides of the equation?" Lamboley's gaze stayed fixed on his own glass, as if it held the secret to how a man might serve his country, his God and his fellow man with honour, all three.

"Not as many who believed they did." Cesario caressed his glass again, aware of the slight tremor in his fingers. Whether it was the storm, or the unpleasant memories acting as a catalyst, he couldn't tell. Please God he wasn't going to have another attack. "If there's a let-up in the rain I think we should take the opportunity to walk back. I'd hate to get soaked."

Lamboley motioned for the waiter to bring the bill. "Not after your bout of the flu. You've hardly had time to recover from it."

They paid, lingering over the last dregs of the wine while the rain petered out. The lull in the storm was long enough for them to get back and for Cesario to reach his bed, but it wasn't guns he heard among the thunder when it returned. All the unpleasant memories of his life were playing out, ones he'd thought were long dealt with, recovered from and forgotten. If he'd been drawn to Cabourg to find peace, it was continuing to elude him.

Chapter Nine

A visit to Ascension was the lesser of two evils. Better to face Beattie; at least then Orlando could keep his feelings under control with the sort of iron will he'd employed in the front line, those nights he'd been yearning for Jonty and had wanted to call out for him in the darkness. Certainly it would be easier to employ self control than have to face up to a loving mother and say, "It seems quite likely that your son ran away." He imagined someone saying such a thing to Mrs. Stewart—it would have been slanderous, of course, but some swine might have whispered it from spite and the speaker would have been laid out by one great blow of fist or handbag. Orlando would make sure he was well out of Mrs. McNeil's reach when he spoke his piece.

He decided to cycle, enjoying the hint of warmth in the air as he took the long way round from Bride's. Across the backs to Grange Road, right the way up to the bridge, down past the Bishop's Cope and along the little back road to Ascension. He made a point of chaining his bike to the railings, securely padlocking it as you couldn't be too sure what the students were like at this place. If they were anything like the ones at *the college next door* then perhaps he needed to chain and padlock his trousers to his legs while he was at it.

Beattie was in his room, waiting, and appeared delighted to

find Orlando when he opened the door to his knock. "Dr. Coppersmith. This is splendid. Would it be too early for a sherry?"

Jonty's voice, the one which hadn't spoken to Orlando quite so often these last few days—not since he'd taken on the McNeil case—said it was never too early for sherry and that to refuse would be insulting. "That would be most welcome, thank you. There should be ample time for both a sherry and this business before I have to get back for hall."

Beattie smiled, pouring out the perfect quantity of what was clearly a superior vintage into an elegant crystal glass. "I got your message very quickly, not like the usual labyrinthine and laborious lines of communication. The innovation of having a telephone in the porters' lodge has put a real spark into them."

"Bride's had one years ago." Orlando couldn't resist a little pride in his college. "We had it before St. John's did, I believe." He was surprised that Ascension wasn't still employing papyrus to convey its messages on.

"Well, where Bride's leads, we should follow. Maybe we'll have our Sherlock Holmes yet." Beattie handed Orlando a glass then lifted his own. "Your good health."

They drank the toast like old associates, too much so for Orlando's liking. He kept the conversation on business. "Wiggins was...interesting. I think I've picked out the truth from the fantasy but I'm not sure I'm any further forward." He told the tale of Wiggins, Eoin O'Leary, "that's *EOIN*, or so Wiggins was at pains to point out," and the elusive and now late, lamented Paddy Rice.

Beattie nodded. "And how can I help you with this trail that's fizzled out?"

Orlando would have shrugged, but that was vaguely

impolite in the circumstances. Too familiar a gesture. If this had been Jonty's study, Jonty's sherry, they could have talked the details through and Jonty would have made some insightful comment, inspiring them to find either a solution or a route to it. "Can you find me a needle in a haystack?" That's what it seemed like. Finding one small man in the expanse of the continent. "All I know is that McNeil was never caught, unless he was found using another name, then shot and buried with it. If we assume he's alive then how on earth can I locate him? I'm presuming he hasn't returned home as that would risk exposure and disgrace."

"You've presumed? Isn't that a risky strategy for a mathematician to employ? Don't you always deal in absolute facts?" Beattie smiled again, offering a top up of sherry, which was politely refused with a groan; this was all getting too near the truth.

"I wish I could deal in facts. I'd give half my kingdom for some solid, decent leads, some way to start along the trail."

"You have a kingdom to divide, then?"

"Not quite, but let's say half my chair in the Senior..." Orlando stopped, feeling the blood rushing up across his cheeks. That chair, its significance—how could he have made game about it with a stranger? He had to focus on the case, or else he'd be betraying Jonty as much as his country had betrayed the man. "I digress, I'm sorry." He pulled himself up in his seat, his body assuming a formal stiffness. "I have no facts, nothing I know for sure except that Daniel McNeil left the wood where he'd first hidden."

"Isn't the key question whether he was following or leading the other soldier?"

"If it is, it remains unanswerable. Even if he went to help O'Leary, or draw him away from where he was causing danger to the rest of his men, he didn't return to his platoon when the man was killed."

"Is that what you'll tell his mother?" Beattie may not have had Jonty's acuity but he'd hit the nail on the head.

"I'll paint it all in the best possible light, but in the end..." In the end it all smacked of desertion and Mrs. McNeil was no fool. "Here's a question for you, Dr. Beattie, almost unanswerable but I'll ask you it just the same. Where might a man go at such a time of duress? Is there some sort of pattern of behaviour he might follow?" It was a long shot but those had been profitable in the past. One had paid off in this very room when it had provided the name of Wiggins.

"I wish I could say for certain. Anywhere he could hide would be the logical answer—it would appear that the rational thing would be to return to where one felt safe, but among families and friends would be the first place the authorities would look, wouldn't it?" Beattie ran his hand along his jaw in thought. "And if this Wilson-Gore chap had his suspicions, then McNeil wouldn't risk suddenly appearing and saying 'sorry, it was all a case of mistaken identity, I was in hospital, suffering memory loss' or some such twaddle."

Orlando sat up even more rigidly. "Some of us did suffer memory loss, sir—not everyone faked such things."

"I'm so sorry. I didn't realise." Beattie's face had paled, genuine contrition written all over it. He hung his head, hands between his legs like some errant schoolboy—Orlando found himself touched despite all his misgivings.

"No, I should be the one to apologise for snapping—you weren't to know and too often people *have* put a convenient medical label on things which didn't deserve it." Orlando held out his glass. "Am I too tardy or too far in the doghouse to belatedly accept your offer?"

"Of course not, on either count." Beattie leapt from his chair to fetch the decanter. "And you're absolutely right, you know. If there's one thing I've learned these last few months it's been that 'neurasthenia' is a nice convenient catch-all term. And that what might be called neurasthenia in a captain from Westminster might well be called cowardice in a private from Leeds." He topped his own glass up and they drank in silence, in thoughts of officers they'd known and ordinary Tommy Atkins types who'd been twice the men their superiors were. And vice versa. "And the thought anyone could have made their way home—if there was any welcome to return to—does seem beyond belief. Although who's to say it hasn't happened? Like the old question about who should get the title of the cleverest murderer in history. How could we ever know, as he or she would have been too intelligent to be caught?" Beattie stayed on his feet, looking out into the court and smiling at something he'd seen there. "Can you honestly say your man couldn't have returned home?"

"Clearly not as..." Orlando stopped, suddenly turning the case on its head as he and Jonty had done many a time before. "Ah. You mean some elaborate double bluff? His mother knows he's deserted and is trying to deflect attention by starting up an enquiry, knowing full well I won't succeed in finding him."

"I could imagine such a case. People will do all sorts of things in extremis." Beattie kept his gaze fixed on the court and whatever fascinating things were occurring there.

Orlando thought for a long moment, then shook his head. "No. Unless Mrs. McNeil is the best actress I've had the privilege to see perform. She's genuinely distressed."

"So we'll assume her son didn't come home." Beattie turned, staring at his desk and still not at his visitor. "And if he stayed in France or slipped into another country, there would be no family there unless he'd holed up with some lady who was free with her favours. Or a family who took pity on someone who seemed to them no more than a boy. A substitute for and remembrance of their own son, perhaps."

Orlando shrugged. "Maybe. Or he's living rough. Or working on a farm. Perhaps men are in as short supply there as they are here and an extra pair of hands is always welcome." An extra man to warm the bed as well, he thought but didn't say. "There are many farms in France, and vineyards and orchards. We're no further forward."

"If I were in your shoes, I would look for somewhere he was happy. Any man might seek comfort after those bleak days. You say he went to France as a child, on family holidays?" Beattie suddenly turned the full force of his stunningly handsome smile on his guest, almost winding him in the process. "Find out the places they went to where he was most content, where he might find most consolation. It *is* like finding a needle in a haystack, but at least you can try the most likely stack first."

It made sense and Mrs. McNeil would be able to guide him with names—not just locations, but favourite hotels, beaches, nooks and crannies. Just as Mrs. Stewart could have pinpointed to the exact inch where her youngest son had passed his happiest hours. Outside of Orlando's bed, of course. "So be it. I'll take my courage in both hands and hope that I don't drop my intellectual faculties in the process." Orlando rose, immediately stayed by his host raising an elegant hand.

"Will you not stay awhile and talk? It must be a good quarter of an hour before you need to leave."

Orlando sat again, uncertain of what he wanted to do. The room felt uncommonly hot, or perhaps that was just the effect of his collar, his neck sweltering like it was ablaze. He remembered this disoriented sensation, he'd been acquainted with it when first he met Jonty; he wasn't sure he wanted to feel it again. Beattie had taken the seat opposite, his face more handsome, now that the sherry had worked its strange enchantment on Orlando's perception, than when he'd been cold sober. The man's initials were G.S., or so the board at the bottom of the stairs had said. George Beattie? Geraint?

Whatever it was, it wasn't Jonty. Orlando would never address anyone by that blessed name again, even if Lavinia and Ralph had a third child and called it after its dear departed uncle. George or Gerald, or whoever Beattie was, was talking—had been talking a while. "I'm sorry, could you say that last part again? I was miles away."

"I was thinking about you facing Mrs. McNeil and pondering on the nature of courage. You and I were both on the front line—could you define valour except in terms of what men did or didn't do?" Beattie passed his hand over suddenly weary eyes. "I have a story I heard. I wish to share with you as it seems pertinent in some way to your case, although I'm not sure how. It's about a man who deserted—or perhaps he deserted, there's another word to define—not from the front but from the train home to England. He'd got a 'Blighty one' but he never got home to have it treated."

"I don't follow."

"It's an odd story. That October, that blighted October." Beattie stole a quick glance at the picture of the officer which graced his mantelpiece. "This soldier, Beaumont, got separated from his platoon, from his whole company. Fell in, with his pack, with the first regiment he came across, saying he'd return to his own regiment when things were quieter. *There's work still to be done and I'm not bothered who I help do it.* They came across a platoon of German soldiers attacking a group of Tommies and this chap absolutely set amongst them—fought like a madman, driving them back almost single handed. He got himself a ruddy great cut to his cheek—almost to the bone—but it didn't stop him helping the injured back to our lines, almost carrying one poor lad who'd been hit in the legs. Then this Beaumont just passed out, totally what my little nephew would call sparko."

Orlando remembered waking in the German hospital, very frightened and very confused. Sparko indeed. "I hope he got the commendation he was due."

"He did that. They patched him up, said they'd recommend him for the Military Medal and packed him off home. Somewhere en route to the coast he went walkabout." Beattie spread his hands. "It's hardly like he deserted, is it? In the event. He wouldn't have been returned to the front even if it wasn't a bad enough wound to keep him out of action. Not with the timing."

"He wouldn't necessarily have known that." This diversion just added another layer to the confusion Orlando suffered. "Something made him go." As *he* wished to go, out into the fresh air where a man could think clearly and get his facts straight. Where he wasn't tempted to ask anyone what their Christian name was and have to reveal his own. "Who knows what motivates another man to do anything?" He leapt to his feet again. "I must go. I have to talk to Dr. Panesar about...about Italy."

"Italy?" Beattie evidently could see straight through the hastily improvised lie.

"Yes." Orlando carried on with what Jonty used to call social excavation. "The Coppersmiths hailed from there, hundreds of years ago." He stopped, furious at how he kept revealing more than he'd intended. He needed to leave right now, but Beattie was effectively blocking his path to the door.

"I'm very fond of Italy. Have you ever been there?"

"Yes. In search of family history." Orlando suddenly

remembered walking through olive groves with Jonty, shafts of bright sunlight crowning his hair with an aureole of gold. It had brought out the olive tones in his own skin, or so Jonty had always assured him, making such fun of the Mediterranean streak in his blood that neither of them had known about until he'd gone thirty.

Well I'm blowed. I always fancied having a continental lover and then I find I've had one all this time. Bellissimo Orlando, caro mio. The words rang clear, stinging even at a distance of over a decade. Orlando had hushed him at the time, of course, embarrassed even though they'd been lovers for three years. He'd been equally embarrassed to hear Jonty speak soft Italian words to him under the olive trees when they'd been lovers for nearer five.

"I've never been." Beattie was speaking again, intruding on private joys and griefs. "I had great plans for travelling but they were rather curtailed, as you can appreciate. And it's never the same without the right companion at your side."

A horribly treacherous voice—maybe it was the sherry, it certainly wasn't his own idea—within Orlando tried to make him say, "We could go together. I could show you where the Coppersmiths, the Artigiano del Rames, came from." He ignored it, ignoring also the other voice—definitely Jonty's—which said, "You should take your chance before you have it snatched away. It may not be a sniper's bullet but it could be a runaway horse on the Madingley Road and you'd be just as dead, you know. Seize the day." He mumbled something about, "Yes, it's as well not to travel alone," and hoped Beattie would let him go. Or at least change the subject.

"Maybe we should..." But whatever it was Beattie was going to suggest they should, a knock on the door brought the suggestion to an end and let Orlando escape. He almost hugged the petrified little student who stood outside the door, an essay clutched in his hands, but decided against it, not just on grounds of propriety. What might you catch from a dunderhead, especially one from Ascension? By the time he'd got to the porters' lodge and secured his exit from the college he'd almost stopped shaking.

He got his thoughts back on the case, wondering if the story of the soldier who'd half run could possibly be that of McNeil, but that seemed too farfetched. Nice thought, though, to be able to tell his mother that he'd turned out a hero, or at least mostly a hero, in the end. Nice thought but unlikely to be utilised. Although, try as he might to focus on the case, the uneasy feeling about Beattie, the one he was desperately trying to subdue, lingered until he was in college and had his nose in a nice, safe book on integral calculus.

Friday afternoon, as soon as he could get away from Cambridge, Orlando was on the train to London, anticipating the second disagreeable visit on his agenda.

Mrs. McNeil's house wasn't quite as fine as her cousin's had been, but it was pleasant enough and beautifully maintained. The front garden was as neat as several new pins, the hedge was elegantly cut and the paintwork on the windows was fresh. The domestic staff—or the tradesmen employed to do the same job—must be solid and workmanlike. Or perhaps there was a Mr. McNeil who was in charge of such things. Maybe retired and turning his hand to things domestic just as Mr. Stewart had occasionally turned his hands to things which were technically far below the station of a Lord, even one who refused to use the title.

Strange how Mrs. McNeil had never mentioned a husband or a father for Daniel. There'd been one in Wilson-Gore's photograph, Orlando remembered—although he couldn't bring the man's face to mind. Not a striking visage or one to linger in the memory was all he recalled—and maybe the man was gone now too, as other males of the family had departed.

He knocked at the door, was answered by what looked like a gentleman's gentleman, and shown to the drawing room. The family was a little later than anticipated finishing dinner, or so he was informed, and Mrs. McNeil apologised for keeping him waiting. She would join him soon and in the interim would he like a drink? He accepted the apology and the offer of a coffee if that were available, although he held out no great hopes for its quality—a misgiving he hoped his tone of voice didn't reveal to the man who went off to get it.

The evening sunlight slanted through the windows in such a way that Orlando tried to work out whether the whole house had been designed and aligned to capture the rays at a perfect angle. While the mathematical part of his brain made tentative calculations and formed cautious theories about the optimum time of the year to be in this room, the detective portion was more concerned with the feeling it evoked. Time standing still, a picture frozen in time, as if the room were rarely used although kept immaculately clean. Like *his* study had been while he'd been away—and like Jonty's was now. Had this been Daniel McNeil's favourite part of the house?

"Dr. Coppersmith, I'm so sorry to have kept you waiting." Mrs. McNeil entered, wearing a smile—a brave smile, the sort that mothers and sweethearts had worn all those middle years of the decade, seeing off their lads on draughty stations or standing at their gravesides, those who had proper graves to stand beside.

"Entirely my fault, ma'am. I believe I was early." He wasn't, but it seemed a gracious way out of the situation. His hostess looked drawn, perhaps dreading this meeting as much as he'd been. "It's good of you to consent to answering my questions." They both sat again.

All Lessons Learned

"Good of me? I hardly think so. I was the one who commissioned you—of course I'll answer your questions. Ah, thank you, Mary." A servant, perhaps the parlour maid, had sidled in bearing a tray, as silently as a ghost; Mrs. McNeil indicated that she might go, leaving her mistress to pour from the coffee pot.

Orlando caught the look in the girl's eye as she left. Worry? Awe? Certainly a sign that something out of the ordinary was going on, or maybe a significant event had occurred. The use of this room, perhaps? "What I ask may seem odd to you and I fear it will be indicative of the direction my enquiries are taking." Orlando heard the long words rolling out of his mouth and could guess what Jonty would have said if he'd been there to hear them. *Forgive him, ma'am, he always talks like this when he's being serious.* Somewhere he could hear the rumblings of a deep voice, deeper than that of the valet who'd shown him in; the elusive Mr. McNeil, somewhere in the house calling for post-prandial port and cigars? "Did Daniel ever mention a chap called Jones?"

"There was a Jones who acted as his officer's servant or whatever they called themselves. Do you mean him?" The hard edge in Mrs. McNeil's voice was surprising.

"I do. He deserted, was caught, court-martialled and shot." It sounded so bleak, the difference between life and an ignominious death summed up in seven words.

"Daniel spoke about him in one of...one of his last letters. It was a shameful business."

"I understand that your son attempted to represent Jones— he seemed determined to try to reverse what must have seemed the inevitable outcome of the process." Wiggins's words rang in Orlando's brain, the repeated litany that McNeil had tried but it had been no use. "Did he tell you about it?"

119

The crumpled expression on Mrs. McNeil's face made her words unnecessary. "I had no idea." She gripped the arm of her chair, knuckles as white as if she'd been Orlando in Jonty's car when he'd been at his most adventurous. "He never told us. His father would have..." She stopped, avoiding her guest's eyes.

"Would have what?" Orlando broke into what was becoming an uncomfortable silence. At last the elusive Mr. McNeil had warranted a mention and there seemed to be a wealth of information in both that half-finished sentence and the quiet that followed.

"He wouldn't have been at all happy. He doesn't approve of not doing one's duty—or of officers who don't enforce discipline." Mrs. McNeil seemed to remember her duty, passing her guest his coffee, her hand making the delicate china shake.

The significance of the phrase—the secret connotations it had for him and Jonty—still made Orlando's stomach turn. He brought his mind back to the task in hand, away from memories of *doing his duty* in various beds but always with the one, the only, partner. "And did your son ever talk about a soldier called O'Leary? One of the men who served in his platoon?" Orlando wished he had a third hand, to cope with cup, saucer, notepad and pen.

"O'Leary?" The effect was electrifying. "Daniel spoke about *him* during his last leave. Got into a blazing row with his father."

"Might I ask the cause of this row?"

"What we've just been talking about. O'Leary would get himself into a funk, on occasions. Upset the other men as well as himself. Daniel showed some sympathy towards him, wanted to help him get home or some such mad scheme." Mrs. McNeil looked up. "My Daniel and his *sympathies*."

Orlando had never seen his hostess display any other

emotions than sadness and anxiety for her son; now she seemed on the point of righteous anger. "I'm sorry to have to touch on such things, but it's essential. Believe me." He studied his notepad, afraid to write, even if they were getting somewhere at last.

"No, I'm the one who should be sorry. You weren't to blame. You weren't to know." She sighed, all anger subsiding again. "Daniel and his father don't exactly see eye to eye on a number of things. Social reform, the role of women—name a subject and they'd be at loggerheads."

"Does he know that you've consulted me?"

"Good lord, no. I mean, he knows you're fulfilling a commission for me, but not its exact nature. He believes..." Mrs. McNeil smiled, unexpectedly, "...you're helping out my elder sister, who had a rather foolish entanglement many years ago, before she married. Audrey's a widow now, and a party to the deceit, so my husband's neither scandalised nor any the wiser."

"And what happens if I find your son?" That could hardly be laid at the feet of Audrey and her dalliances.

"I'll take that fence when I come to it. I'd be so overjoyed to have such a challenge to attempt that the difficulties would be welcome." Mrs. McNeil's face was suffused with burgeoning excitement, as if she were already at that point, son at her elbow and trying to effect a paternal reconciliation. "Perhaps if my husband understood what drove some of these young men to get into such a state...?"

Orlando wasn't sure it would prove that easy, if the day ever came. "Can you tell me if there are any places in France, or elsewhere on the continent, where you might have gone when your son was younger? Somewhere he'd been happy or knew very well."

"Somewhere he might have found a bolt hole, do you mean?" Twin spots of colour flamed up on Mrs. McNeil's cheeks.

"I never meant to imply that, necessarily." Orlando was blushing, now. Too soon to have changed the subject—he should have stuck with O'Leary and the arguments.

"Please don't feel the need to apologise, Dr. Coppersmith. We agreed at the start that you would have free rein to find the truth, whatever it may be, and I haven't changed my mind on that." She shut her eyes, composing herself before carrying on. "You've concluded that Daniel is still alive."

"Unless he has died subsequently, then yes. I don't believe he was killed in action as your cousin said." Orlando laid down his coffee cup—the brew was good but he had no inclination to enjoy it now. "I have no proof to back this up, but the evidence points to Daniel being so upset about Jones that..." he searched for the right word, "...he lost his ability to think clearly." That was a pleasant, harmless little euphemism—it would do. "It was in that state of mind he left his men. Possibly to bring O'Leary back, as *he* went off at the same time." There was no way to sweeten that bitter pill. "O'Leary was killed, but it would seem probable that Daniel remains on the continent."

Mrs. McNeil nodded. Maybe she'd got all this worked out already and Orlando had only been asked in to validate her conclusions. "And will you look for him there, for me? I can hardly expect my husband to believe that Audrey's business would take me gallivanting abroad."

Orlando suddenly saw clearly what had been forming in his head since their first meeting; he really didn't like Mrs. McNeil. He didn't like being part of her conspiracy and would happily throw up the case and tell her to do her own investigating, if not for two things. Some strange obligation hung over him to pursue this matter as far as he could—not just to McNeil, but to

Wiggins and Paddy Rice and poor scared O'Leary and Dr. Beattie with his wistful-looking friend. And there was an equal obligation to Jonty, at least to his memory. He'd taken a commission and it had to be seen through—it was the right and proper thing to do. "I suppose I could take some time in the long vac if I could narrow down an area sufficiently to make my travels worthwhile. I would be limited to a week or so and if I had no success I'm afraid we'd have to call it a day." That much was fair to all parties and would salve his conscience.

"I would be extremely grateful for any time you could spare. And I'd pay all your expenses." Mrs. McNeil looked frail again, a mother struggling with grief, guilt and shame.

Despite his misgivings, Orlando's stance softened. "No, I couldn't ask you to do that. If I succeed, then make a suitable donation to a suitable cause. A home for old soldiers, maybe."

"I promise you I'll make that donation whether you succeed or fail. Now, what can I do to help?" Turning attention to practical things seemed to have galvanised her into action. Orlando could imagine Mrs. Stewart responding in the same way.

"You could answer my original question. Were there places in France, for example, where Daniel could go to regain some happy memories? Assuming he had the resources to do so?" The thought of Daniel McNeil penniless, begging at doors or working his fingers to the bone on some farm to earn his crust, had been haunting Orlando's mind.

"He would have had resources, Dr. Coppersmith. At least in the short term. Daniel inherited some items of jewellery from his great aunt—small trinkets but extremely valuable. When I checked his things I found they'd gone. I can only assume he took them with him, that last time he was home on leave."

Took them with him? That degree of premeditation put a

different complexion on things; this no longer seemed to be a spur of the moment thing, a man suddenly buckling under extreme pressure.

"And he could live by his wits, taking on tutoring duties or something similar. His French is excellent." Mrs. McNeil hurried on, no doubt aware of what her guest must be thinking and probably having the same thoughts herself. "He wouldn't stick out like some sore thumb."

"I still need that list of places, please." Orlando was starting to believe that the delay in answering his question was deliberate.

"How well do you know France? Will the names alone mean much?" Mrs. McNeil's face, increasingly drawn as the conversation had moved on, now looked defeated.

"It would depend upon which part. I've been to Paris, Trouville, the Riviera—anywhere else I'd need a map."

His hostess rose, went over to a little bookshelf and fished out what appeared to be an old atlas. "This was Daniel's. Always fond of poring over maps and imagining adventures, wondering if there really were monsters out there to be discovered if the old maps said so."

Here there be monsters. The stuff of many a schoolboy's dreams. Was McNeil in search of them now, or were the only monsters the ones of his own making, living not beyond the boundaries of the known world but in his own head? "I can understand the appeal—I did the same myself."

"Normandy." Mrs. McNeil opened the book at a well thumbed page and drew her finger along the map. "All this coast here. That's where we took him as a child." She outlined the area from Honfleur southwards.

"Ah, I know some of this quite well. Can you narrow my target down more?" Orlando circled his finger between Lisieux and Caen. Some indication of inland versus coast at least might constrict the size of the haystack.

"Trouville." Mrs. McNeil's fingers were trembling now. "He loved the beach there. And Cabourg, the same. I'll have to find the names of hotels, if they would help you. I really don't remember them, but I'll have a record somewhere. Strange how the memory of exactly where we stayed has faded, when I can see Daniel as clear as day, sitting on the sand in his little shorts with a bucket and spade. I'm sorry."

"No need to apologise for tears." She was lucky to be able to let her emotions out—women didn't realise how blessed they'd been, not to be ridiculed for showing emotion. Orlando wished he could so easily weep out all his grief for Jonty. "I've taken enough of your time. If you could send me that list I'd be very grateful. And if you can think of any other places where he was particularly happy, like that beach, it would be helpful too." He rose, feeling a cad at leaving his hostess when she was so upset, but he had a train to catch. And that was a good enough excuse to absolve him from having to witness her heartache. "Please don't assume that he was anything less than brave." Orlando avoided using the word coward, irrespective of whether he thought it was the most apt term. "Illnesses of the mind can be just as debilitating as those of the body. He might have been as unwell as some of the people I've seen." He thought of Wiggins, poor Wiggins. "I couldn't necessarily condemn them."

The train journey back to Cambridge no longer felt a novelty—how many of these had he taken, on his own, these last few weeks and months, and how many of them had been spent deep in thought? Had Daniel McNeil been planning his escape from the front line? Orlando would be charitable and give the man the benefit of quite a large doubt—maybe he'd taken that jewellery because he wanted to set up a new life on the continent once the war was done, away from an overprotective mother and an overbearing father. Scurrying around on the edges of this case were two new potential motives for Daniel disappearing; not just getting away from constant rows at home, but helping O'Leary to get away from the front. Maybe there was still some honour to be found for him.

Another thought ran around the fringes of his contemplation, one which had been forming since he'd seen Matthew Ainslie. Jonty had often spoken about the Isle of Wight. *We'll take the steamer across and hire bicycles or go on the train and then walk. We'll walk miles, Orlando, and see the kingfishers and the castles and the fossils.*

Orlando had indeed seen kingfishers and fossils with Jonty, more than he could shake a fist at, in plenty of other places but never on the Island. He'd been inclined to go there this last Christmas, for want of anywhere else to spend his time, but what was the point of seeing any of them when there wasn't the one person you wanted at your side? The one person to whom you could say, "Isn't it lovely, Jonty?" He now had the idea to make a sort of last pilgrimage there, to put a final seal to things before he could be tempted to sully the memory of his lover.

He'd find out about Mrs. McNeil's boy and that would be his swansong, the last great commission. Once that was solved, then he was free, with nothing else to keep him tied to Cambridge or even to this earth. Jonty was gone, Mr. and Mrs. Stewart were gone—all those he'd loved, who'd made his life worth enduring—and there was nothing to fill his days now. Even his beloved mathematics meant nothing, nor his family ancestry, nor sleuthing; all the things he'd once put his faith in to make his life worthwhile were nothing but ashes and gall.

Strange how things had worked out—he'd always vowed he'd see Normandy again. Jonty had dragged him, unwilling, to Deauville and Trouville, and as far down the seaboard as the

All Lessons Learned

point where the Greenwich meridian swept over the French coast, but no further. They'd vowed to come back there, together, so going there to find McNeil—if he was lucky enough to stumble over him—would be an appropriate way to end things. Once he'd been successful Orlando could take a solitary evening walk, then he'd make it look as if he'd simply slipped and fallen down some convenient cliff, so there could be no disgrace to St. Bride's and he'd not have to go on living this confusing and increasingly frustrating life.

See Paris and die? Maybe see Cabourg and die would be more fitting.

Chapter Ten

Lavinia Broad, the only female child of the Stewarts and very much her father's daughter, had wanted to take her own children to Normandy as soon as they were big enough to enjoy the experience, but the war had put paid to all her plans. It had nearly put paid to her husband Ralph, as well, when the zeppelins had come over London and he'd been in the wrong place. She'd loved the beaches here as a child, the cream and cheese and wonderful apples, the smell of the sea and the sound of the gulls. She still had a huge scallop shell she'd collected when not much older than her George was now. Ten to his nine, perhaps, with Jonty about the same age as Alexandra, younger by a couple of years.

How Jonty had loved it here, all along the coast. But then he was always at home at the seaside, never happier than when dragging his bucket, spade and net along to dam some little inlet or catch shrimps. He'd been happiest in Cabourg, digging and scooping to create great earthworks—sandworks—on the beach, their elder brothers Clarence and Sheridan helping with a labyrinth of canals and watercourses, whole cities emerging under the Stewart family's hands. Papa had been part of the construction team, as well.

Rome wasn't built in a day, you say? Lavinia could hear his voice as clearly in her mind as if he'd been speaking in her ear.

That's because they didn't have me on the team. Neither he nor his youngest son would have the pleasure of turning a spadeful of sand here again. And strange that Jonty had ended his days surrounded by a rabbit warren of wet, dank earthworks—would he have remembered these happier times and appreciated the irony?

Young George showed suitable enthusiasm for civil engineering, and he bore his late uncle's trait of filling his pockets with shells and stray creatures, the mucky pup. He'd nagged his parents ever since their arrival to be allowed to go to the beach, but the previous evening it had been too late and the mist had lingered late this morning. Now the weak sun was coming through and they could explore the promenade, even if George had insisted on bringing his kitbag along, stuffed with bucket and spade in case parental minds were changed.

"This afternoon," she and Ralph had promised, "this afternoon you can have the run of the beach." For now, to work up a proper appetite for lunch, they were taking the air, and wonderful it felt. Other people were about, even though one might term this early in the year "out of season". One man in particular, up ahead, was pacing a similar route to theirs, often halting to look out to sea, so that the gap between them lessened all the time.

The figure looked vaguely familiar. Not the beard, which was plain even from a distance, because Lavinia couldn't think of anyone of her acquaintance who bore quite such a distinctive cut of hair on his face. But she recognised the gait, somehow—or at least it reminded her of someone. Papa had always said that even if a man or woman changed their clothes, or hair, or appearance or voice, nine times out of ten the way they walked would nullify the disguise. The way they carried themselves would always give them away, unless they were actor or actress enough to dissemble it. This man's bearing wasn't so distinctive that she could immediately put a name to it—like a way of walking she had once known well, but which was now stiffer somehow, more constrained or under the influence of an injury. Just so Jonty might have walked if he'd survived.

"Mama? What is it?" Little George Broad squeezed his mother's hand, clearly concerned that something momentous must have happened to make his mother halt in full stride.

"A headache, dear, that's all. It's come on rather suddenly." Lavinia tried her best to smile and seem brave. "Ralph, my dear. George and Alexandra have been exceptionally good this morning. Would you take them down to the beach for a treat? I think I can see an old friend of ours over there and I might go and pass the time of day with him. Anything to help clear this wretched head." She indicated the man along the promenade with a nod and wasn't surprised to see shocked recognition on her husband's face. "He's an old soldier, George, and he won't want children running around him just at the moment. You'll understand."

George nodded. "Of course." Somehow all of old Mr. Stewart's sympathetic manner, his innate understanding, had jumped a generation and appeared in his youngest grandson, who was his physical image too. "Come on, Alexandra, there must be stones and shells to be collected and we need to fill our pockets with them before anyone else can. Then we've a castle to be making. Papa, do come along or you'll miss all the best ones." George took his sister by one hand and his father by the other, marching them to the little steps which led down to the beach.

Lavinia took a deep breath, drawing on all the courage she'd inherited from her formidable mother. Maybe she was wrong. This all seemed so unlikely it just had to be a case of mistaken identity or else…or else so many certainties were toppling around her. A treacherous part of her wished she could be wrong, fearing the huge number of complications which would ensue should this miraculous thing come to pass. Her parents' voice, deep within her, countered the argument. *What will be, will be and you must be thankful for it.* Yes, her mother wouldn't have hesitated for a moment.

As Lavinia lessened the gap, she could tell the man still hadn't spotted her. The beard looked all wrong, she could tell that from a mile off, but the steely blue of those eyes, unmistakable in intensity when the man turned to face her—and the look of absolute shock and guilt on his face—sealed all the argument.

"Jonty." She stood stock still, two paces remaining between brother and sister and neither of them capable of narrowing the gap.

"Lavinia. Dear God. I'm so sorry."

"Stupid, stupid boy." Lavinia burst into tears; suddenly she was in her brother's arms, that powerful embrace which had always consoled her, even when he was only a scrap of a thing and his arms had been like lithe wires. Younger brother he might be, but he'd been her rock and her shield before and now he was being it again. "What on earth's going on? How did you get here?"

Jonty held his sister tighter, like he'd never let her go. "I was happy in Cabourg, as a child. I never thought I could be happy again but I hoped to find some peace." He caught sight of his niece and nephew playing on the sand and must have remembered all the last generation of Stewart children there, as clearly as if he could see a newsreel playing. "I was drawn to this place, Lavinia, as surely as if a great magnet was working on me. All through France Cabourg called to me, when I couldn't hear any other voice. Above the memory of the guns." He stroked her cheek. "Maybe you were drawn here too."

"We said we'd come, don't you remember?" Lavinia was surprised at how tremulous her voice sounded. "Back in 1915, all of us at dinner. Saying that the first spring after the war was done we'd come back to Cabourg, all the Stewarts, for one great holiday and to celebrate victory. We were so optimistic then." She rummaged in her pocket for a handkerchief, her other arm firmly entwined around her brother's waist.

"I'd forgotten that." Jonty thrust one of his more substantial and practical handkerchiefs into his sister's shaking hand. "I'm afraid I've lost a lot of what happened during the war." He fingered his cheek.

Lavinia gasped. The red, livid mark couldn't be entirely hidden by the beard which grew around and over it. "Dear God, what happened?"

"To my face or to me?" Jonty fought back the tears. "I'm so sorry, Lavinia. It's been absolute hell."

"I know." Lavinia held him tight again, drying her tears on her brother's coat. "It's been hell for us too." The sound of George shrieking with delight, chasing his sister along the beach and shaking a large crab at her, caught their attention. Lavinia pointed a shaking finger at her offspring. "Especially for *them*. They worshipped their Uncle Jonty, still do. How could you be so callous?" The shock was starting to ease, the relief at finding she still had a younger brother was being overtaken by a growing sense of anger and injustice.

"Callous?" Jonty's voice faltered. "I didn't think..."

"No, I don't suppose you did. Why couldn't you let us know you were alive?" Lavinia's tears began anew. Ralph and the children looked up from the beach, as if they could tell something was wrong with their mother, but she put on a brave face, waving her handkerchief—Jonty's handkerchief—as if she'd got it out just for that purpose. "Look at them. If you couldn't do it for my sake why not for theirs? I know mistakes happen in war but we were all so sure you were dead."

"I was dead. A walking death, where nothing really seemed to matter anymore." Jonty took Lavinia's hand again. "Not even them." They couldn't face the children yet, not until they'd bridged this seemingly unbridgeable void. "Will you let me tell you my story? At the end you can tell me to go away and never come back, if you want, but please let me say my piece."

Lavinia nodded. Her words may have been harsh, but still she clung to him.

"I went out to check on the smell of petrol."

"From the leaking tank. I know that." Lavinia clung to what few certainties she had. "The story we had was that there were two of your platoon there, smoking."

"Not quite. There *were* two of my men there, and one of them was in a shocking state. Lost his head completely. He'd taken off some of his uniform, even flung down his discs. Hadn't lost his lucifers, though, and the idiot was trying to light a cigarette. Boyce—I think the other lad's name was Boyce—was trying to stop him." Jonty rambled on, as if forcing Lavinia to understand and then forgive him. "We couldn't have stayed there—I had a feeling a bombardment was going to start at any moment and we needed to get back to the main trench. We tried to persuade Beaumont, that was the one who'd gone doolally, to come back with us but he wouldn't. He kept fighting us off and shouting—made ourselves a nice target. I sent Boyce back to get help and tried to calm Beaumont down, at least keep him quiet. I gave him my jacket to keep warm as he refused to put his back on."

"They found your jacket, folded up and hardly touched, afterwards." Lavinia's voice was softer, a slow thaw in her feelings sounding through it.

"He must have taken it off, the silly sod. Sorry, Lavinia, I won't talk like that in front of the children." A hint of the old Jonty appeared in his face and voice. "I suppose they identified the body as mine because of it?"

"You knew you'd been reported dead, then?"

"Of course. I managed to get hold of the English newspapers in the early days of my travels and found a mention of my departure. I suppose he wasn't recognisable, Beaumont. I saw the foxhole go up like one of Papa's best bonfires."

"They thought what was left was you." Lavinia fought to keep her voice steady. There was too much still unexplained, too distressing to contemplate. "I understand the jacket, but surely you had identity discs?"

"Of course I did." Jonty fumbled in his pocket, producing a little metal object. "Look."

"These say Beaumont." The treacherous objects trembled in Lavinia's unsteady hands.

"I know. I didn't realise until afterwards that I had the wrong ones." Jonty took them back, holding them up to glint in the light. "Beaumont went mad again, when Boyce left. He grabbed me, tearing at my clothes and hair. He ripped off my discs in the process and I had to quiet him again. When I'd finished and retrieved them, it was too dark to check that I'd picked the right ones up. By then the bombardment had begun and all I could think of was my men and how I really had to get back to them in one piece, and how I couldn't leave Beaumont."

"Dear God." Lavinia, stunned, assimilated the information and tried to make some sense of it. "I see now, yes. But you did leave him?"

"I had to. The shells whizzing over set him off worse than ever. There was no sign of Boyce so I decided I should go and try to get help for myself. I'd made it to the next hole and was waiting to move again when the whole shooting match went up." Jonty's face was like a ghost's. "I felt so helpless. I'd not been able to save him and the way things were going I wasn't sure I was going to have any men to return to, even if I could get back to the main trench. And I'd made Orlando come out to France and I'd failed him as well and it was all so bloody hopeless. I suppose his death was the beginning of the end for me."

"But Orlando isn't dead." Lavinia put her hands to her mouth; she hadn't intended it to come out so bluntly.

"Orlando? Are you mad?" The words died on Jonty's lips. It seemed he could hardly force the words out and when they came his voice was harsh and rattling, like the sound of a young soldier dying a slow and horrible death in the mud. "He's dead. I was told he was dead."

"He wasn't the day we left—I spoke to him on the telephone. I call him every week, just to see that he's taking care of himself. Oh God, you really didn't know, did you?" Lavinia caught her brother as he stumbled forward. "Here. There's a bench just a little way along. Easy. Let's find you a seat and get some blood back into your poor old head." She sat next to him, hugging him tight like she'd done when he was barely five and his favourite hound had broken its leg and had to be shot. How could she be angry with him, now that it was clear? No wonder he'd not wanted to come home.

"I was told he'd gone, missing presumed dead. No word came to contradict it."

"It wouldn't have done, not to start with." Lavinia squeezed her brother's hand. "Shall I tell you now or do you need some more time?"

"Tell me now, please." Jonty blinked back his tears.

"I suppose everything goes back a long time." Lavinia spoke

softly, like she was telling the children a bedtime story. "Mama and Papa's deaths affected him greatly, I don't need to remind you of that. I suspect he lost his sense of reason for a while. You know how prone he's always been to getting upset and storming off."

Jonty nodded. "Of course, the great idiot. Dear God, Lavinia, I can imagine him blazing away, leading his men in some inferno of anger and grief. My poor boy."

"His platoon was smashed to pieces. *Smithereened,* George used to call it when playing with his tin soldiers and a more apt word I can't think of." Lavinia shuddered. "Not that he plays with them that often, now. He was injured, your Orlando—out for the count, picked up almost for dead and put into a prisoner of war camp. He couldn't get word back, not until weeks later. He was lucky not to have been left there to rot."

"A night in the open might have finished him. The cold sometimes achieved what the bullets couldn't." They sat in silence, taking in everything by slow degrees. The world had turned upside down; it would be a while before they really found their feet.

"He was stumbled upon, quite literally, by a German officer. Rather than bayoneting another annoying Tommy, he made his men take Orlando back to their sick bay. Apparently the officer was a very decent chap, not like some I've heard about since. They cared for him well enough and when he could be moved he was sent to the camp. That's the first place he has a clear recollection of, or that's what he told us."

Jonty guessed what might be coming next. "Did he lose his memory again?" His sister's embarrassed nod told him more than fifty words might have done. It seemed to be another way that Orlando coped with pressure, a fortunate bout of amnesia. "But surely he had his discs with him?"

"Of course. It all came back to him once he was *compos mentis* enough to think clearly but by then it was too late. He'd been presumed dead, like so many of his men, swallowed up by mud." Lavinia's face paled but she carried on bravely. "That's what we all believed. We should have known better and clung to hope, but after Mama and Papa hadn't made it I'm afraid I had no hope left. It was ages before his letter came through and by then we'd heard you were dead and I had to tell him so."

"Hope was never a quantity in great supply, those years." Jonty stroked his sister's hand.

"What happened after the foxhole? Did you..." Lavinia couldn't finish the sentence. The sudden import of what had happened must have swooped in on her.

"Did I run?" Jonty interlocked his fingers, winding them round like he'd done as a boy when he wasn't going to lie but wasn't going to tell the entire truth, just yet. "I don't know if you'd call it running. I fought on, but it wasn't quite the same."

"I really don't follow." Lavinia reached for her brother's hands, both of them trembling.

"I'm not sure I do, either. I'll tell you it all, every bit, later on—only let me get my head around Orlando being alive, please." He caressed his sister's fingertips. "I think my most cowardly act was not writing to you and Ralph, but I couldn't bring myself to talk to anyone. I clammed up, tight as a limpet on a rock and just as hard to prise open. I couldn't face coming home, not even for my sister, not even for George and Alexandra. I've been in another world."

Lavinia nodded, evidently trying to understand. "I can see why you needed time to think, why it would have been painful to talk to me. I know how much you loved Mama and Papa. Oh here, silly boy." Lavinia fished in her bag for a clean handkerchief, pressing it in her brother's hand as she might have pressed it in George's. She smiled, a wonderfully maternal smile, the miracle of motherhood late blossoming but evidently fruitful. She'd found her niche in life, it suited her and it had mellowed her with it; the old Lavinia would have hit her brother by now, rather than dried his tears. "They'd have been heartbroken to see you like this. I'm not sure they'd have understood, the same as I can't yet understand it. I will though." She rose, holding out her hand for him to join her. "Come on, better face the others straight away rather than brood over it. You'll have a few of these reunions to cope with."

Jonty sighed, taking his sister's hand and escorting her across the esplanade and down the little steps to the sand. Ralph—always keen eyed, the man who could spot a mile off where everyone's golf balls had come to land—had clearly recognised him from afar, beard and all. He was already in the process of rounding up the children, an incongruous hen with his brood under his wings. He'd his hand ready to offer before they'd even got within ten yards. "Ralph. It's good to see you."

"Old man." No use of names yet, clearly for the youngsters' benefit. Alexandra looked puzzled, although George wore the beginnings of a smile.

"How fares the castle?" Jonty pointed at the work of engineering which was under construction.

"Fine, so far, but I think it would be all the better for you giving a hand with it, Uncle Jonty." George's delighted grin, accompanied by his thrusting a small wooden spade into his uncle's hand, lit up the scene.

"Are you sure that's Uncle Jonty?" Alexandra's tones were so like a younger version of her grandmother's that all the adults drew in a sharp breath. "I thought he was supposed to be dead." It was a statement of fact, as the youngest of those present understood it. She looked offended that someone might have been keeping secrets from her—the same look Helena Stewart could well have given her offspring when they were suspected of purloining pastries from the pantry.

"Well, he was *supposed* to be, of course." George laughed at such typically adult ignorance. "Although he clearly isn't. I never believed it for one moment." He squatted down again, making important adjustments to a corner tower of the curtain wall.

Jonty turned to his sister, but only received a shrug in answer to his questioning look. She was clearly as surprised as he was. "How could you be so sure, George?"

"He used to say that, every night over prayers." Ralph's voice, uncharacteristically quiet, cut in before his son could even look up from his civil engineering. "He used to pray for his mother and father—didn't you, Georgie—then his Uncle Orlando and various assorted Stewarts and Broads. And then his Uncle Jonty."

"That's right." George carried on working, his sister joining him while the adults sorted the muddle out.

"And I'd say he didn't need to pray for you, as you were already in heaven."

"You forgot to say the bit about causing a nuisance to the angels." George looked up brightly; a boy, with a boy's persistence. "Father said you'd be making them all play rugby."

"Quite right too." Jonty could feel the years dropping off his shoulders, the almost unbearable load of the last few months gradually easing.

Ralph must have been trying to ignore the fact that his cheeks had turned bright red. "Anyway, Georgie always used to reply that you weren't in heaven just yet. He seemed to have got it into his head that you were on a mission somewhere, investigating."

"Will you tell us all about it, over dinner?" George got up, wiping his hands just as his father always did after taking three shots to get out of a bunker. For him, a Lazarus-like return was clearly something quite commonplace.

"I'll tell you everything, but don't get your hopes up about high adventure. There's been precious little of that." Jonty took his nephew's hand and endeavoured to scrape some more wet sand away. "Very prosaic and mundane, these few months have been."

"Of course, Uncle Orlando will need to be told. It'll be a great surprise to him." Most parents would have been horrified to hear their child speak so, but both George and Alexandra had been brought up the Stewart way—to speak the truth and air their opinions among family, even if they had to be seen and not heard when with the rest of the unenlightened world.

"Mrs. Trimble says that if you believe in something enough you can make it come alive." Alexandra's words shocked them even more than George's had; even her parents, who were used to her spouting the great pronouncements of their cook, were speechless. She shrugged at the cook's opinion, at the absurdity of grown-ups in general. "I suppose that's what's happened. Uncle Orlando has wanted something so much it's been given him."

Jonty swallowed hard but couldn't even begin to reply. Out of the mouths of babes and sucklings may come praise, but he'd not expected anything so profound to prowl there. Because even if it wasn't a case of Orlando wishing so much that he'd made Jonty appear, the reverse held true. Maybe all those cold long nights praying to a God who'd suddenly seemed to have stopped listening to him, or whose still small voice had been muted by the guns, had come to fruition? He'd wanted so much for Orlando to return, Odysseus like, sweeping away all the pain and putting right what seemed unrightable. And now he'd get his wish.

"Come on. This calls for tea—if we can get a decent pot of the stuff—and the best pastries in the world. My treat." Jonty put out his hands, taking hold of one hand each from his niece and nephew and racing with them up to the promenade, like he was a boy again.

"The world's gone mad, old girl." Ralph linked his arm through his wife's, following the rest of the family at a properly stately pace.

"No, it hasn't. I think for the first time in years it's showing a degree of sanity."

Chapter Eleven

Lavinia presided over the tea pot just as her mother had on many occasions at The Casino hotel when they were children. Jonty watched his niece and nephew, seeing in them the reflection of his sister and himself at the same age. History repeating itself—although the circumstances had never been so strange before, Lazarus taking tea with Martha.

"Uncle Jonty, how did..."

"No more questions for the moment, Georgie. Can't you see your uncle's in need of his whistle being wetted?" Ralph clearly had some questions of his own he wanted to ask and was restraining himself manfully. So far George and Alexandra's enquiries had centred solely on Jonty's journey through France; what he thought of Honfleur, what he'd seen in Paris, whether he too thought the Venus de Milo had been modelled on a man as Uncle Orlando insisted was the case. Nobody was touching on what really mattered.

"I promise I'll answer everything to the best of my ability—" Jonty held up a small square buttery biscuit, as if he was in court and taking an oath on it, "—if you'll let me get outside of at least two cups of tea. More if it's a decent brew. Allow an old soldier some comforts, please."

He got his tea—and pastries, which were even more consoling than the brew was—while Lavinia and her brood prattled on about school and how George had to remember not to be too frank when they discussed Shakespeare in his English lessons. Jonty was so comfortable, so ridiculously happy, he wanted to curl up and doze like a great contented cat right there in the chair, but he'd have to earn that privilege. Too much had still been left unanswered and how close "the best of my ability" was going to come to the literal truth, he hadn't decided.

"What gets me is how you've managed to survive financially all this time." Ralph, practical as ever, couldn't keep the question in a moment longer. His tone also implied the bit he didn't actually say—that Jonty clearly hadn't been on his uppers nor had he been going door to door, begging.

"Ah. It's a bit embarrassing really." Jonty saw the sudden flush rising on his sister's cheeks, her sideways glance at her children. "Nothing to offend the ear, Lavinia, I hasten to add." Maybe she'd got it into her head he'd been acting as some sort of a gigolo? "I'd had it planned, you see. I had no intention of returning home—not to *live*—if Orlando was killed."

"Oh." The wind was taken out of Ralph's sails. "That seems a bit...cold blooded, old man."

"Not so much cold blooded as a case of survival. I couldn't have gone back to Cambridge if he wasn't there to keep me company. I'm not that brave." Jonty laid down his cup, wondering whether he'd need something stronger to see him through this ordeal.

"Uncle Orlando's gone back there." Alexandra looked to her brother to have this simple fact confirmed, as if the grown-ups were too stupid to have remembered. "Back to St. Bride's and his old chair." The sudden haste with which her parents, uncharacteristically, "shushed" her made the girl jump.

"It's fine." The tremor in Jonty's voice must have told

everyone it wasn't fine. The mention of the college—and the sacred chair, the cause of his and Orlando's meeting—had unmanned him on a day when he felt vulnerable enough. "Well, good for him." He fought to regain control of his voice. "I'd never thought he'd have that much guts—I'll need to revise my opinion." They had always constituted Orlando's home though, that college and that chair, before Jonty had steamed—or steamrollered—into his life, and it wasn't unreasonable to think of him returning there. And, if not happy to be back, then at least at ease in his old stomping ground.

"What would Grandmamma have thought?" George voiced what all the others were probably thinking. "She'd have spifflicated you if she'd caught you."

"She knew all about it, Georgie boy. Well, don't look so surprised, all of you—do you really think I'd have dared attempt anything like that if Mama hadn't been in the know?" The outbreak of slightly constrained smiles and laughter confirmed that none of them would have been so foolhardy. "I sorted it all out before we went out to France. The way the war was going I had very little hope that we'd both return. I made sure my will was up to date and then told her about my scheme."

"And she sorted everything?" The keen glint in Ralph's eye left no one in any doubt that he expected the answer "yes".

"Can you envisage a situation in which she wouldn't? Got her man of business on it, all hush hush, and set up the means by which I'd be able to access the funds Grandmother Dewberry left me. Wherever I happened to find myself, this side of heaven, I'd be able to get by."

"Did Orlando not know?" Lavinia was evidently unhappy at the machinations of her dearest family members.

"Of course he didn't. Think of the fuss he'd have made." He'd have appealed to Mrs. Stewart to put a stop to the nonsense, for a start, and she'd have probably sided with him, as usual. "I'm surprised he hadn't twigged yet, though. Surely my estate has been sorted?"

"It's still stuck in probate." Ralph caught a waiter's eye and quietly ordered a bottle of decent white. He too must have felt the need of fortification. "And Orlando doesn't seem to be doing anything about moving it forward. When last we spoke he'd not really enquired into your business—I'm not sure he even wants to get hold of any of the money."

"He wouldn't." Jonty hoped the bottle would come soon.

Lavinia turned to her children, with a look in her eye that Jonty recognised from when it had lodged in his mother's. It said, *I mean business*. "George, Alexandra, would you like to go up to your room for a nap before dinner? It's been a long and exciting day."

"Any day less extraordinary I'd say, 'yes please, Mama', as I'm terribly tired. But might I beg that we be allowed to hear what happened to Uncle Jonty?" George sounded so like his grandfather that a shiver shot along Jonty's spine. "He'll be telling you everything and then he'll only have to explain it all over again, poor thing." He cast a sideways look at his uncle.

"Would it be a great trouble to let them stay, Lavinia? I really would rather say it just the once, for now." Jonty sighed. "I'll be made to retell it plenty of times over the next few weeks, I guess. There's nothing they can't hear. Nothing."

Lavinia nodded, almost imperceptibly, and her brother ploughed on. He took the story up to the point where he'd left it with his sister, sitting in a muddy hole in his shirt sleeves with another man's discs, a man who'd been killed in front of his eyes, despite Jonty's best efforts to save him. If he bowdlerised the minutiae of warfare slightly, his sister and brother-in-law must have appreciated his discretion.

"They mistook this Beaumont for you." Ralph had sent back one bottle of wine—horribly corked—and approved its replacement. At last they had a glass in their hands to strengthen them. "That's the poor chap lying in your grave in Sussex."

"I have a grave at home?" Jonty's fingers trembled around his glass. "It never occurred to me that Beaumont would be anywhere but under the fields of France."

"You can thank your Orlando for that." Ralph grinned. "Very persistent, as you can imagine."

"It's a super memorial, Uncle Jonty." George sipped the lemonade he and his sister had been treated to, drinking it from wine glasses like the adults.

"I bet it is. You can take me to see it." Jonty laid down his glass, afraid the tremor might grow and he'd spill it. "I suppose we'll need to find his relatives and tell them about the mistake. I'm sorry to have caused so much trouble."

"It's not your fault he died. And he would still be under the French fields, I bet, if they hadn't thought he was you. They wondered if he'd run, you know, the man who was in the foxhole with you. Someone said they'd seen a figure without a jacket scrambling out—that must have been you, trying to get help." Lavinia had laid down her glass too; this fence had to be faced without Dutch courage.

"I remember getting out of that foxhole and almost the next thing I knew I was on the way home. I was wearing another man's jacket, carrying another man's pack and gun and I'd got this." Jonty touched his face, tracing the scar beneath the beard. It was pretty near the truth and the rest would wait for Orlando's ear alone. "I wanted to get back to my regiment—my real regiment, not the mob I'd ended up with—but they said I'd possibly got a Blighty one and needed to be tended to at home for a while."

"But you didn't come home."

Jonty had the awful feeling he was five again and his big sister was interrogating him about the disappearance of some biscuits. "No. I wasn't sure there was very much for me in England anymore." He saw the look of disappointment on his niece and nephew's faces. How much it must hurt them to hear such things. "You see, Georgie, it's not been an adventure I've been on. There wasn't any big investigation or espionage for me to boast about. I didn't know that your Uncle Orlando had survived, you know. I thought he was dead and what with your grandmamma and grandpapa and the flu, it was all a bit too much for me. I got myself a bit confused."

George nodded, but didn't speak. Alexandra dabbed at her eyes with her sleeve.

"So I thought I might try and get a bit of thinking time—it wasn't easy to see things clearly among all those people. I was due to go home anyway, so it didn't feel wrong just slipping away when I had the chance." Maybe he should dab his own eyes as they might betray him at any moment. "And then, you know, I found I couldn't just return to the East Surreys. They'd have thought..." He spread his hands, his eyes pleading with Ralph and Lavinia not to make him spell it out in front of the children.

"They wouldn't have understood, Uncle Jonty." Alexandra piped up amongst her sniffles. "It pains me to say it..."

Dear God, that's Mama speaking, as sure as eggs is eggs.

"...but some grown-ups can be awfully dense at times. They can't see the truth for the explanation they want to put on things."

"Is that what Mrs. Trimble says?" Ralph smiled, clearly besotted with his offspring—and who could blame him? What a shame that St. Bride's would probably never see the sense of taking women into its bosom; Alexandra could already have put some of the dunderheads to shame.

"Of course she does." George cut in. "She does speak some sense, sometimes. Anyway, Uncle Jonty, what did you do then?"

"I found out I was dead. Or should I say I heard I was supposed to be dead." Jonty grinned. "I ran across someone who'd been at Cambridge. It was in a café of all places, when I was trying to get my head into a decent nosebag. I started chatting to him about the old place and he said that he'd been at *the college next door*. I was stringing him along a bit, about to boast about the many virtues of St. Bride's, when he said that he'd heard things about 'the college across the wall'. That's what they call *us*, Georgie, the swines, and I'd never realised. Anyway he said that for the first time he felt sorry for St. Bride's as it had suffered worse than many of the other colleges and that even the famous sleuth Dr. Stewart had been killed. Rather took the wind out of my sails."

"And that's why you carried on travelling. You were effectively a dead man, so why not find a new life." Lavinia nodded, as if it were starting to make sense.

"That's right. A new start." Jonty shut his eyes, hoping that they could move on now; he was happy to discuss the days since then.

Ralph's practical streak came to his rescue. "And what have you been doing with yourself? Haven't you been terribly bored?"

"There was no time to be bored at first. I spent some time just finding my feet." Best not to be too specific about those early days of ducking and weaving, still keeping out of sight and trying to make sense of all that was going on. The armistice had helped, of course, as had the beard and the scar. He didn't really look like Jonty Stewart any more. "As soon as I could, I got my financial plan into operation. I had some things with me, items like my cufflinks and watch that I could sell and keep myself going until everything was on an official footing." He glanced down at the ring Orlando had bought him when they'd known each other a year. He'd never have sold that, even if he'd been on his uppers.

"That sounds like the sort of thing a real spy would do," George chipped in, earning himself a harsh look from his mother.

"I don't think I could ever entertain the idea of being involved in espionage, Georgie—sorry to disappoint you. Anyway, once I had some money..." Jonty shrugged, then laughed, realising that the Gallic gesture had become ingrained. "I did a bit of sightseeing. A lot of thinking. A bit of tutoring young lads, to stop my brain rusting entirely—and they've been worse spotty Herberts than even you and your schoolmates are, Georgie." Trying to find peace without success—although now it seemed peace had come along and found him.

"And will you come home now? With us?" Alexandra said what everyone was probably wondering.

Jonty thought for a while, then nodded. "I think so, if not with you then eventually. If England will have me again."

The hubbub which erupted in the hotel lounge threatened to become a miniature riot, with everyone talking at once and assuring their uncle, brother, brother-in-law, that he was always welcome back home—could come and live with them if nobody else had the sense to make a place for him. Several stern looks from the other guests and Lavinia's raised hand, which seemed like it was on the verge of delivering a whack, calmed the situation.

"I think I'll have to come home, by the sound of it, or you'll truss me up and stuff me in the luggage rack all the way. Mind you, St. Bride's may have given my post to someone else." St. Bride's might not want to touch him with a barge pole. *No smoke without fire*—his mother had always said it was the most evil saying in the English language. No matter how he could try to justify what he'd done, someone would always be whispering those words he feared behind their hand. *Coward. Traitor. He ran. Should be shot.* Jonty shook himself and came back to the present. "And I suppose Orlando will want to murder me for all the heartache I've caused him. He always said he'd devised two or three foolproof ways of doing so and not being caught—now I suppose I'll get to find out what they are."

"We really should ring your Orlando." Ralph wouldn't let any of the practicalities rest until every t had been crossed and i dotted. "The sooner we can put him out of his misery the better."

"I know." Jonty swallowed hard. Poor Orlando; what would he be feeling? Jonty had gone through all those emotions himself these last few months, helpless and hopeless. Now he'd found the possibility of happiness again and Orlando should be given the same ray of hope. "I'm not sure how I should tackle it, though. Don't want the poor lad having a heart attack and pegging out on me when he hears my voice down the line."

"I'll ring him." Lavinia's voice was authoritative. "If you spoke to him, out of the blue, we couldn't answer for the consequences. I'll tell him to get leave from St. Bride's and get himself over here as soon as is possible. I won't say what it's for—he can work that out for himself."

"Is that playing fair?" Ralph often seemed to regard the complexities of life as being akin to a game of cricket or golf.

"Of course it is. He likes a nice puzzle to occupy his noddle and he'll have a few days to fathom it. This may not be the kindest option but it might be the only one." Lavinia's lips settled into a thin line. "We have to get him here, don't we, Jonty, and then see what happens?"

"I think you're right. There's no fair way to play this."

Orlando was sitting over a rapidly cooling dinner plate, wondering whether he should talk to Ariadne Sheridan before he spoke to her husband. The long vac seemed far away but he wanted to start to get his plans clear, especially if he never returned from France—there was a lot of subterfuge to be undertaken in getting his affairs straight.

He was preparing the list of what he needed to do in preparation for his one-way journey, even down to the items he needed to pack—his "everything and the kitchen sink list", Jonty used to call it—when the telephone rang.

"Orlando?"

"Yes." Who else could Lavinia have thought was living in the house? "Are you having a nice holiday?" Orlando immediately regretted the pleasantry—what if there'd been some disaster, one of the children taken seriously ill or something equally unpleasant?

"Smashing." Lavinia sounded happy enough, although there was an edge to her voice which suggested the chipper manner was rather strained. "Look, I know this is an absolute imposition, but could you come out to Cabourg for a few days? I appreciate it'll mean having to take a few days away from the college, but Dr. Sheridan would surely let you go if it was important enough. And it is, I promise you."

"I'd have more chance of persuading him if I knew what it was about." Orlando's brain was whizzing, trying to figure out what was going on.

"I can't tell you, my dear. You'll just have to trust me on this." *My dear.* It must be serious. Those were the words she'd used when she'd told him about Jonty. Had it turned out that Ralph had a mistress, meaning he and Lavinia had parted brass rags on the seafront at Cabourg and she needed a reliable escort home?

"I'll get onto it first thing in the morning. Don't worry." Orlando took the name of the hotel and other useful contact details, determined that he'd be off as soon as the occasion allowed. Jonty would have expected him to come to his sister's aid, as would Mrs. Stewart, and neither of those could be let down. It was neatly logical that it was the right part of France, though. Maybe after he'd sorted out whatever the mess was—he was sure there would be a mess—then he could have a look around for Daniel McNeil while he was at it. And, on the plus side, he could go and plead with Dr. Sheridan that he had a family crisis to deal with—that would be far more likely to result in the required leave being granted than pursuing one hundred missing sons.

There was something at the back of his brain, something vague taking form, as an object might have its outline clarified with the daylight waxing at dawn. Unable to get it to clarify itself at the rate he wanted, Orlando made his usual evening visit to Jonty's study, taking his pudding from dinner with him, such was his mental state. He sat in Jonty's chair, as he'd done at roughly this time of night every day he'd been in residence since returning home, snuggling into the depression still left where his lover's not inconsiderable buttocks had made the upholstery sag. It wasn't just an act of sentiment, some means of reconnecting with the impression that Jonty had left on both furniture and Orlando's heart. It was an affirmation that what had been between them still lived on. He ran a finger along the desk then over the familiar piles of articles, the mess and disorder that Jonty Stewart always left in his wake.

Bloody Jonty, his college gown *still* lay over the top of a little cabinet, where he hadn't bothered to hang it up their last night here, the untidy little toad. If he was such a slattern at home, why the hell had his last gesture been to fold his bloody jacket and leave it as neatly on the battlefield as a valet might place it on a chest of drawers? The sudden importance of that incongruous piece of evidence hit Orlando like a bolt of lightning, all the more shocking for the fact that he should have realised its significance months ago. Jonty *never* folded his jacket and war wouldn't necessarily have taught him any different; there'd be an officer's servant to keep him in line in his billet.

Daniel McNeil wasn't dead—what if Jonty wasn't, either? What if he'd taken fright, the awful terrors of his schooldays, the ones he'd thought had been cured of, having re-emerged in the hell of the trenches? What if the thunder of the guns had reminded Jonty of thundery nights when he'd suffered so much? Might he have given up and fled and some kind soul, a friend of Richard Stewart or an ex-suitor of Helena, covered things over for the sake of family honour?

Orlando thumped his thigh with his fist. Jonty couldn't have done such a thing. He wouldn't have done such a thing. He'd come through desperate times still smiling, still brave and gallant; surely even the front line couldn't have broken down that heroic spirit? Orlando wouldn't even let himself think about it, not just because such a thought besmirched his lover's honour, but because it raised his own hopes unnecessarily. Jonty was dead, as dead as Marley and not even his ghost would be returning.

Orlando opened the window, letting the fierce breeze sweep over his face, wishing it would blow all the niggling doubts from his mind.

A logical trail of thought, started by the phone call, worked its way through his brain, culminating in a simple assertion, even if the line of logical reasoning wasn't yet foolproof. Orlando would have bet his last five pounds that someone else had been wearing that jacket in the foxhole. *He'd* worn it, *he'd* taken it off and *he'd* been the one killed, no matter what the evidence of the identity discs said. They could be logicked away later. There was another man in the story, the one who'd been seen leaving the hole—was that Jonty? And had Jonty run?

His thoughts raced back to everything which had crossed his mind in London and this time his unease couldn't be ignored. Now he had two men to find, even if he only had one name to clear; Daniel McNeil may have deserted but it was Jonty who had to be proven not to be a coward. There would be a logical explanation to what had happened, of course there would. He'd have got tangled up in some train of events beyond his control and felt himself unable to return to dishonour the Stewart name, or anyone's remembrance. Orlando wouldn't entertain for a moment that there was any other reason why Jonty hadn't come back to him, that their great love could have been blown to smithereens on the front line.

Assuming Jonty actually knew he was still alive, of course.

Dear God.

Orlando found a piece of paper and a pencil, then started scribbling madly—dates, time it took for letters to get home, for replies to return again. It was possible, more than possible it was *likely*, that Jonty wouldn't know he'd been captured rather than killed. He could check it all with Lavinia—except he wasn't sure he dare check anything with Lavinia as that would give rise to speculation. Unless...

He sat in Jonty's chair again, Lavinia's words echoing in his brain. *I can't tell you, my dear. You'll just have to trust me on this*. Did those simple phrases envelop the greatest thing that could have happened in his currently fruitless life? Was this what Jonty, in his coarser moments, used to call an attack of the bleeding obvious? There was only one reason Lavinia had summoned him, only one cause he could be expected to drop everything for, and he had to act right now. He had to find Mrs. Sheridan. She'd have done anything for Jonty in years gone by and Orlando bet she'd do so now. He would tell her everything—he'd have to tell her—and she'd make sure he was given as much time as was needed. Daniel McNeil would have to wait; whatever had happened to him, there were other priorities, now that Orlando had convinced himself there was still a chance Jonty was alive. And if Jonty was alive, then Jonty needed him.

He left his list discarded on his desk, his pudding uneaten on its plate, got out his bicycle and set off for St. Bride's. He had to catch Dr. Sheridan tonight and head for the coast in the morning. If he was right then there wasn't a moment to lose.

Chapter Twelve

Orlando looked out over the sea with eyes that barely took in the glorious sights in front of him. The sun was glinting on the waters, the light breaking into a thousand shimmering diamonds, the sky was piercing blue with not a cloud to sully it, and there was just a chance that those dots in the water were seals, breaching the top of the waves to gaze curiously at the ship as it passed. As the ferry headed for France it passed the Isle of Wight which, while not as lovely as Jersey, was turning out to be every bit as beautiful as he'd been promised it would be.

How long ago had that been when they'd first talked about it? All of ten years, but it seemed like yesterday. The island looked even more beautiful now that he had a flicker of optimism in his heart, a little spark that there might just still be something worthwhile left for him. He thought of his vow—his stupid suicidal urge—and thanked the God in whom he still didn't really believe that Lavinia's call had come when it did.

He watched the waves coursing along the sides of the ship, more at ease on the water these days than when he'd first gone to Jersey with Jonty and disgraced himself over the side on more than one occasion, seasick beyond all measure. He was a better sailor now, since his discovery of ginger ale and its therapeutic effects, even if he preferred a large ferry to a small yacht. Jonty had loved sailing, as his father did before him.

Orlando remembered the pair of them taking him to a mill, not far from Portsmouth, constructed from the timbers of a captured American frigate. He'd gone along under sufferance and been amazed to see the enthusiasm the old man had shown. Mr. Stewart had been there when younger, a lad with dreams of being a naval captain, fascinated by all he saw. "I always used to wonder, Orlando, that if walls have ears, as the old expression had it, then would beams and lintels? I used to dream that they'd hear the mill wheels turning and remember the capstan working." Mr. Stewart's bright, nostalgic smile was as clear in Orlando's brain as if the man was pacing the deck beside him. "Too many iron ships these days, my boy. The rush of the sea along the sides isn't the same any more."

Nothing was the same any more, was it? England's wooden walls had become metal ones, tanks and armoured vehicles would succeed horses—and thank God for that—and... Orlando shook himself out of his slough of despond. The world had moved on and he could either spend the rest of his days, long or short, moping about it, or he could get on with life. He set his gaze southwards, trying to force the French coast into view by willpower alone and ignoring the darkening and deepening clouds out to the west.

Honfleur was a known quantity, the stepping stone into France that he and Jonty had trodden years before, but Orlando wasn't as happy as he should have been, landing there. He was frustrated that he couldn't make much further progress once he'd disembarked, but the storm which had hit the ferry about twenty miles out from the coast was now virulent. Plans to find a coach to take him to Deauville, from where the train line snaked along to Cabourg, were put on hold and the best he could hope for was a nice dry bed in a decent hotel. He found both, and got a decent enough meal inside himself, but sleep was elusive, even as he began to warm through. Tomorrow he would find out what awaited him with Lavinia; he would know then, one way or the other, and the day had the potential to be the best or the worst of his life.

By the time the dawn was edging over the rooftops he'd fallen into a fitful sleep and allowed himself to rise an hour later than intended. The bleary face and reddened eyes that greeted him in the mirror were no encouragement—how could he let Jonty see him in such a state, if Jonty were still alive? Orlando took some breakfast then determined to find a barber to get a really good shave and be spruced up a bit; the last thing he wanted was Jonty to take one look and decide that he didn't fancy his erstwhile lover any more. He was recommended one by the hotel concierge—despite what a certain little toad used to say about Orlando's French, he could speak and read enough to get by—got the directions and strolled there in the watery sunshine which followed on the heels of the storm.

It was a beautiful morning, the sort which might fill any man with optimism, and Orlando didn't hurry to the barber's shop, content to feel the warm rays on his back. He took his time in the chair too, pleased to see that with every moment he was becoming more human in appearance and less unappetising. He tipped the man with the razor and towels handsomely, then decided to have a coffee before he set off for the station. He was at a pleasant corner café, halfway through his second cup, when he could no longer try to pretend that he was just enjoying the morning. He was prevaricating, the urgency of the previous day being replaced with something akin to reluctance.

The part of him which wanted to get to Cabourg within the next five minutes was being gradually supplanted by the dread of being wrong, of finding out the only crisis was Ralph breaking his leg and Lavinia having no one else to turn to for help. There was even a hint of something treacherous: even if Jonty was alive and Lavinia was trying to organise a blissful reunion, Orlando wasn't certain he wanted to meet his great love again. At least not yet.

Why hadn't Jonty himself rung? What if he didn't want to meet his old lover? What if he'd known Orlando was alive all along but had seen the war as his chance to make a clean break?

The voice of Mrs. Stewart came ringing into Orlando's mind, clearer and louder than if she'd been on the chair next to his on the little pavement table. *When they gave you brains, young man, they may have dolloped the mathematical bits like cream onto a scone but there are parts they left sorely lacking. You can't know if you don't go and find out and even then what's the very worst which could befall you? A bit of disappointment and a few days on the beach with George and his bucket and spade. Courage, my lad.*

Suddenly a great smile broke over Orlando's face, a wave of decision followed by a tide of happiness such as he'd not felt in what seemed years. Courage? He'd show the world who had courage. He left some money on the table and his coffee half drunk—this precipitate leaving of the nosebag was becoming habitual—and strode back to the hotel to get his suitcase.

The surge of bravado lasted all the way to the point Orlando's train pulled into Cabourg station, remaining strong as he made his way along the platform, into a cab and off to the hotel. It started to waver a bit while he was checking in, putting his bag in the room Lavinia had booked for him, and going down to the hotel lounge to meet her. The ebb tide began in earnest when he saw that she was alone and looking drawn.

"Orlando. My dear." She let him kiss her hand but didn't seem to know what to do or say next.

"I came as soon as I could." Orlando bit the first bullet. "Ralph and the children keeping well?"

"Never been better." Lavinia smiled and her almost-brother-in-law shivered inside. It couldn't be a heart attack, then. "They've gone out mackerel fishing or something equally outlandish. George will probably be sick everywhere." There seemed to be no more forthcoming, Lavinia watching Orlando and seeming slightly dumbstruck, smiling at him and rather lost for words.

He broke the silence at last, in case he burst from any further delay. "Why did you ask me here?"

"I can't tell you." She was like a child, desperate to share a secret and knowing she shouldn't, afraid to say too much in case it all spilled out. "You have to be at the seaward side of the Casino at four o'clock. That's all."

A place and a time—it could only mean a meeting. A sick feeling in the pit of Orlando's stomach—half excitement, half nerves—threatened to overwhelm him. He fought it down with the steely, fiercely logical resolve which had seen him through plenty of difficult times, both pre- and post-Jonty. "Tell me where to go, and I'll be there."

"Hello Orlando, lovely to see you."

Orlando ignored the voice behind him, just for the moment; he still wasn't going to get his hopes up, even at the appointed place at the appointed time. He kept his gaze fixed out to sea, over the beach and the running waves to the distant horizon.

He'd heard that voice in his head before—and many others—just as lifelike.

"Orlando, I know it's a shock but will you please turn around and look at me? Even if it's only to tell me bugger off?"

Orlando couldn't have turned if his life depended on it—he was frozen to the spot, incapable of controlling any of his movements. What if this was all some hallucination? There'd been times in the past he'd felt he was being haunted, prey to some cruel jest of heaven to make him suffer even more than he already was; he wouldn't turn and face the demon. So the demon came round to confront him—only it didn't bear a devil's face, but one of an angel, a heavenly messenger with what seemed to be a great livid scar across his right cheek, hidden under a grizzled blond beard, and with blue eyes that spoke of fear that all hope had been lost.

"It's me. Honest to God, it's me." Jonty's hand shook as he touched his one-time lover's arm. "I'm so sorry. I thought you were dead."

Orlando reached out a hand—trembling uncontrollably, the fingers like wild things—to touch Jonty's jacket, his sleeve, his hand. Taking an inventory of evidence that this was no illusion and that every hope had come to fruition.

"If you don't say something soon, I swear I really will die."

"If you're real, if you're my Jonty, then where the hell have you been all this time?" The initial mixture of euphoria and incredulity had been superseded by anger. And the gnawing worry about what had happened in Cambrai. Now Orlando couldn't hide any more from all the questions why. "Why did you make me endure such grief? I was beyond myself with sorrow. I would have gladly lain down and died right there in St. Bride's but Mrs. Sheridan forbade it. *Live for him* she said, *make him look down on you and be proud.* So I did—I had no idea that all that time you were alive, that you were hiding yourself away from me..."

Fingers were pushed against Orlando's lips and as swiftly taken away. Maybe if they'd been in the privacy of a room then Jonty might have done more, used his physical affection to overcome his lover's doubts, but in public it wasn't possible. Maybe the rendezvous had been chosen for that very reason, so that no underhand tactics could be employed. "Sh. No. You have no idea, none at all. Be quiet. Let me explain, please."

"You'd better have a damned good explanation." This wasn't how Orlando had imagined the scene playing out, last night as he'd lain sleepless. He'd envisaged a sweet reunion, tears and embraces, maybe kissing of cheeks—they were in France after all and who would notice? Now he couldn't do that; the unease had built up again, the sense of betrayal was too strong, and until he understood entirely what had gone on they would remain as far apart as when the Channel had divided them.

"God alone knows I have an explanation, but I'm not sure it's good enough for me, let alone you." Jonty ran his hands through his hair, clasping them behind his neck. "Where do you want me to start? I didn't know you were alive, I swear. I was told you were missing presumed dead, and I'd never come across anyone in that position for whom the presumption of death hadn't turned out to be true. Our lieutenant colonel always used to say it definitely meant you'd had it." His hands dropped to his sides, fists clenching and unclenching.

"Is that why you didn't come home?" Orlando could barely control his voice.

Jonty nodded, body still shaking. "I didn't have anything to return home for."

"Please tell me this." Orlando caught sight of his own hands and was stunned at their pallor. He looked at Jonty

All Lessons Learned

again, saw the shock there, but ploughed on. Like a man encountering a ghost, or one in deep dread of something—an operation, an examination, the opening of Pandora's chest. "I know that you've never lied to me, although you may have let the truth seep out drip by drip at times, for my own good, I'm aware of that. Tell me that's not the case now."

They stood without speaking for what seemed an age, each holding the other's gaze, disconsolate at not finding there the swiftly resurrected love that they'd expected. "I'm not sure I understand you..." Jonty was lost now, swallowed up and tossed about by eddying emotions, a great riptide of feelings.

"Did you desert, Jonty?" Orlando had broken eye contact and seemed unable to address anything but his shoes. Thirteen odd years had slipped away and they were almost back to those early days when he'd been hardly able to talk about anything which really mattered to him. "Are you going to spin me a tale to cover over the fact that it all got too much?" He looked up suddenly. "I wouldn't condemn you, I promise. God knows I appreciate what it was like. What changes the conditions could work on the best of men. I just need to know the truth so I can come to terms with it."

Jonty gently touched Orlando's arm with a trembling hand. "I could never have just cut and run. I won't deny that there were times I thought about it, when things got so much on top of me. The cramped conditions, the guns at night like thunder..."

Orlando returned the touch. They both understood the significance of small cold rooms and stormy nights, days that Jonty thought had been overcome and left behind in his schooldays, never to return to haunt and hurt him again. "Was it like that when you were in the foxhole with the petrol fumes?"

163

"You know about that?" Jonty shook his head, frustrated at his own idiocy. "Of course you do. Lavinia knew the story as well, or at least half of it. Let's find a seat and I'll tell you the rest." They strolled on, along the seafront and away, although they didn't stop at any of the resting places they passed. Somehow it was easier to talk as they walked, the movement oiling the wheels of speech. "There was this man called Beaumont..." He told the story of the foxhole simply, Orlando chipping in with questions, clarifying points as if he was dealing with a witness, although the strained emotion in his voice showed that this was far more important than any testimony he'd ever had the privilege of taking. They soon reached the point where Jonty had left the story with his sister. "I was there, in the open, with Beaumont's discs and unable to get back to my platoon. Lavinia and her family think that the next thing I knew I was on the way home. That I tried to get back to the East Surreys but gave up in case they thought—well, what you thought, old man."

Orlando linked his arm with his lover's—they could get away with that here, the continental holiday atmosphere allowing them an extra degree of freedom. "But you didn't tell them the truth, not the whole truth?" He tightened his hold, unwilling to let Jonty escape either the questioning or his grip.

"Not entirely. I do remember some of what went on—I certainly recollect knowing I had to get out of the open so I inched back to a little depression in the ground. Then all hell broke loose and carried on for what seemed weeks, but I guess it was two days. I honestly can't remember all of it..." He gripped Orlando's hand, the one that snuggled in the crook of his arm. "And some of what I do recall I would never tell Lavinia in a million years."

"Will you tell *me*?" Orlando's voice was tremulous again, full of concern, not just at revelations to come. He was worried about being shut out of the intimate part of Jonty's life, the place he'd uniquely held for all those years.

"Of course. It'll do me the world of good to be able to tell someone. But not everything, not yet."

"Enough for now?" Orlando looked so ridiculously like a seven-year-old boy begging for a sweet that Jonty couldn't help laughing.

"Enough for the moment." He steered Orlando slightly away from the sea front, down towards his lodgings. "That first night, in the ditch, I was bloody cold. In shock, I suppose."

"I remember your mother always warning us about shock and how it could kill you..." Orlando stopped, clearly embarrassed at letting his tongue run on. "I'm sorry, I didn't..."

"Nothing to apologise for. Idiot." Jonty grinned, saying the word again and savouring its feel on his tongue. "Idiot. I never called anyone else that, all the time in France, not even the most block headed of my men. You alone deserve the title. And now you're blushing, like when you were in your twenties. There is a God in heaven, I knew it."

"And you've never lost the ability to prattle." Orlando was clearly fighting a smile from lighting his face—if he succumbed to the grin he really would look like a flaming idiot, one with red cheeks to boot.

"I've not had much of a chance to prattle, so I have to make the most of this glorious opportunity." Jonty stopped in front of a tidy and well maintained pension. "Would you like to come in? My landlady will find us some excellent coffee, or tea if you prefer—really very civilised."

"Landlady? Why aren't you in the best hotel in the town?" Orlando bit his lip again, perhaps afraid that he'd spoken out of turn once more. Post-war Jonty might not have the resources that his pre-war incarnation had.

165

"I was, but I got bored with it. Ah, I recognise that sceptical look, Dr. Coppersmith. No, I'm not in penury, I just fancied something which smacked of home rather more than the Hotel Casino." Jonty pulled his friend with him through the front door, met the landlady in the hall and begged her for some refreshments. The glint in her eye when she saw Orlando clearly meant she was impressed and that the pot of tea would be the best she could produce. They settled down on the bench in the garden, warming tired legs and flagging spirits in the late afternoon sun. The story soon resumed. "I had company that night, in my ditch. Two soldiers, dead as doornails. One was—well if I say that he was in pieces need I say more?" Jonty shut his eyes at the memory then opened them again, fleeing the picture that had filled his brain. "I never want to see anything like that again."

"Please God neither of us will." They sat in the sunshine, the need for words suddenly gone—all they really wanted was the glow of the other's company. Anger and mistrust, fear and doubt had begun to subside beneath the tide of true, deep love.

"I took one of the chap's jackets and cap—he wasn't going to be needing it any more and I'm sure he wouldn't have denied a fellow soldier a bit of warmth. Found some food and a water bottle in his pack, fags and lucifers too." Jonty pressed his knuckles to his forehead. "I got through that night still alive, despite Jerry's best efforts. Not sure I was in a particularly good state up here." He rubbed fingers across his temples. "Worst night of my life and that's saying something, isn't it?" Memories of the horrors of schooldays cast a cloud over the warm afternoon. A huge bumblebee alighted on a lavender bush, filling the air with its industrious hum; Jonty smiled at the happier reminiscences this evoked—his mother's garden, childhood days, Orlando at his side in a bee-loud glade.

Orlando spoke again, his voice barely more than a whisper.

"What about when the morning came? Were you still pinned down?"

"The next day? Actually it's all a bit of a muddle." Jonty sat back, eyes screwed up, trying to feel his way through it all. "When it was light I could see that these chaps had been East Surreys, but with another platoon, and they were pretty well marooned. So were my lads, as far as I could tell, because everyone who had any sense had their heads down. I sat tight, getting by on the providence of a Mrs. Lodge who'd sent her husband a nice little parcel for his birthday. I suspect he'd been sharing it with his mate when..." Jonty shivered; he'd never get that image completely eliminated from his brain. "That night I decided to make a dash for it. There was a lull in the firing and I thought I'd have a chance. Took Lodge's weapon and the other chap's pack and made a run for it—well a crawl, anyway. Ended up going in the wrong bloody direction."

Orlando reached out to caress his friend's hand but was forestalled by the arrival of tea and pastries. Madame DesRues smiled sweetly, pinched Orlando's cheek and left them to it.

"You've made a conquest. And gone red again. I never thought a seventy-year-old lady could have such an effect on a man of your tender years." Jonty poured the tea, as if this were an ordinary afternoon at home in their garden.

"Will you ever hush?" Orlando could feel, as the anxiety subsided, his excitement building up. For all that Jonty wore that dreadful beard he was still *his* lover and memories of beds they had known and enjoyed couldn't be ignored.

"I'll be silent when I've told my story. It's quite cathartic, this." Jonty quietened Orlando with tea and cake. "I found myself with another regiment entirely, must have been all of a mile down the line. Don't ask me how I got there because I really don't remember that too clearly. This lot were already involved in a skirmish so I just joined in—I'd never fought with so much venom. All I could think of was that poor chap I'd just left behind, someone's son, someone's lover maybe, in a dozen pieces. There was work still to be done in that bloody war and I wasn't bothered who I helped do it."

"Dear God." Orlando almost dropped his cup, catching it just in time as it slid from his grip. *There's work still to be done and I'm not bothered who I help do it.* "I should have recognised the name Beaumont. I was told your story and I didn't realise it—a story about a soldier who appeared from nowhere and who fought like a man possessed. They recommended him—you—for the Military Medal."

"Did they? Did they really?" Jonty rummaged in his pocket for a hankie and blew his nose. "Well, maybe that medal makes it a bit better. Does it excuse the fact that I didn't go back to my regiment?"

"I rather think the fact you were being sent home with that wound..." Orlando indicated the scar which Jonty's beard couldn't entirely hide, "...excuses everything. There would have been no more war for Beaumont or Stewart, not for the foreseeable future."

"I'm glad you take it in such good spirit. I'm not sure I do." They sat in silence again, the sun moving behind the trees now and the air cooling. The reverie was broken by Madame DesRues asking whether they needed anything more, as she had to slip along the road. They declined, graciously, and watched her amble along the footpath, a basket of wool, and what looked like needles, tucked under her arm.

As soon as she was out of sight, Orlando leapt up, pulling Jonty with him and holding him close. "It's fine. It will be fine now. My Jonty, my most precious thing." Orlando's hands naturally moved to where they'd always gone, caressing his lover's back and hair, resting Jonty's head against his own shoulder. Great shivering sighs came from deep within Jonty's chest, but he didn't break that precious contact. Orlando would have stayed there forever, suddenly happy again as he hadn't been in years.

"It's wonderful to be back in your arms once more but I genuinely can't breathe. You're even more overwhelming than Lavinia and she nearly broke my ribs." This not only sounded more like the old Jonty, the first signs of a genuine Stewart smile had appeared, through what might just be some burgeoning tears. "Come on, let's sit again. The hedge isn't that tall and who knows who'll be passing along in a moment and catching us."

Orlando couldn't have cared less who caught them, but he happily obeyed, nestling himself at his friend's feet and evidently looking so ridiculous that Jonty started to laugh. "You must have a story to tell too. Lavinia's told me part of it, although not exactly why things ended up being in as much of a muddle for you as for me."

"Nothing spectacular, just the usual sort of stupid thing. I lost my memory again and was out for the count over a crucial period of time."

"Oh." Jonty swallowed hard. "Oh, of course. Now I see."

Orlando drew closer, almost resting against Jonty's legs. "It was a bit like before, except this time I knew very little. Then one day I woke up in a prisoner of war camp and I had it all back, as though a great vault had been opened. The greatest treasure was finding you locked away in my heart—such a bloody shame I had to lose you again so quickly."

Jonty laid his hand on Orlando's head, sitting with him in a thoughtful silence. It was good to once more work through his feelings down labyrinthine paths of thought, as was his wont.

Orlando had to be allowed to think everything through methodically, assimilate and evaluate every new piece of information or emotion. Jonty suddenly ruffled his friend's hair and laughed. "There's a grey one here. In fact there's a whole clump."

"There is not!" Orlando swatted the hand away, exceedingly offended, then burst out laughing himself. "God, I've missed you. I don't think I've really said how much I love you and I want to make it absolutely clear that this is the best day of my life, without compare." He snatched the hand back, kissing it along the knuckles. "And if my hair is greying, then these are getting knobbly."

"Idiot. Can you bear another question, one I hope won't break your bubble of joy? You must have read that last letter I left for you. Did you ever think of finding someone else, as I'd asked you to?" Guilty thoughts of the attraction he'd felt for Lamboley were soon dismissed to the boundary of Jonty's brain. Nothing had happened between them and he had plenty to hold himself to account for without adding that to the receipt.

"Never. I would never have taken anyone else into my heart. You were always irreplaceable to me." Orlando picked up a handful of grass, tipping it from hand to hand. Jonty suspected that the answer had been a bit too quick and forceful to be the absolute truth, but not enough to cover anything but a relatively minor misdemeanour. That would be a story for another day too. "I still can't believe you're flesh and blood. I keep thinking that this is just a dream or a haunting. How can I know that it's really you?"

Jonty made a swift reconnaissance of the territory, but it was empty—at least within spying distance. "Ghosts can't do this, Orlando." Jonty turned Orlando's face up to his and gently kissed him. "And if it was a dream it wouldn't taste so good. I know—I've been dreaming about you endlessly these past few days, since Lavina told me the errors of my ways. Made it distinctly embarrassing sometimes." They kissed once more, savouring every little taste and sigh, then drew apart. They'd used up all their luck for the moment, twice over.

"Dear God, I love you, Jonty. There's still so much to ask you but I don't feel I can until you let me kiss you again."

"Is kiss a euphemism for going to bed?" Jonty grinned, tousling his lover's hair. This was so wonderful, the sunshine and unexpected romance creating what seemed like a foretaste of heaven itself.

"Of course it is." An inane grin covered Orlando's face. "Although I suspect that the location of said bed will present a bit of a problem. I don't suppose your landlady would approve and the chambermaid would die if she caught us in my bedroom at the hotel."

"Perhaps we've got a guardian angel or two minding us again. Madame DesRues will be out for the rest of this evening—I suspect she has a fancy man although she insists it's a meeting of ladies who crochet blankets for orphans. All her lodgers have to fend for themselves come knitting night." Jonty grinned in return. "Come on. I've a lovely room here. Only a single—couldn't face a double, not alone—but it has a lovely view and it'll be secluded."

Orlando pulled himself up, face so shining with contentment that the years seemed to have dropped away and he looked twenty-odd again. "Perhaps we should use the back entrance, if there is one, so no one can stumble over us. And what is *so* funny?"

"You, my great gormless boy. And if you can't work it out I shan't tell you, not until afterwards." Jonty ran his hands down Orlando's lapels, a last lingering touch before they reached a place of safety. "It's clearly been far too long."

They negotiated the distance between garden and bedroom without meeting anyone to either wonder about them or hinder their progress, something for which Orlando in particular was grateful even though the distance travelled was barely more than fifty yards in total. A man couldn't be too careful when he was wearing trousers with so tight a cut and his excitement must be sticking out like a sore thumb. He wasn't sure he could last out much longer, like a callow lad again, desperate and with little control. How he'd cope with Jonty naked and close to him, his distinctive scent in Orlando's nostrils and flesh against eager flesh, he couldn't imagine.

They entered the room together, barely through the door before the kisses began again—wild, impassioned, reckless, glorious kisses, like those they'd shared when they were first in love. They were lost for ages, aware only of themselves and the distant sounds of life out in the streets. Orlando's hands tugged Jonty's shirt free and found skin, stroking it and moaning as if he were the one being caressed. "Now, come on, now." Orlando's fingers fumbled at his lover's flies, making a mess of things in his haste.

Jonty smiled. "You look like my nephew at Christmas back in 1910, when he got everything he'd asked for and he said it felt as wonderful as when he'd only wanted it. Same old Coppersmith—you always were insatiable once we'd unleashed the inner beast. I shan't complain, though. This will be like the greatest gift and one I never thought to enjoy again."

"You have no idea how delighted I'd be to share it with you. If only you'd bloody well let me get about it." Orlando kept fumbling, fingers shaking like wild things. "Damn, there's a button gone."

"One of yours or one of mine?" Jonty fiddled with his flies. "Mine, I should have known. Is there no room for a slow romance any more?"

"Maybe tomorrow, or the next day. I'll take all the time you want then, but I need you now, Jonty, and I think I'll die if we don't do it soon. Oh hell." Orlando had managed to get his trousers unfastened and sat on the bed, fiddling ineffectually with his shoelaces.

"What's the matter?" Jonty's shoes were off, discarded with the laces still done up—the sort of thing his mother would probably have whacked him for. It had become automatic, taking them off at the first hint of hanky-panky. It didn't help Orlando's physical composure, having his ear nibbled and his neck licked, but Jonty seemed to care as little about that as about his knotted laces. This was mad and wonderful. "Got a problem with those boots?" He worked his tongue along Orlando's ear.

"No, although I will if you keep doing that and it won't just be a problem with my boots. Feel for yourself if you want to." Orlando took a deep breath.

Jonty moved his tongue away. "Don't need to feel it—visual evidence is amply sufficient." It would be nice to be excited to fever pitch, but if there was a premature discharge of his weapon then it would all be in vain. At their age there was no longer the capacity for a quick sponge and reload. "So what's the cause of consternation if it's not just your boots and your magnificent firearm?"

"I've not got anything with me. You know. Like Vaseline or something."

"Ah. Keeping the old gun oiled, you mean?" Jonty moved away from the bed, abandoning trousers and drawers on the way, his muscular and still attractive backside barely covered by the tail of his shirt.

Orlando breathed deeply again at the sight. "I wouldn't have put it so crudely. But the gun needs oiling if it's to fit into the carriage without undue incident." And without shooting at random and too soon.

"I've got some salve here. I use it for chapped skin on my feet. Well, don't turn your nose up, it's better than nothing." Jonty produced a little jar, loosening the lid. The aroma of lavender and other herbs filled the space between them.

"Better than nothing, if a bit lacking in romance. Foot ointment." Orlando rolled his eyes. "Smells nice, though. Would you like to do the honours?"

"Looking at the state you're in, I think if I tried to do anything with your poor old gun I'd set off an explosion. Worse than mine sweeping. Sorry, that wasn't in good taste." Jonty sat on the bed, sighing in frustration. "Making a bit of a mess of this, aren't we? I'd rather hoped for a wonderfully romantic union and this is just too prosaic and problematical."

Orlando put his arm around his lover's shoulders, kissing the top of his head. "Prosaic will do just fine. It's taking some of the edge off my disobedient cannon down there. Maybe he'll behave himself long enough to get onto parade properly and do his duty like a good little soldier."

"Not so little." Jonty sighed again, but took the sturdy soldier in his hand and admired his fine carriage. "I would say this is one of the most magnificent specimens I've ever seen and I saw more than I wanted to when it was wash day. You have no idea how much I've missed teasing you, almost as much as I've missed doing my duty with you." He stopped, a great shiver working up his body. "Actually I'm not sure I have the heart to call it 'doing my duty' any more—lost its special meaning, somehow. Not sure I want to call him 'my brave soldier' or 'your old gun', either."

"We've both seen too many guns and soldiers—too much duty and not enough common sense." A sudden silence fell between them, as threatening as the sound of cannon fire out on a dark night. Orlando felt Jonty shuddering against him. "What's up?"

"Wash day. A line of men lining up to clean some of the filth off themselves. A quarter of them dead five days later." Jonty's shoulders sagged in poignant remembrance and his voice sounded as if it was on the verge of tears—whether of sorrow or frustration wasn't clear. "Some of them had probably never had a girl—or a man—in all their lives. It doesn't feel quite the thing to be here, with you, and those poor sods are all food for the worms..." Jonty rubbed his hands over his eyes, twisting out of Orlando's grip. "It'll never be the same, you know."

Orlando swallowed hard. Never be the same? Had any future chance of intimacy been blown away in a bombardment of remorse, the awful guilt that Jonty had survived while his men hadn't? "They wouldn't begrudge you a bit of happiness, you know."

"Maybe not." Jonty's great sighs seemed as if they'd stemmed from the depth of his being. "And I won't begrudge you a bit of happiness too." He slipped his hand between his lover's legs again. "Afraid I've lost the inclination for the moment."

Orlando didn't even need to look to assess the physical problem—Jonty had never been that excited and *he'd* been too wrapped up in his own needs to really notice. Now he wasn't aroused at all. "I'm sorry. I've been selfish." He took Jonty's face in his hands, smoothing over the unfamiliar beard with gentle thumbs. "Perhaps it would be best to leave it for today." He leaned in for a swift, tender kiss. "I've been in such a tearing hurry. Maybe tomorrow and a slow wooing will work better."

"Maybe. But let me sort you out, please. It would be lovely to make you come again." Jonty returned the kiss, skilled hands working their way up and down Orlando's abdomen and in and out of his legs.

"No, no. Not if we can't be together." Orlando breathed deep again, trying desperately not to climax.

"Please don't say that. If you don't let me do this for you right now I'm going to go mad. Honest to God." Jonty stroked more insistently, taking a firm grip until any resistance was overcome and futile. "I love you, Orlando. I need to show you that feeling's not dead, even if half the world is." He pressed his lips to Orlando's ear, murmuring the declaration of love over and again as the ripples of pleasure flowed through the man's body.

They lay together, arms wrapped tight around each other, holding close for what seemed an eternity, as if the pair of them were afraid that if they parted for a second the other man would disappear. "I'm sorry." Orlando's ecstasy had turned to tears. "It should have been better. For you."

"Hush. I've got you again. How could anything be better?" Jonty snuggled into his lover's embrace, maybe trying to shrug off their failure, if not the guilt. "We've got time again, as well. I'll meet you tomorrow, after breakfast." He made no further promise of what the next day would bring, perhaps just in case it was a pledge his body—or spirit—couldn't guarantee to keep.

"It will be fine, Jonty. We've known hard times before and overcome them." Orlando's hands drew lazy circles on Jonty's back, caressing the shirt if not yet the skin. "I'll take you home again."

"Will you? And will you be glad you did so when they start whispering behind our backs?"

"I think I'm beyond worrying about people knowing we're lovers. We've hid it for all these years, I've no doubt we can hide it for longer."

"Not that, Orlando, although it's scandal enough." Jonty shook himself free of his lover's grip, picking up his clothes and dressing again, disconsolate. "What about when people say 'Jonty Stewart ran away'? Have you thought about that?"

Chapter Thirteen

Orlando had always believed the best thing for improving Jonty's mood was food, especially seafood; it had proved effective in the past in fuelling both his brain and his body. There was plenty of seafood at the little restaurant they found on Cabourg's main street. The menu was awash with it, enough to take a man's mind, even if just temporarily, off what had happened in Jonty's bedroom. Orlando didn't quite drag his friend in through the door and to a table—Jonty never had to be dragged to the nosebag—but he had to fight to muster any enthusiasm in him. The Coquilles St. Jacques they ordered to start, with a delicate little white wine which wouldn't overpower either them or the salmon which would follow, worked a bit of magic on his spirits.

"So what have you been up to?" Jonty's voice sounded forced—almost theatrically airy. Perhaps the wine would soon begin to ease things. "Apart from burying me in the churchyard. Lavinia told me about that."

"Did she tell you about the garden?" Orlando launched into the tale of the work that had been going on at their cottage, inside and out. Mundane, domestic considerations, safe to discuss and unlikely to take them into dangerous waters. This reunion wasn't at all turning out to be how he'd expected it. He took another sip of wine and turned to matters investigational.

"I have a commission going on, as well. Or I was supposed to have before I got sidetracked." He rummaged in his pocket for the picture Mrs. McNeil had given him. "He disappeared and his mother wants to know where he is."

"Ah." Jonty topped up their glasses, then put on his own spectacles to better study the picture. "Tell Uncle Jonty all and he'll use his impressive powers of deduction to find the flaws in your analysis."

Orlando resisted either kicking his friend under the table or making some barbed retort. Whatever was causing the roller coaster of emotions that Jonty was undergoing, it was a positive sign to hear him make such a frivolous remark. That was like the old Jonty, pre-France, pre-Room 40, pre-everything bad. "It started with Matthew Ainslie—he brought me the case as a present, I think. To cheer me up."

"Dear Matthew, bless him—and bless his honey buzzards. Tell me everything, from the beginning."

The story lasted through the entrée and into the second course, Orlando's elegant and methodical narrative being constantly interrupted by someone else's piercing and sometimes ridiculous questions and comments. Despite how closely Jonty must be feeling the parallels with his own experience—and the occasional wince showed that he did feel them—discussing the case seemed to be improving his mood, not dampening it.

"Matthew Ainslie, Collingwood, Uncle Tom Cobley and all." Jonty clearly savoured the names on his tongue. "When I think of them I think that there's a chance everything will be well again, one day. Smacks of England and home and basic decency. Matthew still tupping that American lad?"

Orlando swatted Jonty's arm. "That's hardly a decent way of putting it. You've spent too long with the common foot soldiery and I'll have to wash your mouth out with disinfectant. Matthew is still partners with Rex. In more ways than one." He couldn't resist the addendum, nor the grin that went with it. "Let me finish the story."

The possibility of pudding was hull up on the horizon by the time Wiggins and O'Leary and all had come into play. "I even wondered if Beaumont might have been McNeil—we've had stranger coincidences happen to us—and then of course it turned out to be odder still, because it was you, you little tinker." Orlando scooped up his last morsel of food and let part of his mind wander to Crepes Suzette. Discharging his weapon—no, they were going to have to find a better term for that—always made him hungry, as did sorting out a mystery or trying to make Jonty happy once more.

"Will you ever find him, do you think?" Jonty looked at the little photo again. It seemed like his appetite had returned too, and not just for food. He had a dreamy look in his eye which had been missing earlier.

"Will *we* find him, don't you mean? We've always investigated together and it's brought us good fortune."

"I thought you only believed in logic, not luck." Jonty sat back, smiling almost happily, the candlelight creating strange highlights in his beard, hints of auburn and silver winking amongst the dusty blond.

"I've begun to believe in a lot more than just logic these last few years. And I'm not sure logic brought you to me again—that was pure luck, your Lavinia's, or maybe my grandmother acting as guardian angel again as you used to swear she did back home." Orlando sat back as well, swelling with an emotion that could only be described as overwhelming soppiness. If he'd ever forgotten one iota of how much in love he'd been with the man sitting opposite, he recalled it all now. Love to the point of pain.

Love even more painful because of the distress of bereavement which had preceded it. He took another drink of wine, although the consumption was being paced—if that look in Jonty's eye meant anything, there was still a small possibility of relations being resumed this evening and he wasn't daft enough to risk brewer's droop.

"Can you imagine Grandmother Coppersmith and my mother in cahoots? They'll have sorted out all the Archangel Michael's problems by now and be setting about Gabriel. And poor St. Peter will be prostrate with shell shock. Oh, that wasn't really called for was it?" Jonty began to laugh, a deep bubbling incongruous joy welling up and overflowing.

"No, laugh about it—the only way we'll prove to ourselves that we've left it all behind us is to be able to see the funny side of things. We can't cry and fret forever or else we might as well be buried in the ground with all the lads who never made it. We owe it to them to laugh."

"My lads used to call it sticking two fingers up at fate. Well maybe we're sticking two fingers up at the war and saying it didn't finish us off." Jonty wiped his eyes, drained his glass and looked out of the window. The evening light still lingered over the sea, although it seemed much darker looking out at it than walking home in it would be. "Maybe we should leave poor Daniel McNeil alone—stick two fingers up at his fate too. I can't condemn him, Orlando, it would border on hypocrisy. And if going home scares the hell out of me, how must he feel?"

"I understand, but I have his mother to face. If you leave the son in peace would you condemn her to uncertainty and misery at the same time? If it was your mother alive now wouldn't you want her mind put at rest?" Orlando gave his friend time to think, time to figure things out rather than leap, in his Kildare Fellow of Tudor Literature way, to some hasty conclusion.

At long last Jonty spoke. "No, you're right. She'll welcome him home with open arms and they'll pass it all off as neurasthenia or something. He was an officer." The sudden bitter edge to Jonty's voice made Orlando's spirits drop; the roller coaster still ploughed on, clearly. "Can't see how we do it, though. Will this be the only mystery Stewart and Coppersmith will ever have to leave unsolved?"

"Coppersmith and Stewart. I hope not. I even hoped that, finding you again, you'd have come across some clue. I've drawn two bows at a venture and hit the target on this case, so I was sure it would happen a third time. Especially now I have you again, my talisman." Orlando briefly caressed Jonty's sleeve.

"I don't think he was just trying to escape from his father." Jonty's fingers walked across the table cloth, in a ridiculous mime of someone running away. "The little escape fund notwithstanding. McNeil would have gone off to the Sorbonne or some other respectable place and continued his studies, like a sensible lad, and not risked being on the run the rest of his life."

"You've not met his father..."

"Neither have you, or so it appears, so don't presume. This chap O'Leary's at the bottom of it all, mark my words." Jonty lifted his fork in an eloquent gesture. "Now, I've had enough of talking about times past for a while. I need some eloquently presented petit fours and then you can walk me home."

Orlando could barely concentrate on his crepes nor on the St. Bride's small talk which flavoured them. Even bewhiskered, Jonty by candlelight was beautiful, his cornflower blue eyes a deep sapphire and the blond of his hair aflame with subtle shades. There was nothing likely to be more enjoyable than sneaking him back into the Hotel Casino and exploring the delights of a bed together, except that risked being discovered and—worse than that—another failure to bring Jonty to completion. Returning to the pension was just as likely to be a disaster, with the memory of recent failure and worries hanging over it.

As if his thoughts had communicated themselves directly into his lover's brain, Orlando was jolted into the present by Jonty leaning over the table conspiratorially. "We could try again, you know. That which we attempted earlier with so little success." Something resembling a smirk broke over Jonty's face although it was hard to tell the subtlety of the expression below all the fungus.

"If you could suggest a suitable location I'd be more than willing to make the effort. Unfortunately both of the obvious places seem to have insurmountable problems." Even though they'd been speaking English—except for placing their orders—a certain amount of verbal subterfuge still seemed necessary.

"Then we need a third place." Jonty lowered his voice to hardly more than a whisper. "Surely there must be some little pension where we could take a twin-bedded room just for the one night and no questions asked? Madame DesRues will assume I've found myself a nice little soubrette to spend the evening with and the Hotel Casino probably won't even notice you've just left your bag in your room. You've paid for the place—it's up to you what you do with it."

"And Lavinia?"

"Lavinia is far too sensible—and sensitive—to ask where you've been and what you've been a doing of." Jonty grinned. "And Ralph would be far too embarrassed. Come on, finish up like a good boy and I'll pay the bill. You can pay for the room."

"If we ever find one." Despite his irritable words, Orlando set to the last of his crepes with alacrity. When his plate was almost spotless he pushed it away and refused the offer of coffee, simply calling for *l'addition*. "And talking of you paying the bill, how on earth have you managed for the old filthy lucre all these months?"

"Ah. I'll tell you that story en route—there's a little back road I've strolled along that seems to have one or two places which might suit. It's just far enough for me to relate the tale, so long as you promise not to be cross with me." Jonty rummaged in his pocket, producing a prodigious quantity of francs.

"As long as you've not been acting as a gigolo, I think I could forgive you anything tonight."

The story lasted almost the perfect amount of time, from restaurant to the front door of a clean looking if very modest boarding house. Jonty did the honours with the landlord, pleading that they'd arrived later than expected and needed a room just for the night while they awaited their baggage catching them up. The wonderfully innocent look on Jonty's face wouldn't have fooled his mother but it took in the elderly man who was the keeper of the house. He showed them up to a humble but scrupulously clean room, with two small beds, a dressing table, jug and bowl for water and—an unexpected touch—a small vase of fresh flowers. It was homely if very plain and it felt like heaven. Jonty murmured something to the landlord, pressed some coins into his hand and let him depart, leaving the door ajar.

"We should close that." Orlando eyed the door uneasily.

"No. Not for the moment. I've asked our host to run me a small errand." Jonty smiled enigmatically, and Orlando didn't have to wait long to find out why the happy look was on his face. A boy appeared, carrying a jug of steaming water which he tipped into theirs, then the landlord came with a razor, brush and soap. Last of all in this strange procession came what must have been his wife, bearing a small, soft towel and a pair of apple brandies on a tray. When they'd all departed again, the door was firmly closed.

"What's all this?" The brandy Orlando could understand but the rest of the rigmarole made little sense.

"I've struggled to come to terms with these whiskers, but they've seemed a necessary evil." Jonty weighed the soap in trembling hands. "If you can cope with my face as it really is, then it'll be a sign there's still hope for things to turn out fine."

"Idiot." Orlando steadied his friend's hands. "Is the brandy for before or after the operation?"

"After, I think. Just in case you can't stand the shock." Jonty smiled again, but the tremor in his voice betrayed him. Maybe this, as much as the story of his fall from grace, had been preying on his nerves. Could the scar be so bad?

"Whatever the outcome I think I'd prefer you clean shaven. I don't think I could ever get used to those whiskers."

"I thought I never would, either. Used to wake in the morning and think another man was staring out of my mirror at me. Perhaps he was." Jonty ran his hands over his chin, with a finality of movement. "Maybe it's time for this to go, in allegory of the old Jonty trying to come back and Monsieur Cesario having outlived his use."

"Cesario?"

"That's been the name I've used. Think about it—when you're less befuzzled it'll make sense." Jonty took Orlando's hand, dragging him off the bed in the direction of the jug and toiletries. "You can do the honours."

"With what? I can't use my fingernails—did you forget to ask our host for a razor?"

"Brought my own." Jonty lifted a little velvet bag from his pocket and tipped the contents onto the dressing table top. "Just in case the evening took a turn for the better—better than in my room, that is."

Orlando hadn't seen Jonty pick up the blade nor put it into a bag. Sleight of hand or sleight of tongue? Maybe he always carried the razor with him, for the moment he took the plunge and rid himself of his facial disguise. "What's this? I never thought I'd see Jonty Stewart use a safety razor." Orlando twirled the sturdy metal in his hand. "After all that fuss you made when your father first tried one."

"It was much easier to use in the trenches. I wasn't going to make my servant have to use my old cutthroat on me and he'd have never deigned to let me *perform the service on myself*, which was his usual expression for anything he disapproved of me doing." Jonty took the brush and worked up the shaving soap into a satisfyingly creamy lather in the cup of his hand.

"I think we should prune some of the fungus first or we'll never make it through to the skin. Do you have some scissors?"

"Ah, no. Bit of an oversight." Jonty stopped in mid stroke, his face half lathered.

"Luckily I have the ones on my old penknife. Here. Wipe this lather off first." Orlando handed Jonty the towel. "And sit on the chair, please—let the dog see the rabbit."

"Will that old thing be up to the job?" Jonty looked uncomfortable, as if he was facing Sweeney Todd.

"I should think Mrs. Ward's pinking shears are hardly up to the job. Or the gardener's scythe."

"We have a gardener now, do we? There's distinction." Jonty swallowed hard and shut his eyes.

"I could do with him here." Orlando set to with the scissors, cautiously at first, not wishing to nick his lover's flesh, then

All Lessons Learned

with more gusto as he realised there was what seemed like miles of the stuff to penetrate before terra firma was reached. "I feel like the prince in Sleeping Beauty, carving my way through the brambles to reach my loved one."

Jonty sighed. "You always did have the most romantic way with words. I'll keep my eyes shut and dream, then you can claim me with a kiss when you're done."

"Don't fall asleep. I'll need the moral support." Orlando hacked at a particularly wiry clump of ginger tinged whiskers. "I could be hours." As it was, the initial part of the operation hardly took more than a few minutes, a rather wary Jonty eyeing himself in the little mirror on the wall once part one was complete.

"I resemble a leprous badger." He turned one particularly scabrous cheek towards the glass. "Most unenticing. You'd better hurry up and get the rest done." He swallowed hard and the troubled look in his eye gave Orlando pause. Jonty wasn't looking forward to having his scar exposed, but he was putting his bravest front on things—had he the same glint in his eye when he was about to lead his men over the top? They worked up the lather again in silence, Jonty holding the foam while Orlando smeared it on his face. With gentle strokes, as tenderly as if he was handling a baby, Orlando drew the razor over his friend's cheeks, exposing the soft skin that hadn't seen the light of day for months. He avoided the scar, skirting around it until the last possible moment.

"Would you rather I did the last bit?" Jonty grabbed Orlando's now trembling hand.

"Perhaps. I'm afraid I'll hurt you." Orlando gave up the razor.

"You could never hurt me, old man." Jonty fingered the last remaining whiskers. "Actually, I'd prefer if you did it. Distance of this mirror and all that..."

"You don't want to put on your spectacles do you, vanity-thy-name-is-Jonty?" Orlando grinned then, steadying his hands, took back the razor and began to work. "It would serve you right if I sliced part of your nose off for being so vain." Whatever the threat, there was no risk of it being carried out, Orlando being even more careful in his ministrations. When cold water and then a towel were applied, Jonty was entirely clean shaven and as beautiful as he'd been when they'd first met.

Orlando reached over, edging a finger towards the scar and gently tracing its lines. "I think this makes you even more striking than you were fourteen years ago. It adds a dignity and gravitas I'm not sure you ever had before."

"I don't believe a word of that, but I'll pretend it's true." Jonty turned his good side to the mirror. "I'll just have to face everyone this way on in the future, except for young George. He'll be impressed, if no one else."

"He thinks his Uncle's a hero and quite right too." Orlando held up his hand to delay any further argument. "But me no buts this time. It's too precious a moment." He caressed the scar again, then sprinkled a line of kisses along it.

Jonty leaned back into his lover's embrace. "I should let you shave me more often—it was incredibly stimulating. I do feel rather like you deflowered me." He turned his face so that he could return the kisses. "And if the contents of your pants aren't deceiving me, I'd say you found the process equally exciting."

"I find everything about you exciting. Haven't you got that into your noddle yet?" Orlando bent down and placed another tender kiss on Jonty's lips. "I do love you."

"And, remarkably enough, I love you too. Maybe there's a

chance the world is all right, after all." Jonty's tongue edged along Orlando's lips then thrust into his mouth, hard and insistent. As hard and insistent as they wanted something else to be when it got its chance. "Would it be indecent to ask you to take me? Right now?"

"How can I refuse you anything?" Orlando pulled Jonty from the chair, hefted him up and carried him all the way—the entire three paces—to the bed. Jonty would have his wooing and his romance, even if it risked his lover pulling a muscle in the process.

Jonty tousled Orlando's hair then pulled him onto the little bed alongside him. "Well there may be a sprinkling of snow on the roof, but there's plenty of fire in the hearth, I can tell that."

"There's not a flake of snow on this roof, Dr. Stewart—your eyes must be worse than ever. And as for the hearth, the fire's been out for years. You've laid the kindling again, the second time today." Orlando studiously ignored the fact that a certain Dr. Beattie had at least reminded him that he possessed a hearth—and a heart—to warm. Only Jonty counted, as only Jonty had always counted. He gently peeled off his lover's waistcoat and shirt, the jacket having been discarded before the shaving had begun. He wanted to see flesh, the magnificent chest that was usually kept hidden away under tweed and linen, although he started to bridle when Jonty tried to remove *his* shirt. In the heat of the moment he'd forgotten about *it*.

"Whatever is the matter, man—I thought that we had the same end in view? Although I'm not getting to view anything, at this rate." Jonty grinned, getting to work with even more determination. "I don't know why you're suddenly so..." He found out as soon as he lifted Orlando's vest. The great livid mark swept down almost from clavicle to diaphragm; red, nasty. "That's one hell of a scar—I suspect it's the most startling thing I've ever seen. Like a huge medal ribbon. Is that what happened before you were taken prisoner?"

"It was. It's pretty well superficial, I guess—nothing vital got touched apart from a few ribs that were nicked, but I lost a lot of blood. I've wished plenty of times since that the blade had done its job properly and gone all the way in. I don't wish that now." Orlando leaned to start the kisses again, tender at first and then more insistent, tongue probing and darting.

Jonty sighed. This was better, so much better than before—the heady rush towards instant gratification replaced by proper romance, the sort he'd always craved. And funny how all the important details flooded back, how lying bare chest on bare chest made Orlando so happy, where and when to touch. Where and when not to touch and risk another disaster. Jonty deliberately refrained from some of Orlando's favourite delights; the man was hard and excited enough already.

"Glad to see you're still *interested.*" Orlando's hand slipped down between his lover's legs, caressing and coaxing.

"You'd better loosen your grip or all the good work your devastatingly romantic words have done will be lost. Ah, thank you." Jonty took a deep breath, calming himself before any premature storm could break; there couldn't be a greater contrast to the last time. "Are you going to get prepared for me or will this fine moment go to waste? I'm ready. Right now." If they didn't get about it soon, he couldn't be answerable for the consequences.

"Are we going to have to use that soap?" Orlando was breathing heavily now—still in control but barely.

"Not when Uncle Jonty's in charge." He rummaged in his trouser pocket again—not only had the razor been brought, just in case, but the little tub of salve had managed to find its way here as well. "Let me do the anointing. Roger needs to be tended to."

"Roger?" Orlando lay back and let himself be ministered to.

"Yes. If we're to have no more talk of doing our duty or oiling our weapons then we'll have to call it rogering. Rogering with Roger." Jonty grinned and wiped his hands on Orlando's chest. "You always seemed to have an affection for those terms, old boy."

"Old boy? I'll show you who's an old boy." Orlando grabbed his friend, rolled him onto his back and mounted him, slowly and sensitively uniting their bodies. Jonty was certainly ready, yielding himself with a long, languorous sigh. Orlando murmured into Jonty's neck some tender words which might have been ancient French or even Swahili for all the sense his lover could make of them. But the essence was clear—loving and being loved in return. And when they came, almost in unison with mouths pressed against each other's skin for fear of crying out, the first steps towards healing had really been taken. They weren't whole again yet, either of them—might not be for years—but at least the possibility was there once more and the path towards the light had been found.

Any daylight was all gone now, even the distant glimmer from a window across the street had disappeared, the lamp put out or the candle snuffed. Not even a sliver of moon to illuminate the little room, but it wasn't necessary. They had known every inch of each other's body before and needed no lighting to find their way around that landscape. Orlando traced the scar right along Jonty's cheek, adding a new feature to his mental map as Jonty had already taken in every detail of his scarred chest, although this time with his tongue. He fingered the rest of Jonty's face. "You're no less handsome than you ever were. This scar's as striking as your Military Cross and as fine a symbol of your gallantry. But this..." his fingers slipped down to Jonty's chest, hovering above his heart, "...is the most beautiful part of you. Your brave heart."

"Idiot." Jonty's fingers closed over Orlando's hand. "But you're the most wonderful idiot in the world."

Orlando lay in a cocoon of contentment, afraid to move in case he broke whatever spell had woven itself around him, maybe to wake up and find that these last few days with Jonty had just been another dream, the sort he'd had regularly since the previous October. He had to speak, though, release some of the pent-up dam of emotion. "I've been in hell the last few months. With a hole in my heart that couldn't be healed and that ached like rats were gnawing at it continually."

"Only rats? I had filthy great tyrannosaurs eating away at mine." Jonty twined his fingers with his lover's. "That's been and gone now, though. All done."

Orlando wanted to say, "I wished every day that I'd died with you in the mud," but he refrained. Jonty's mood was lighter now and he wouldn't risk it darkening. Each day had to see them creeping forward, another step on the slow road to complete recovery and rehabilitation. He thought of Wiggins, of the other men in St. Judith's and how Jonty could have ended up alongside them; might still end up alongside them if he couldn't overcome his fear of returning home. If it took the rest of Orlando's life—if it took everything he had to give—he'd see his friend cured and if that meant keeping his own pain to himself, so be it. He certainly wouldn't tell him yet how he'd intended dying by the green fields of Normandy, slipping down a conveniently precarious cliff. That would wait until next spring or the one after. Or maybe the spring twenty years down the line. "You have no idea how many times I cursed your God for taking you away from me."

Jonty rubbed Orlando's shoulders, clearly trying to ease away any residual pain or despair. "And you have no idea how often I thanked him for bringing me safely through and reminding me of where my heart lay. Especially the last few days." He lifted Orlando's head, looking straight into his eyes. "Till death us do part. It tried very hard but it didn't succeed—I pray to God that it won't for many years yet."

Chapter Fourteen

They slept soundly, more deeply and contentedly than either of them had managed these last few years, despite the awkwardness of the bed. The pair nestled close together as they'd done the first time they'd shared—Jonty wedged against the wall and Orlando wound about him. An owl roused them in the night, perching in a bough just feet from the window; waking in pitch darkness, and with the rustling sounds of life outside, unsettled Jonty again.

"Did I wake you? I'm sorry, I was a bit cramped." Orlando whispered against his friend's neck.

"I thought I was back *there*, when I woke. Like I used to think I was back at school." Jonty didn't elaborate—they both knew what he meant. "It's been happening on and off since the war, regressing in my mind to unhappier times. It's not your fault at all. Nice to have you here. My hero, my champion." They drew closer, warm skin against warm skin.

"I was never a hero. That was your job."

"A hero? Was I?" Jonty was weary, wearier than their passion earlier or the interrupted sleep had warranted.

"You know you were—they recommended you for a medal, for God's sake." Orlando held his lover tighter, nestling Jonty's head under his chin. No one could reach them now; nothing would ever again take away their chance of happiness, unless it was their own bad dreams.

"Oh yes, a medal. Did the citation say it was for leaving his platoon under enemy bombardment, because I sure as damn it didn't lead them as I should have done." The sudden tension in Jonty's body—every inch of it coiled up like a spring—was palpable.

"That's not what your obituary said."

Jonty's laugh was bitter as his words. "It's a lucky man who gets to see his own obituary. I wish I'd had the opportunity to read it."

"You can, if you really want to." Orlando reached for his jacket, making sure he didn't lose hold of his friend in the process—he was never letting Jonty out of his sight, or metaphorical grip, again. Fumbling in the pocket, he produced an envelope from which he shook out a small piece of newspaper, folded small enough to keep with him always, among the other things which were constant reminders of the best thing he'd ever had in his life. "Let me find a light."

"There are some matches in my pocket." Jonty found his spectacles while Orlando lit a candle.

"Look." Orlando pressed the cutting into Jonty's grasp.

Jonty held the paper in trembling hands, adjusting his spectacles to make sense of the closely typed print, while snuggling Orlando closer to him again. He was gentle, smoothing out the folds with tender care, as tenderly as he'd caressed his lover's flesh. "Well I'm blowed." It wasn't from the Times or anything so grand—it was from the local Sussex paper, the one read upstairs and downstairs in the Stewarts' country home. Local pride it may have been, but the encomium couldn't have been more glowing, to a glowing local man. The report of his career was entirely accurate, Jonty wouldn't be able to deny that—Orlando had verified every detail as his first task on returning home, warming him with pride over the long cold midwinter evenings.

"It still doesn't sound like me." Jonty could hardly control the shaking in his hands. "Not the me I've had to live with. Not the me who ended up miles away from his platoon and has no idea why."

"But it is you. You can't argue that you didn't earn that first medal fair and square."

"Do you carry my Military Cross in your pocket too?" The sudden reappearance of a smile, another touch of the old Jonty, was a sign that not all hope had been lost.

"That medal's still in your study along with the rest of your mess. There should be a Military Medal to lie alongside it. I've not seen the citation but I've heard the story." Orlando carefully replaced the little slip of newspaper. "The Jonty Stewart I know couldn't have run. The Jonty Stewart who was his parents' son would never have been so disloyal. If you'd stayed in that foxhole you could well have been dead. Maybe your God and his angels gave you a second chance and you took it—you went into action again as soon as you could, for goodness sake."

"Don't make me talk about it, please." A great shiver racked Jonty's body. "Not now. I can't bear to even think about those nights. Put out the light and hold me. Remind me that we're both alive."

"Would taking me drive away the bad thoughts?" Orlando slipped his hand down the bed, desperate to find anything which would elevate his friend's mood. "That salve's still here, waiting."

"Orlando Insatiable Coppersmith. Is that what they christened you?" Jonty let himself be aroused again, even if his mind only seemed half on the process in hand. At least his body was fully employed in their lovemaking—diligent, tender, careful, as if Orlando were made of crystal, not flesh and blood. Two bodies united, two souls in union, two against a world that had made little sense of late.

They slept like stones, Orlando's innate clock making sure he was up and in his own bed before there was any risk of being discovered. Even though they'd woken early, they were refreshed and restored—new men even if the old Adam had made its presence felt the night before. And they woke to the sound of birdsong, in warm, comfy beds and with the smell of coffee and brioche drifting around the door jamb, like a foretaste of heaven, a dispensation of grace. They didn't linger over their toilette, just making themselves and the room presentable enough before taking their voracious hungers to be sated at the breakfast table in what was evidently the landlord's parlour.

"Is the hawthorn good this year? Or has it all gone and left not the merest scent behind?" Jonty broke his brioche and applied a little strawberry compote—not too sweet and extremely sticky, just as he liked it.

"I'm not sure I noticed." Orlando took a draft of coffee and smiled; this stuff was excellent, probably better than he'd get at the hotel.

"Not noticed?" The brioche was used to make an admonitory gesture. "Forsythia Cottage is always overrun with flowers, especially when the wind gets hold of the petals." There'd always been an amazing profusion of hawthorns edging their plot, their heady scent swamping their senses as they tended their garden. They'd developed their little piece of land together, chosen many of the shrubs and perennials, weeded and dug and sworn and sweated side by side.

"I've not really looked at things since I got back. Not in the same way."

"No." Jonty didn't need to say more. He remembered how Orlando had once found some very late tulips looking rather sorry for themselves, to which he'd showed no mercy and they'd ended up in flaming row about it. So stupid, such things seemed now.

"I care about your plot though." Orlando fished out his wallet and the little photograph with it. "It doesn't give a very good idea—still in its early stages."

"It'll be magnificent. Not many men get to see their own memorial." Jonty laid down his food.

"Less a memorial now, than a celebration. What's the matter?"

"It was thinking of home, the cottage, Mrs. Ward—Mrs. Sheridan! How on earth am I going to face everyone?" Jonty pushed away his plate. "I've been so happy this morning I completely forgot."

"Well, it's not *you* for a start. It's us. And we won't go home until you're ready and we've got your story all sorted out." Orlando risked a quick squeeze of his friend's hand. And a smile, a smile fortified by thoughts of the night before and his extreme gratitude.

"You're not suggesting we lie, are you? Papa would be known in heaven as revolving Stewart, he'd be turning so much in his grave." Jonty's face was ghostlike. "I won't lie."

"A mathematician would never lie, not like a historian." Orlando tried to erase the face of a certain historian from his memory. He'd never be able to go down to Ascension again and would have to thank Dr. Beattie—and tell him of the extraordinary coincidence regarding his story—by letter. "It would be presenting the best theorem to fit the facts, the best story. And if you're coming home with that scar and you wear your Military Cross, who's going to doubt you? And if anyone did they'd have me to answer to."

Jonty suddenly grinned, stretching like a cat in the sun. "I'd forgotten what a magnificent knight in white armour you make."

"Knight in armour, on a white *charger*, thank you. Ow." Orlando rubbed his shin. "And I'd forgotten what it was like for you to whack me. Dear God, Jonty, never leave me again, please. I wanted to die. I was going to come here and kill myself, you know." He stopped, cross that he'd poured out so much, words tumbling from him and exposing every part of his soul. In the past Jonty would have had to winkle out such gems of candour.

"Good God. Really? No," said Jonty, placing his hand on Orlando's arm, "don't answer that. I know it's true if you say it is. I know you too well." They finished their brioche in silence; all that needed to pass between them had already done so. Love would deal with the rest.

They made their way back—separately—to hotel and pension, to assure people that they hadn't died or run off to join the navy. Madame DesRues tried to feed Jonty a second breakfast, probably having convinced herself that he'd spent the night in a young lady's arms and would need building up after his exertions. He refused the food graciously, tried not to let the cat out of the bag in answering his landlady's questions and finished certain she couldn't have fallen for his story of helping out an old friend in need.

He spent the afternoon both staving off enormous yawns that threatened to overcome him and attempting to drum some more English into his charges. He could have cancelled, of course he could, pleading a cold or some such nonsense, but it was the sort of thing his mother would never have forgiven. And anyway, Orlando had gone off to try to make some sort of explanation to Lavinia and Ralph about why he'd not been around the previous evening. Jonty guessed *he* was having the easier time of it with his pupils.

Of course, Orlando was having no such thing as a hard time. He'd met Lavinia and her family over lunch, having changed and made himself slightly less raddled looking. Before he could even begin to try out one of the many explanations he'd put together for the previous evening, George had taken the wind from his sails by apologising that they'd not been around to entertain him, but the whole family had been to see a moving picture show. While he and Alexandra told the story of the evening and the film in excruciating detail, Orlando tried to look interested and not too relieved. Lavinia and Ralph just seemed slightly discomfited, as if they had known exactly what had been going on between him and her errant brother.

They'd all met for afternoon tea, the children falling on Jonty as if they'd not seen him in years and regaling him with another long-winded explanation of the wonders of the cinema. When they'd finished—or at least drawn breath before a second assault on everyone's patience was essayed—Ralph managed to force a word in. "Will you both join us for dinner tonight? The children are having an early supper and an early night as we were a bit late getting home yesterday."

Orlando cast a quick glance at his lover but bowed to the inevitable. Jonty evidently also realised there was no escaping this summons and that sharing a bed tonight was going to be improbable if not absolutely impossible. Tea and conversation about the doings of St. Bride's gave way to getting children an early supper and getting adults into their best bibs and tuckers. The conversation over dinner turned to the more serious matter of Daniel McNeil.

Ralph and Lavinia hung on every word Orlando had to say, which he found agreeable—there was always part of him which, bashfulness notwithstanding, enjoyed being the centre of attention. Ralph had been on the fringes of their investigations before, an enthusiastic and perceptive player when he'd been allowed to play, and now his ears pricked up like a racehorse sighting the winning post.

"There must be a chance he's gone to ground here." Ralph twirled his knife in the air—the sort of sloppy manners his late mother-in-law would have upbraided him for, but allowable in the heat of the chase.

"If he has, I bet my dear landlady would know all about it. It seems she has the same infallible means of finding out about things that Mama possessed." Jonty laid down his cutlery with care, in case he was tempted to make Gallic gestures with it. "I'll ask Madame DesRues in the morning, although I don't hold out much hope. Needle in a haystack doesn't begin to describe it."

"I had this mad idea, this morning..." Orlando was suitably embarrassed at such a revelation. He was the man of logic, after all. "That the forces of coincidence would strike another time. I've become almost used to it these last few weeks."

"And this mad idea was?" Jonty delighted at every occasion when the irrational took precedence over the forces of reason.

"That you might have come across him on your travels. Or heard a story about him, like when I found someone who'd known about McNeil defending his servant."

"Just because I've been wandering France, it doesn't mean I've met every other waif or stray along the way." Jonty touched Orlando's arm, briefly caressing the sleeve of his jacket in as intimate an act as they could risk over the dinner table. "I'm sorry. It's a big country and a man could lose himself forever if he didn't want to be found and he had help."

"Don't I know it?" said Orlando, putting his head in his hands. "There's nothing the trail of reason and common sense can do—we either get a blinding stroke of luck or it's all up." The party sat in silence, looking at their plates and studiously avoiding Orlando's gaze. It seemed such a shame to disappoint him. The meal ended quietly, with both Orlando and Jonty trying desperately to hide their yawns and Lavinia and Ralph trying not to catch each other's eye and giggle.

"I'll just walk Jonty back to his lodgings." Orlando kissed Lavinia's hand and shook Ralph's.

"You do that." Ralph nodded. "But don't stay out too late. Barometer's falling and I didn't like the look of the sky, earlier."

"I'll make him take a brolly back here if the heavens open." Jonty kissed his sister's cheek and cuffed his brother-in-law's shoulder. "And you *will* come back here tonight," he whispered as they went through the hotel doors. "I need my sleep." They walked side by side along the front, the evening having the smell of rain in the air but still mercifully dry.

"That mad idea of yours..." Jonty's voice broke the companionable silence which had enveloped their stroll.

Orlando's ear pricked up like a greyhound in the slips. "I like the sound of 'that mad idea of yours'. It's the sort of thing which usually means you've just had your annual profound thought."

"Blow me, if there's one thing I've really missed it's you talking such rot. If I didn't love you for your handsome face or beautiful body or the wonderful way you roger me stupid I'd love you for your wonderful insults." Jonty grabbed Orlando's hand, swinging his arm then letting it go, like they were children at play. "And I suppose that's rather useful isn't it, on the grounds that your looks might fade and your body might either go stringy or run to fat but you'll always have a way with words. Ow. And a way with pinching my backside. I can't work out if I missed that or not."

"You did and you know it. And I suppose I'll have to grudgingly admit that I quite missed your endless prattling waffle. Life has been far too quiet." Orlando wiped his nose with his hand. "Sorry. Old soldiers shouldn't sniffle."

"Why not, Orlando? We've seen enough to make us weep." Jonty's arm slipped over his friend's shoulders, to remain there until they reached his pension. "Cheer up. I really have got a tiny little gem to share."

"Will you tell me your wonderful idea or will I have to pinch your backside black and blue to get it out of you?"

"I'm not sure it's that good a thought... Ow, stop it. I'll tell you—I really don't want to have my bottom resembling a map of the Himalayas. It's still a little delicate after last night," Jonty added, *sotto voce*. "It's the merest little molehill of a thing so don't go making a dirty great mountain of it. I've made a friend here, a painter called Lamboley. Served with the Flying Corps and is...well I'm not really sure what he's up to. Wandering around France looking for peace, he says."

"Maybe he's like McNeil, and has his reasons not to return home."

"I don't think so. I mean, he has his reasons, but they're different—his young lady died of the flu and I think it would break his heart to go back there just yet. I suspect when he finds love again, he'll find courage with it." Jonty's hand caressed Orlando's arm, the contact speaking volumes. "He's out at the beach almost every day, taking advantage of the light and making his sketches. Perhaps we might be lucky enough to catch him tomorrow, creating a picture of the fishing boats in the rosy-fingered dawn. Then you can interrogate him."

"You've not given me a reason yet to want to interrogate him. Being in the army hasn't made you any less woolly headed. Ow."

"You deserved it. Actually I think I need to administer knuckles to your bonce more often—you've done without for long enough and the effect on your manners has been highly detrimental." Jonty smiled and caressed the head he'd just attacked. "Lamboley told me this rather peculiar story. Your case has been full of peculiar stories so maybe this is the next little bit of coincidence you need."

Orlando nodded. Why shouldn't a twist of fate have this Lamboley—a slight spark of jealousy flared, quickly extinguished when Orlando remembered how he'd been attracted to Beattie—tell Jonty a story that might turn out to be about McNeil?

"He was in Trouville and he saw a bloke sobbing his heart out in a church. Someone who was racked with guilt because he couldn't save his men. Two of them had been shot for desertion or something and he felt like he'd done the deed. What a bloody mess, eh?" Jonty's voice was constrained, reverberating with sudden anger.

"Was this man in the church English?"

"He may have been. And he may have equally been over-dramatising the whole 'I'm responsible' part and covering up his own cowardice. Lamboley wouldn't commit himself either way." They stopped, having reached the pension but reluctant to say goodnight. "I'll ask him to give us all the details he has, but it seems awfully unlikely that there's any connection."

"We could at least try to pick up the trail in Trouville—I'd like to see the old place again, and a few more days away from St. Bride's would be justified. On all sorts of fronts." Orlando briefly caressed Jonty's hand in the dark. "We could take a suite or just another little room with a pair of beds. Then I wouldn't have to leave you on the doorstep."

"Like a pint of milk?" Jonty leaned close and kissed his friend's cheeks, one then the other. "This is one advantage of living here in France—couldn't risk that sort of greeting on King's Parade. Trouville sounds splendid, although I feel obliged to have another day here to resign my tutoring post and to spend some time with George and Alexandra."

"We did promise them sandcastles tomorrow morning." Orlando returned the kisses. "The day after it is. I'll get the hotel to organise our transport and make a forward booking."

"You do that, my boulevardier." Jonty slapped his lover's shoulder and was off through the door, whistling some continental sounding tune, leaving Orlando to wander back to the Hotel Casino in a warm and almost optimistic haze.

Chapter Fifteen

Trouville was even lovelier than Orlando remembered it. The sun was shining, the train journey had been pleasant, and the hotel Clerc, where they'd dropped their luggage, seemed absolutely perfect. A two-bedroom suite had been reserved for them, and the rumour had it that one of those rooms had a double bed. Whatever the day held in store, the chances were that the night would hold a lot more. They'd taken lunch but resisted the temptation of a post-prandial snooze in favour of a walk in the sunshine and doing some proper detective work.

Jonty wore a smile as they strolled along, a smile that had grown more relaxed as the last few days had worn on. His young charges at Cabourg had declared his scar the most magnificent thing they'd ever seen—although one had asked if he'd got it at Agincourt—and it hadn't seemed to produce any untoward reaction as he'd been out and about. Ladies still held his gaze just a little too long and some of the minxes dropped their handkerchiefs as he passed. Business as normal, at least regarding outward appearances.

He tapped Orlando's arm. "I can't quite believe this story of Lamboley's will turn out to be anything but a mare's nest, although I'm trying to keep my faith in our guardian angels."

"Are we going to have the big coincidence versus guiding hand debate? Again?" They'd argued this out plenty of times before but this time Orlando's tone showed he wasn't ready for a big fight. It had all been said before, of course. *He'd* talk about all the hundreds of little events that happened over the course of a day—a week, a month—and how some of them were bound to link up. It wasn't fate, it was sheer volume. And Jonty would usually sniff meaningfully and say, "Believe what you want, I think there's more to it."

"Only if you want to bow to my superior debating skills. And please don't give me all that nonsense about random events clustering." Jonty grinned, the sun on his back and his lover at his side and Trouville looking magnificent. What more could a man want for the moment? Even a nice sturdy dispute paled into insignificance. "I've heard it before and it's terribly unromantic."

"But they do. Because they're random. You see it's a case of..."

"Shut up this minute or I'll throw you over the side of the quay." They were sufficiently close to the edge, where the river wandered down to the sea and the boats could moor up, for a well judged charge to do the honours and Jonty was pleased to see his friend sidle away from the danger zone. "It's irrelevant in this case."

"Ah but it isn't." Orlando had worked himself the other side, closer to the road than the water, confident enough to pursue his point from a place of safety. "Now, you said to me a couple of days ago that it must have been God and his angels that made you and Lavinia end up in Cabourg at the same time."

Jonty remembered the exact circumstances in which he'd said it and blushed to the roots of his hair. Orlando had been in the height of ecstasy and he'd not been far behind; he'd never appreciated how much attention his friend must pay at these sorts of times. He was at least gratified to see that Orlando had turned scarlet as well. "Better pass quickly on to the point you want to make." He lowered his voice. "I'm not sure it does to remember that moment in too much detail. It's giving me ideas." They stopped, finding a little wall to lean on, one just the right height to hide any untoward embarrassment.

Orlando's voice was barely audible. "Just because we've been apart for all this time—it doesn't mean you have to make up for every single missed encounter at once. You'll run me ragged."

Jonty grinned even more broadly and leaned closer to the wall. "Concentrate on the matter in hand, then. Lavinia was drawn to Cabourg."

"Nonsense. She came to France because of that vow we made about having a family holiday here—she's the sensible sort of woman who'd take that sort of promise as binding. You probably went for the same reason, if subconsciously. I'd have gone there too. It was second on my list after Villers-sur-Mer."

"Not top? You're losing it, old man." Jonty turned sideways on to Orlando. Curse light summer trousers and the revealing way they outlined your every part. "What made that the place of choice?"

"Those blessed fossils you used to go on about. The ones I keep seeing every time I go in your study." Orlando, evidently in a fit condition to proceed along the road, did so. "I had a feeling you'd be down on the beach with your little hammer, filling your pockets with them."

"If you'd come a few weeks ago I would have been. I have a whole box of fossils in storage back at the pension if you'd like to see them. Madame DesRues says she'll keep everything until needed. I might donate them to the paleontological boys. If they'll have the things, of course." Jonty was suddenly rueful again. "If they'll have *me* back at Cambridge, come to mention it."

"Can you doubt that Mrs. Sheridan wouldn't exert her influence?"

"Could she influence everyone, Orlando? Wouldn't there be talking behind hands down at Ascension and at *the college next door*? They'd love to rake up some scandal."

"Are we back there again?" Of course they were. This wasn't something which would blow over like a squall—there'd be no resolution until they were back in England and saw what befell them. For all that Orlando could remind his lover that they'd faced a damn sight worse in their time together, Jonty wasn't going to be mollified, either by food or affection, both of which had taken his mind off his worries but neither of which could solve them. "Come on. We're not going to go looking for McNeil with you in this mood. He's waited long enough, he can wait a while longer—you need some rest."

Jonty was about to argue, but settled for a shrug. Maybe 'rest' was a euphemism for "rogering", although Orlando's face indicated he was likely in for a disappointment. A man had to replenish his ammunition. They walked in virtual silence, only resuming something like a conversation as they lay side by side on the well-appointed double bed of their well-appointed suite.

"Did you have anyone over in England, Orlando? When you thought that I was gone. I remember our exhortations to each other, to try to love again." Jonty lay on his side, fingers doodling on the counterpane.

"No." The answer came slightly too quickly for comfort. Even if Beattie didn't count as he'd been just an inclination, one day Orlando was going to have to confess all, for his own peace of mind. Even if he'd be ribbed mercilessly about it. "Did you find a..." he struggled to say the word, "...lover? I wouldn't be resentful if that's what had happened."

Jonty threw back his head, but his usual laughter didn't come. "How can you say that? You'd be beside yourself with jealousy. No, there were no lovers, even when I thought myself in widow's weeds."

Orlando breathed a sigh of relief; as usual Jonty had known him too well and of course he'd have been overpowered with resentment if there'd been anyone else. Not resentment at Jonty of course, he'd remain inviolate, but against whoever it was who'd seduced him. The little spark of ready-to-be-jealousy which had kindled in his mind ignited something else. Jealousy always went hand in hand with desire in Orlando's heart—the first time he and Jonty had done anything that resembled making love was with envy of a past lover stoking the flames of Orlando's lust. It had its usual effect now. He snuggled closer, fingering Jonty's shirt buttons.

"I heard that sigh—you might as well have 'I'm so relieved' tattooed all over your forehead. Such a great pudding." Jonty kissed the top of his lover's head and caressed his ear. "But my very own pudding."

"The crown prince of romantic language." Orlando turned his face up for a kiss, drawing Jonty's body closer and realising that, whatever emotions were going through the man's brain, his body was ready for action. Maybe both of them were capable of replenishing their ammunition more quickly than they'd assumed. He risked another kiss and had it returned with interest. This was like being young and reckless again, wanting to make love at any and every opportunity. But didn't they have months—years—of abstinence to make up for? And both were now more aware of the importance of seizing the day, of never assuming that another opportunity would always be found just around the corner.

"Shall I put out a 'Do Not Disturb' sign?" Jonty's soft voice tickled his lover's neck. "I thought I'd run you ragged."

"You have." Orlando drew his hand along Jonty's side. "It'll have to be a slow race, not a sprint."

"Then a sign seems essential. I'll help you with the French so it can't be misinterpreted." Jonty took some of the writing paper from the bureau and crafted a message, his concentration not helped by an extremely frisky mathematician nibbling at the back of his neck. Not entirely run ragged, then. "Hang that out while I perform my ablutions."

Orlando did so, checking a dozen times up and down the corridor to make sure the coast was clear before displaying the little sign. He eased the door shut, taking a deep breath of anticipation and stilling his excitement. How long was it since they'd last made love?—barely thirty-six hours, but he was ravenous again. Things had better settle down soon or he'd have a head full of grey hairs and sciatica before the week was out.

Jonty emerged from the bathroom looking like he could run an Olympic marathon, shirt off and nicely muscular chest on display. Whatever the condition of his mind and spirit, his body belied his age. Only pausing to ensure the door really was locked, Orlando took Jonty in his arms, drawing him as close as still allowed for breathing. "Turn or turnabout?" Secret code, of little meaning to anyone but them.

"Turn, I think. Unless turnabout would be less raggedifying?" Jonty drew his fingers down his lover's back, touching each little ridge along the backbone.

"That's another word you've made up. You're worse than Shakespeare for doing that." Orlando let his shirt be stripped from him, so that Jonty could better caress his vertebral processes, or whatever they were called. "But there's one word which you didn't have to make up. Love. As in I love you." Orlando landed a succulent kiss on Jonty's waiting lips. "Sometimes I think it's the only word that matters."

"More than integral calculus?" Jonty returned the kiss, gently caressing Orlando's chest as he did so.

"More than anything. It's taken me a long time to understand it, but I've grasped it at last." Orlando pulled Jonty towards the bed, encountering no resistance. "Turn it is, then." He started work on his lover's trouser buttons, slowly edging his clothes down and revealing the delicate and eager flesh underneath. There are no right angles in nature and each curve of Jonty's body—more substantial now than when they'd first been lovers but still trimmer than many men of his age—arced more elegantly than any graph of sine or cosine. No integral flowed more perfectly than the line from Jonty's waist to hip.

"Are you thinking Maths again?" Jonty pulled Orlando closer, making a mime of listening at his lover's ear. "Ah, yes. There's a horrible lot of numbers and incomprehensible signs parading through your bonce."

"How do you always know?" There was only one way to stop Jonty teasing and even that didn't always work. Even in the height of passion he could find a *bon mot* to share and jolly unsettling it could be. "I was comparing your body to a gracefully flowing curve." He traced the line of Jonty's flank. "Lovely."

"Away with you." Jonty smiled and leaned close for another kiss, a passionate and desperate kiss, the sort which usually marked the boundary between the entrée and the main course. Bon bouches were all very well, but this was the point where a man wanted more substantial fare. He let his hand trickle down Orlando's body and found what he seemed to be looking for.

When they'd first been in love this next part of the banquet had always passed too quickly, like dishes so delicious they had to be consumed without delay. The dessert—the perfect ending to the feast, the gloriously sticky, all encompassing pudding of delight—always used to arrive too soon, but now it was often deferred, kept at bay by both willpower and expertise.

The delights of stroking and fondling, resting and renewal of contact, union and dissolution couldn't be underestimated and if they took all afternoon, they had the time. "I love you." Orlando lay back, arms stretched behind his head, letting himself be caressed and excited. *I love you.* They may be the most important words in the world but they sounded meagre spoken into the mild afternoon air. Not enough syllables to express entirely all that they contained and represented.

"Well, by an amazing stroke of coincidence—as you would call it—or the working of powers beyond our ken, as is probably the truth of the matter, I love you too." Jonty's lips worked up his lover's chest, along his neck and over his face. "Isn't it extraordinary?"

It was. Too extraordinary to let mere words interfere with the rest of the process. And by the time they'd both reached the peak of ecstasy, Orlando wasn't sure he had a single coherent word left in his head any more, let alone the ability to string together a sentence. Only when the last little ripples of bliss had left his body could he even think about crafting some words, but by then Jonty had curled up and was asleep, so communication was left at a cuddle, which probably spoke louder than mere words might.

The sun was sinking now, and by rights they should have been getting changed for dinner or at least have been rebooking their dinner reservation for a later time. But Orlando and Jonty didn't at this precise moment care about the hotel dining room, anyone or anything else, or even having good manners. They were in a bed together again, entangled one in the other's arms, both spent, both tired and both incapable of moving apart even if they wanted to. The only concession to decency was the sign hanging on the door asking the chambermaid not to disturb them as Dr. Coppersmith had a terrible migraine.

The subterfuge of the last few days—so long unnecessary since they'd first bought Forsythia Cottage—had added a frisson to their encounters, especially this last slow pas-de-deux, Orlando taking his lover in an unhurried and complicated dance of love. Thank the lord the chambermaid hadn't burst in on them, spare key in hand. Now the only interruption was the sudden, urgent rumbling from Jonty's stomach, reminding the rest of his body, and anyone else within earshot, that it was time to put on their nosebags. Despite the fact—the wonderfully romantic fact—that they'd become one flesh, one soul again, a man couldn't live by rogering alone.

They had a church to find in the morning, and maybe a priest with it. Questions to ask and a mystery to solve. If they could bring about the seemingly miraculous rehabilitation of Daniel McNeil, his reconciliation with family and country, then the return home of Jonty Stewart should be a doddle.

Chapter Sixteen

The church wasn't hard to find, nor was the priest's house, alongside it. Jonty spent a few minutes in a little side chapel, lighting a candle and saying silent prayers, head bowed and an intent look on his face, while Orlando sat in a pew and tried to be invisible. The Church of England was trial enough, but Catholicism oppressed him. Thankfully he was spared the usual circuit of a place of worship, admiring the brasses and translating the Latin for someone whose grasp of the language had become rusty—today business took precedence over Jonty's pleasure.

If pleasure it was. His eyes were still screwed tightly shut, his lips moving as he implored his maker for something, blessing or act of grace. Orlando wished he knew what conversation was going on between man and maker, but he kept his counsel—if he was meant to know, Jonty would tell him soon enough. A hand to his shoulder roused him out of thought. Jonty had done and, whatever the dialogue, it had a positive effect. His face still bore the worried look which had dogged it on and off these last few days but there was also a hint of something else—hope?—which hadn't been there before.

They knocked on the door of the priest's house and were welcomed in by a lady who was evidently the continental equivalent of Mrs. Ward, with a smile that suggested her generosity of spirit would match that sainted lady as well as her physique did. They were ushered into a small study and introduced to Monsignor Nallet. The priest was wiry, spare, with hair that seemed prematurely grey given the freshness of his handsome face. Orlando would have put him in his mid-thirties—perhaps the duty of care for his church and congregation weighed heavy and had silvered his hair ahead of its due time. Maybe some terrible shock or strain associated with the war had produced the same effect.

"We appreciate you taking the time to see us." Jonty spoke softly, as suiting the almost confessional atmosphere of the room. "Our reason for asking for your time is a little unusual, to say the least."

Monsignor Nallet spread his hands in a magnanimous gesture. "One must always try to help one's fellow man, no matter how odd the request. The Samaritan woman at the well must have been equally surprised to be asked for water."

Jonty smiled, visibly relaxing. Another strange coincidence, how this man had picked on one of his favourite gospel stories—the Samaritan woman and Mary Magdalene were as much Stewart family heroes as the centurion who'd had more faith than most of the apostles. "Our request isn't as easy to fulfil as drawing from a well. We are trying to locate the whereabouts of a man named Daniel McNeil. His mother is extremely worried about him."

"And she believes he is here, in Trouville?" Even if the name had meant anything to him, Nallet's face gave nothing away.

"He visited here as a child and was at ease—she thinks he may have returned to recapture that contentment." Jonty's voice dropped. "He may be in need of comfort."

Orlando couldn't speak French with the same fluency his lover displayed, but he could follow more of the conversation than he'd expected. Jonty's face—always as easy to read for him as a book—made up for where Orlando's vocabulary lacked. And how many ways could there be to say, "We need to find Daniel McNeil, has he been to your church?"

"It seems a tenuous link." Nallet folded his hands and leant back in his chair. The light filtering into his little office was dappled from passing through the leaves of the lime tree by the window. This must be a pleasant place to work, to sit and reflect upon life. But now there was a certain element in the air—unease, mistrust, a decision that needed to be made?—that unsettled the atmosphere.

Jonty smiled, although not with his usual friendly expression—this smile stayed at the mouth alone. "It would be tenuous indeed, were it not for something a friend of mine told me. He's fairly confident he saw Daniel here, in your church and in a distressed state." Jonty had stretched the truth as far as it might go without breaking, and been vague about the dates, but there was no room for allowing a loophole, the sort that might let this man slip through their net. Orlando would have bet a month's wages Nallet knew something.

"Are you asking me to break the confidentiality of the confessional, Doctor Stewart, because if you are I'm afraid I have to tell you now, you will be disappointed." Nallet drew his steepled hands to his chin. Orlando was reminded of the game his grandmother had taught him, the one with your hands together, fingers interwoven. *Here's the church, here's the steeple, open the doors and here's the people.* Who or what lurked within Nallet's steepled hands?

"I would never ask anyone to break a confidence, least of all a man of the cloth." Twin peaks of colour rose on Jonty's face, as sure a portent of storms in the offing as the distant rumble of thunder might be. "Anyway, I know what caused Daniel his grief, the sin he would have wanted to confess should it come to it. He was ashamed of what he'd done, abandoning his men in the heat of battle, with some idea about going and telling the world what soldiers' lives were really like. How the fight was no longer—if it ever had been—a gallant war fought in fields of green."

A quick, wary look in Nallet's eyes suggested that another bow drawn at a venture had succeeded. Orlando clung to his belief that it was no more than that; neither an angelic Mrs. Stewart nor equally angelic Mrs. Coppersmith was manipulating events for their own purposes. The priest spoke again. "*If* you find this McNeil, what would you do with him?"

"Do? We're not proposing we do anything with him, Monsignor. We both fought at the front and I would never condemn a man who found that he couldn't cope under extreme pressure, no matter what many of my fellow officers might say. Are you suggesting we've come to you under false pretences, bent on bringing Daniel McNeil to justice?" Orlando must have had angels on the brain, because that's just how Jonty appeared to him. He'd seen it before, his lover in the guise of St. Michael or some other avenging spirit, clothed in the light of righteousness. It almost shone from him again, now. "A mother may ponder many things in her heart and know more about her child than anyone else. Even unto death." Jonty cast a sideways glance at the crucifix and Orlando had to hide a smile at the patently dramatic gesture. His Jonty—how he loved him.

"I'm sorry that I misjudged you. I always tell my parishioners it is wicked to make assumptions and here I am, breaking my own rules." Nallet suddenly smiled, and the air of warmth which Orlando had expected from a priest—although he wasn't sure why, plenty he'd known had been sorely lacking in the milk of human kindness—appeared for the first time.

"We just want to be able to tell his mother that he's safe and well. If she wants to come to him, she can, and the rest we would leave to the pair of them." Jonty's voice had softened. "It's as I would have wanted it, had my mother still been alive and looking for me."

Nallet's shrewd grey eyes looked into Jonty's bright blue ones, as if penetrating the window into his soul. "You clearly have a story to tell there. Come, I'll ask my housekeeper to bring us coffee and we can drink it in my garden. If you will tell me your tale—and I will treat it with the same respect as if it were told me in the confessional—then I will share what I know with you. Is that, as you English would say, a deal?"

Jonty glanced at Orlando to get his assent then held out his hand. "It's a deal."

The garden was even lovelier than they'd assumed from the little glimpse of it they'd had through the partly-shuttered window. Late spring flowers bejewelled the flower beds and a lime tree gave a shaded nook which must have been delightful in the height of summer. For now they sat in the sunshine, under an open, south-facing window, in little wooden chairs that reminded Jonty of holiday time. He would bring Orlando here again, all down this coast, when this business was completely settled and they were at ease. All the way past Caen and onto the coast at Arromanches—that would be wonderfully peaceful.

The coffee they were served was lovely too, as were the little butter biscuits which accompanied it. Maybe if they lingered long enough calvados might appear, but that might be asking too much from what was already turning out to be an unexpectedly good day. Jonty told his story, in the version he'd told Orlando—the full, unexpurgated version, avoiding only the true nature of their friendship. David and Jonathan would do for now, rather than Adam and Eve. Nallet listened intently, sometimes closing his eyes in thought but clearly with his ears and mind alert. He asked incisive yet sensitive questions, always concentrating on bringing his guest's actions into the best possible light.

All the nuances of the tale revealed themselves, as if Jonty's heart was being laid bare on the altar, sprinkled and made clean. Jonty's Protestant soul made some mild protestations about the nature of confession but he couldn't deny the cathartic value of what he was doing, whatever the means of facilitation. Clichéd it may be, but he really did feel as if a weight had been lifted from him, a new sense of grace bestowed, even if he'd received no official absolution—that could only come at the gates of St. Bride's or in the confessional of the SCR. To have Orlando at his side to witness and take part in it was another blessing. "And so you have it all, Monsignor." Jonty spread his hands in supplication.

Nallet nodded. "I do. And it makes more sense to me than many of the stories I've heard these last few months. You have nothing but my admiration at how you've tried to work your conscience and your duty in tandem—I have no doubt I wouldn't have been able to do the same, in the circumstances."

"My duty continues to call my conscience out, though." The words were as harsh as any Jonty had used these last few days but he felt more at ease, less frightened of the trials which lay ahead of him. "Did I do right?"

"Tell me one thing, Dr. Stewart, if you can. The key point in all this was after you took up another man's rifle and pack. All the rest, before and after, can carry no implication of wrongdoing. Did you really go astray or did you leave your platoon deliberately?"

"I...I don't remember." Jonty tried to control his shaking

hands by twisting the fingers into some Gordian knot.

"Try, please. You've done this before, when we've worked on cases. Shut your eyes and take yourself back there." Orlando spoke in English, laying his hand briefly on his lover's arm—if Nallet objected, so be it. There were more important considerations.

"Go back? I've been going back on and off since the armistice." Jonty shut his eyes, immediately opening them again. "Whole days and nights at a time, hearing the guns, seeing the faces." He faced his friend, eyes awash with fear. "Must I suffer it again? Would you torture me so?"

Orlando thought he might just disgrace himself by throwing up in the forsythia bush. The idea of Jonty suffering once more, the bad dreams an echo of the terrors he'd experienced because of his schooldays, sickened him. But they had to go through it, as they'd gone through the deepest darkness to help cure Jonty of the pain he'd had before, like the pangs of childbirth leading to new life and new hope. He steeled his resolve. "If it's the only way to make you well, then we have to do it." Orlando cast a glance at Nallet, wondering how much of the conversation he could follow and whether he could risk some convoluted and obscurely worded declaration of love. Discretion would have to count and a look would have to work as effectively as words. "Trust me, please. Remember what you thought then and answer us."

As they sat awaiting a reply—a reply that Jonty was considering carefully, hands pressed to eyes which were jammed shut—a small bird meandered into the garden, perching in a bush and filling the air with its song. Orlando remembered the day after the war had ended, hearing a bird singing and feeling all hope was gone. Maybe his rediscovered hope had gone too, now that he'd forced Jonty onto a path he didn't want to tread.

"I took Lodge's things because he didn't need them and I did." Jonty's voice was small and tremulous. "I started to crawl in the darkness and I didn't know which way to go." He frowned, eyes still tightly closed. "Someone was shouting my name. I thought it was my father calling me, like he used to when I was a boy and it was time to go and practice my tables. Do you know, I'd forgotten all this."

"Then I hope the remembrance will not distress you." Nallet's voice was as soothing as the wind rustling the lime tree's leaves. "Did you follow your father's voice?"

"I did, although I'd decided it couldn't be my father, just my fevered imaginings twisting my perception. I assumed Lieutenant Colonel Protheroe was calling out and I was getting confused." Jonty's eyes shot open. "No, that can't be right. Protheroe was killed, the day before I went out to try to rescue Beaumont. I didn't find out until weeks afterwards."

"Does that mean you were...dreaming?" Orlando couldn't remember the French word for hallucinating, if he'd ever known it.

"I have no idea what was bloody well going on." Jonty snapped back in English, wiping his face with his cuff, more little boy than grizzled veteran. "I'm sorry, that wasn't called for." He repeated the apology in French.

Nallet spread his hands, an eloquent gesture of absolution, at least for the swearing if not yet for the rest of the tale. "You heard what seemed like your father's voice..." he prompted.

"And I followed it." Jonty's eyes shone with tears. "And when I was clear, and looked around, a filthy great shell hit where I'd been holed up. If I'd stayed that would have been the end. I'd have been dead as a dodo." He ran his hands through his hair. "I'd completely forgotten all the details, and now I see them as clear as day."

"Were you scared?" The question, in Orlando's fractured French, was barely more than a whisper. "Scared enough to just up and go?"

"No." Jonty sounded more certain than he'd ever done, discussing those days. "Scared, certainly, but all I could think of was my men. I kept moving. On my hands and knees a lot of the time, hardly able to see." He rubbed his fingers, as if still getting the dirt of that strange journey off them. "When I could get to my feet, I thought I'd circled round and come back to my boys, only it turned out I was miles off course." His voice faltered. "You know the rest."

"We have no one who can verify the scene, and so we must call on a character witness." Nallet spoke like a judge, but his voice was benevolent. "Tell me, Dr. Coppersmith, can your friend's testimony be entirely relied on? If he says that he acted as honourably as the circumstances allowed, would it be true?" The look in Nallet's eyes made it clear that it wasn't *he* who needed to be reassured, but Jonty himself.

"In the things which really matter, Jon...Dr. Stewart is as honest as the day is long." Orlando kept his gaze fixed on the priest—to look at Jonty would unman him and jeopardise his *own* testimony.

"Even with himself?"

"Especially with himself." Orlando risked a small glance sideways, but Jonty was studying the ground, looking like a little boy whose headmaster is praising him in front of the rest of his house, and who's torn between nervous delight and embarrassment.

"Then I'm happy to state that I can see no reason to say that you were not right to do what you did." Nallet reached for a little silver bell, to summon his housekeeper.

"Could you repeat that without all the negatives?"

Orlando was pleased that Jonty had been brave enough to pose the question as *he'd* got lost after the first "vous"

"I am ninety-nine percent certain that you did nothing wrong. I will reserve the other one per cent as the prerogative of any man who can distinguish faith from certainty. Ah, Madame Poitrenaud, would you fetch us a little calvados, please?" Nallet smiled as the housekeeper inclined her head then slipped away in search of the bottle.

"I'm happy with ninety-nine per cent, although I'm not sure what a mathematician would say." Jonty's eyes were shining, with both tears and unexpected grace.

"Any mathematician worth his salt would regard the odds as statistically significant." Orlando breathed hard, keeping his own emotions in check; he wasn't going to break down in front of a priest, no matter how sympathetic a one. Luckily the calvados arrived to save any further complications. "And so we come back to Daniel McNeil, who may or may not have been in your church."

"Ah." Nallet lifted his glass into the sunlight, the golden liquid shining like a stained glass window. "Now we know what happened to Dr. Stewart and he has emerged with his honour intact. What do you think happened to your McNeil?"

"I believe he acted initially as I did, going out to try to save Beaumont. O'Leary had gone to pieces and McNeil tried to help him, to get him away from the shelling." Jonty sounded so certain of all he said, as if supposition had become fact in this little garden.

Nallet nodded. "Then you have that part of the story correct. Do you know what happened next? I will ask you again to go back in your mind, to when you were with the soldier who had gone mad with fear."

"Beaumont?" Jonty closed his eyes, willing to submit to the

process once more.

"Yes. What would you have done if he had continued to act wildly? To risk your life, the life of his colleagues?"

"What I did. Try to get help." Jonty opened his eyes. "I don't follow."

"I have expressed myself poorly." Nallet spread his hands, in a gesture of supplication. "Imagine if he had been more of a danger to your men, if he was in the trench with your platoon and started to fire his gun, or take out a grenade, for example."

"I'd have tried to overpower him, or got my men to. If he'd gone too far I might have had to lay him out. I thought about it, in the foxhole." Jonty turned, favouring Orlando with one of his wistful smiles. "About taking the butt of my revolver to his head, but I didn't think quickly enough. Good God."

Monsignor Nallet smiled. "He is good—he brings grace and he brings knowledge."

"I don't foll..." Halfway through the word, revelation struck Orlando like a blow to the chest—taking his breath away. "You're not talking really about Dr. Stewart's story, are you?"

"When we have finished our drinks I have someone I would like you to meet." Nallet topped up the little glasses then pointed to the open window. "Clearly you will not need to repeat your own tale to him, Dr. Stewart. So you can relax for a while."

Jonty looked up at the casement, in what seemed like a dumb show of a second revelation. "I see. Maybe I will rest on this seat in the sunshine for a while and Dr. Coppersmith can meet your other guest. I'll be here should I be needed."

Orlando was sure who he'd meet in the little room above the garden. He kept telling himself it was all coincidence and wondering how he'd ever convince Jonty that it was nothing more. The cerebral arguments meant he didn't have anything prepared for when the door opened and Nallet ushered him in. "Dr. Coppersmith, this is, I believe, the man you seek." The priest smiled then left them, the pair standing speechless and uncertain. "Daniel? Daniel McNeil?" Whatever Orlando had expected it wasn't this. He'd a clear mental picture of the man, built up from familiarity with the photograph he'd been given and coloured by the stories he'd heard. The appearance was right, but surely there should be signs of bravado, the cockiness of a man who knows he's got away with things? Or maybe the signs manifest in Wiggins and the other men who shared his ward—wrecks, shells of humanity. The man who welcomed Orlando to the little room seemed almost beatific.

"That's correct, Dr. Coppersmith. Can I offer you a chair?" There were two comfy chairs either side of the fireplace in what appeared to be a guest bedroom. Although there were indications that the guest had been there a while and was making it his own.

Orlando lacked the exact vocabulary to describe the impression McNeil gave, even if he were forging the description just for himself. Jonty would find the right words when the time came—maybe Jonty would also find the right words to break the awful news to Mr. and Mrs. McNeil. The discussions in the garden may have absolved one loving son, but they'd incriminated another.

McNeil spread his hands in a gesture of welcome and then extended one for his visitor to shake. "Have you come to find me? Did my mother send you?"

Such prescience, such far sight. Had McNeil been expecting this visit and, if so, for how long? Orlando remembered a discarded remark that Jonty had made in the train on the way here. *If my dear mama had been alive she wouldn't have slept* until she'd found me. She'd have known I was alive—even if there had been fifty bodies to show her, all of them mine. I'd have known she'd known and would have felt her eyes boring over my shoulder. He'd been castigated for talking rot after that and the subject had changed to a long litany of the occasions when Jonty Stewart had spoken a load of old rubbish. And, as usual, the old rubbish had turned out to be a classic piece of intuition or foresight.

"She did. She's been desperately worried." Orlando held out the photograph Mrs. McNeil had given him. "She could hardly bear to part with this, or any other memento of you, but she was desperate to find out the truth. She refused to accept the official line."

"She would. She knows me too well." McNeil looked up from the photograph. "She knows about the jewellery, I assume? My little running away fund?"

Orlando nodded, unsure of what was going on. Daniel McNeil didn't seem like Jonty had been—wracked with guilt and almost desperate to be punished for imagined wrongdoing.

"I hadn't been sure I'd use it. Please don't think that of me—none of this was premeditated."

Orlando reserved judgement on that account. "Some people might say the circumstantial evidence for premeditation was insurmountable." Long words again; how Jonty would tease him if he could overhear this conversation, as theirs in the garden had surely been overheard by McNeil. "There is no doubt that you didn't return to your regiment." Harsh words now—if he'd ever had any sympathy for this man, Orlando had lost it.

"I won't deny it. Neither will I deny that the circumstances weren't as savoury as your friend's—no paternal voice leading me from danger." McNeil raised his hand as Orlando drew himself up, bristling with anger. "Please, I meant no insult or implication of dishonour. I truly wish I'd acted as admirably."

Orlando seated himself again, restraining the desire to thump McNeil one and have done with it. The level of anger he felt surprised him; why react so strongly over one man dead among so many? A man Orlando had never even known or heard about until a few weeks ago. "You deserted."

"I deserted, yes." McNeil's voice sounded very small. "God knows if I could go back and change things, I would, but..."

"You deserted because you'd shot Eoin O'Leary and you couldn't face your platoon again." The words came out like machine gun fire. "He panicked and you shot him and..."

"Orlando, please." Heaven alone knew how long Jonty had been standing at the door. "Daniel, we might have got this completely wrong, so would you clarify things for us?" The measured tones, the calm voice—Jonty might have been addressing one of his dunderheads to clarify a point in an essay on the sonnets.

"Of course. I have nothing to hide." McNeil offered the newcomer a seat but Jonty preferred to stand by the window, catching the last of the sun before it turned the corner of the house.

"I believe you heard my story, just now. I know what it's like to have to cope with situations you could never have envisaged. To make split-second decisions in circumstances where you can't even think." Jonty's voice shook with emotion. "Did you shoot him?"

"I did." McNeil shut his eyes, sitting back in his chair. "He'd been threatening to shoot two of our men, waving his gun about and being stupid while we were trying to advance under covering fire. Covering fire that seemed to be aimed at us—I think that was the thing that sent him crazy. I got him away into a little copse, it seemed the only thing to do. I was going to leave him there but he started to take aim at my boys, saying he was going to pick them off, one by one. I had to..." Hs eyes shot open again, "don't you see that? I had no choice."

Orlando was about to suggest that every man always had the choice, could always settle on good over evil, when Jonty spoke again. "Did you use your own weapon?"

"No, that's the irony. I was trying to wrest O'Leary's gun off him when it went off. For what must have been a fraction of a second but seemed like an eternity, I thought he'd shot me. The muzzle had turned towards him."

"If it was an accident, why run?" Orlando managed to get a question in.

"Because I was bloody useless. A fat lot of good I'd done for Jones and I'd done even less for O'Leary." McNeil, for the first time, seemed to be registering deep emotion. "They were better off without me."

Orlando was about to deliver the "pull yourself together" speech when Jonty spoke. "And what now? Will you return home to your mother? Is *she* better off without you?"

"I can't go back." McNeil smiled. "No, Dr. Coppersmith, before you get angry again, I'm not that much of a coward that I won't return home to face either my father or the military police. I've taken a vow."

"A vow?" Orlando almost snorted out the words, earning himself an old-fashioned look from Jonty.

McNeil nodded. "Look. I spent months wandering about in a daze, working on farms..." he spread his hands to show the clear evidence of manual labour. "I kept pretending I'd gone a bit odd in the head. Maybe that last bit wasn't pretend. Then I started to work my way here—Mother will have told you about the family coming to Trouville, no doubt."

"Mothers always think of their children as no older than

seven." Jonty's voice was quiet and reasonable. "And of childhood days as the happiest."

"I used to be very content here—and am so again." McNeil closed his hands together, maybe in some unwitting imitation of prayer or maybe to hide the calluses and scars, marks not befitting a gentleman. "When I came to the church I was at my lowest ebb. Monsignor Nallet found me and gave me absolution."

Absolution. Orlando had never trusted the practice of sins forgiven by human intervention—he may not believe in God but Jonty did and Jonty always dealt direct.

"And what penance did he lay upon you?" Straight to the crux of the matter. How Orlando had missed Jonty's direct and insightful approach. What would *he* have got from Wiggins and the rest?

"To take the cross. Monsignor Nallet has good friends among the Benedictines down at Caen and if they'll have me, then there I will go. I have to try to make amends, you see—not to O'Leary or Jones or the men of my platoon but through serving others." McNeil's face began to shine with fervour as he spoke.

"And are we allowed to tell your mother this? Or do we lie and say we found clear evidence that you never survived the winter? Plenty of people have succumbed to the influenza..." Jonty shivered as he spoke. That idea cut too close.

"Tell her the truth. All of it. Better still, let me write a letter and beg you to deliver it." McNeil moved to the desk, opening a drawer and finding writing paper, as if to fit the deed to the moment.

"You'll tell her everything?" There was some disquiet or doubt in Jonty's voice that wouldn't have been obvious to anyone except those who loved him dearly. Orlando picked it up straight away.

"As I have told you. Every word." The pen was already in McNeil's hand. "Perhaps she'll visit me, one day, in Caen..."

They didn't return to the hotel straight away, preferring to walk along the beach, clearing their minds. Orlando had the letter in his hand, turning it over in its sealed envelope and examining it, as if checking that McNeil hadn't pulled a fast one and substituted some travesty of the truth. They'd seen what he'd written; as promised, every word of it was as he'd told them.

"The truth according to Daniel McNeil." Jonty stared out at the sea—his beloved sea—yearning for home again, at last. "All else he takes to the cloister with him."

"I've always found it odd how your cases mirrored each other in so many ways—you often call St. Bride's a scholastic monastery. Strange how you'll both return to the cloistered life." Orlando placed the envelope in his inside pocket, the one for unimportant items, not the one for everything to do with his lover.

"Both of us unable or unlikely to see our parents again, this side of heaven. Do you think the McNeils will try to visit him?"

"Who knows? From what I've heard of Mr. McNeil I wouldn't be surprised if he was delighted with what his son had done. *Sorting out the softies* or some such rot he'd call it."

"Leaves a nasty taste in the mouth, this case." Jonty picked up a stone, casting it to skim over the water.

"You don't believe him, do you?"

"I don't know enough to condemn him out of hand, but

something doesn't add up about that story he told. Think about it—our lads all had Lee Enfields. Takes a lot to shoot yourself in the face with that during a struggle. McNeil would have had a pistol, though."

Of course. Orlando should have picked that up too, but he was so full of defending Jonty that he'd missed the point. "And they said O'Leary had half his face taken off. I can't help wondering if some of that was done afterwards to hide the truth..." He shivered. "I feel like tearing that letter up and telling his mother everything."

"Ah, but we haven't got an 'everything' to tell, have we? We could go back and interrogate McNeil but I'm not sure he'd change his story." Jonty found some more suitable stones and skimmed those too, with a violence that surprised his friend. "And Nallet would plead the inviolability of the confessional. Leave it. It's a bloody mess."

"The last five years have been a bloody mess." Orlando slipped his arm through Jonty's. "We should concentrate on making the next five better."

"Will you tell that to Mrs. McNeil, as well?"

"I think we should send Mrs. Sheridan to explain the situation. I've no more appetite for wars I can't win."

Chapter Seventeen

"You need to go in. Now, quickly." Orlando had his hand on Jonty's elbow, the pair of them standing like two schoolboys come up for interview and too scared to make their way through the hallowed portals of St. Bride's.

Jonty had the feeling his feet had stuck to the pavement. The carriage had dropped them on King's Parade so they could walk the last part of the way, then had taken their things off to Forsythia Cottage, where Mrs. Ward could fuss over them, laundering and ironing to her heart's content, happy to have her boys with their goods and chattels home again. They'd walked the short distance down towards St. Bride's, almost in silence, Jonty reluctant to trust his treacherous tongue. Every faltering word seemed sure to trip him up.

It had seemed so easy back in France, the sharing of the whole truth with Nallet, and then over the telephone to St. Bride's, Mrs. Sheridan reassuring him that all would surely be well. Now, in the hard light of a Cambridge early summer morning, things seemed less certain. Orlando's voice—his eminently reasonable and sensible voice—wasn't helping. Jonty was well aware he had to go in now, for goodness sake—he was scared, not an idiot. He was about to snap then held his tongue, settling instead for a deep breath.

"Dr. Stewart!" It was Summerbee, coming up behind them

at a rate of knots. "They said you were coming back to us, sir, all Lazarus like." He took off his bowler hat and extended his hand. "Welcome back. Blimey." The porter clapped his hands—hat and all—over his mouth.

"*Blimey*, Summerbee?" Despite his fears, Jonty grinned. This at least seemed like a proper St. Bride's porter's welcome.

"I'm sorry, Dr. Stewart, it's that scar took me a bit by surprise. It's a corker, sir, better than anything the lads have got to show." He extended his hand again, achieving a handshake this time. "We've missed you, sir."

"Did you miss me or the crate of beer at Christmas?" Jonty could hear the trembling in his own voice, the strange excitement that things might be all right, if he just believed.

"Both, of course, sir. The college has been far too quiet this last year." Summerbee's face still wore a huge grin. "Will you come and say hello to the lads in the lodge? It seems unfair to have first dibs on you before the Master, but I'm sure he'll understand." He extended a hand and neither Jonty nor Orlando could deny him. By the time they'd been plied with beer and sandwiches—which seemed, mysteriously, to have been prepared in anticipation of the event—and Jonty had told his complete story—with slight Bowdlerising of the bits which concerned Orlando, emphasising the male friendship and eliminating the rogering—they were allowed to escape.

"I'm sorry about that." Orlando's voice was full of concern. "Didn't think they'd fall on you quite so enthusiastically."

"I was expecting the robe and the ring to appear at any moment, once the fatted calf sandwiches came out." Jonty grinned and slapped his friend's shoulder. "No need to apologise. They're honest men, the lot of them, and if I'm not made welcome in the SCR then I'll ask Clough if I can buy a bowler and get a job in the lodge." He stopped, suddenly serious. "I mean it, Orlando." The totally unprecedented use of his lover's Christian name in the public environs of the Old Court indicated the seriousness of the situation and his deep vulnerability. "This city is my home, so long as you're here. I don't care what I do if I can be at your side doing it."

Orlando opened his mouth to reply, but Jonty was never allowed the privilege of knowing the answer, a deep female voice sounding across the court and probably scaring all the delicate dunderheads who hadn't quite realised where much of the power of St. Bride's resided.

"Dr. Stewart!" Ariadne Sheridan came flying over the grass, as girlish in her late fifties as she'd always been. She seemed as if she was going to embrace him but settled for a hearty handshake. "You're here at last. Come home."

"Home is the soldier, home from the mud." Jonty caressed Mrs. Sheridan's hand then let it fall. "I feel as if I'm here under false pretences, though."

"Nonsense." If St. Bride's—and the rest of the university, not to mention the rest of society—had been enlightened enough to employ a woman to teach the dunderheads about vertebrate palaeontology, she'd have knocked some understanding into them. "And before I hear any argument, your sister has told me everything. Well." Mrs. Sheridan looked from Jonty to Orlando with an uncomfortably shrewd eye—uncomfortable for those pierced by its gaze. "Well, she told me everything you'd told *her*, so I suppose thirty-seven per cent of the story is missing or bowdlerised. At least."

"But surely you haven't been keeping my job vacant, just in case I returned Lazarus like?" Jonty thought his poor, tremulous voice might be absorbed by the stones and the grass, drawing his words into the being of the college as it seemed to be drawing him in again, unwilling to let him go.

235

Mrs. Sheridan rolled her eyes, in a gesture so like Orlando might produce that Jonty had to bite his lip to stop laughing. "Ask the Master." She linked one arm through Jonty's left and another through Orlando's right and turned in the direction of the lodge. "Come on, chop chop." Like a pair of four-year-old twins being directed home for tea by their nanny, Drs. Stewart and Coppersmith, ex-officers, veterans of both Room 40 and the front, let themselves be led.

"Dr. Stewart." The Master's welcome was not quite as effusive as his wife's, but then he'd never been half in love with Jonty. "I'm so pleased to be able to welcome you back to St. Bride's. Dr. Coppersmith." Sheridan extended an elegant hand into Orlando's equally elegant one. "Thank you for bringing him home." He indicated the comfortable settees either side of the fireplace and bid his guests sit. Sherry was to hand, and little biscuits; Ariadne Sheridan dispensed them, chatelaine of the lodge in her own drawing room and delighted to be so.

"I feel like the prodigal son." Jonty steadied his hands before they set his glass awry and spilled the sherry.

"You'd only qualify if you spent all your money on loose living." Mrs. Sheridan laughed heartily, like a man, and handed her husband a glass. "If that were the case we might not run to a fatted calf."

"I have been concerned these last few months that you wouldn't run to anything." It had to be said—the question couldn't be avoided any more even for politeness' sake. It had to be stated clearly and a clear answer received—from the Master himself—with no room for misunderstanding. "If there's no place for me here, for whatever reason... Jonty kept his gaze firmly on his glass, "...then tell me and I'll make no argument. I'd be happy to work in the lodge, or tend the library, but if that would be equally untenable I'd understand." He looked up, directly into the Master's eyes. "Not the prodigal son. Lazarus.

And I would understand if you felt I'd be an embarrassment at Mary and Martha's table."

Dr. Sheridan didn't rush to speak. He shook his head slowly, reaching into his inside pocket for what seemed to be a letter. "I believe your sister has been talking to Mrs. Sheridan. Her husband has written to me. Two medals, Dr. Stewart, even if one was earned in a different guise. There are plenty of men at St. Bride's who haven't the one. You are a credit to us. Always have been and always will be."

Jonty swallowed hard; he wouldn't have minded blubbing in front of Mrs. Sheridan, but he was keeping his stiff upper lip in front of the Master. Orlando still sat unspeaking, gaze passing from face to face, probably trying to force a positive outcome by willpower alone. "Let me tell you everything, please." He didn't even wait for a reply, plunging into the story he'd told three times so far, but now in its fullest and frankest version, embellished with all the things he'd remembered under Nallet's gentle questioning. "Can you see why I've felt a fraud?"

Mrs. Sheridan had produced a handkerchief the size of a small sail and had been dabbing her eyes from the point in Jonty's narrative where he'd found himself in a dugout with two dead men. "Now I've heard everything, I'm confident you deserve all that's coming to you." She turned to her husband. "I think we should take this young man to receive his due."

Sheridan nodded, his handsome head inclined like an abbot saying prayers for his cloistered flock. "It were best done now." He rose. "Gentlemen, if you'll come with us."

Orlando could hardly breathe, let alone speak. It seemed as if the triumphal return was about to become a punishment parade, spiteful defeat snatched from the jaws of a tentative victory. They crossed the court without speaking, all four, then went through the entrance into the next court, heading clearly for the SCR. Maybe Jonty was up for the educational equivalent of having his medals stripped from his chest, or some sort of didactic firing squad. The feeling was reinforced as they climbed the two steps up to the SCR, the place where he and Jonty had first met fourteen years before, entering the room to find the great and good of St. Bride's assembled in ranks.

Orlando had avoided looking at his friend, afraid of the anguish he might read on his face. He risked a small glance, feeling sick beyond measure—all Jonty's confidence seemed to have evaporated, his pale brow beaded with sweat and the scar livid against his cheek.

Sheridan was speaking, his quiet voice addressing his fellows as Dr. Peters's used to, in measured, authoritative tones. "...momentous event in St. Bride's history."

Orlando was cross about missing the first part—the Master's tone gave nothing away in terms of whether he was delivering good news or bad.

"Dr. Stewart has returned to the fold and the welcome we must give him is..."

"Oh!" Mrs. Sheridan shrieked as a bullet-like report rang through the air. Orlando turned to Jonty, convinced that he'd been assassinated, but found him red faced and smiling.

"I'm so sorry." Dr. Panesar's handsome face was covered in confusion. "I wasn't supposed to do this yet, but it sort of went off in my hand." He held out a champagne bottle, one which he was struggling to contain.

"This is evidently an occasion when actions speak much louder than words. Can we have the toasts and let the celebrations begin?" The rank of fellows parted like the Red Sea to reveal a table laden with bottles, glasses and trays of savouries; the Marthas of St. Bride's had been hard at work. Jonty was soon lost in a tide of back slapping, hand shaking and—in the case of Dr. Panesar himself—a huge embrace. All doubts dispelled, Orlando took a glass of champagne and tried not to grin too stupidly.

"He's a silly lad, but he's *our* silly lad." Mrs. Sheridan linked her arm through Orlando's. "I'm so glad he's home."

Orlando tried to answer but both voice and words had failed him—he could barely find more than a simple "yes", "no" or "indeed" for the next half an hour, watching while his friend received his deserved welcome. He'd just finished a rather tearful—on Lumley's part—conversation with the chaplain when a familiar hand laid itself on his shoulder.

"Don't know about you, but my legs have gone. Have the seating arrangements changed at all?" Jonty grinned, blue eyes dancing. "Don't want to blot my copybook."

"That chair is your chair, sir." Orlando could barely steady his hand as he pointed out the familiar seat.

"Then I should sit in it." Jonty flopped down, none of his normal elegance on display. The Master was now in conversation with Lumley, and Mrs. Sheridan was being offered tiny little sweetmeats by Dr. Panesar. They'd all drifted away without any further fuss, evidently aware of the significance of the moment. Of the chairs. "There's another one here, beside it—will you care to take it?"

"I will." Orlando slipped his backside into its rightful place. "Forever."

Nine o'clock in the evening, Forsythia Cottage lay bathed in what remained of the late evening sun, and a haze of rather soppy protestations of love. Any plans for cycling to the Bishop's Cope for a nostalgic pint had been abandoned in favour of a supper that consisted solely of lemonade (just what the doctor ordered after the alcoholic excesses of St. Bride's) and chocolates, consumed in the bed that had seen their own first consummation on English soil since 1917. That act had been the very final proof for Orlando that this wasn't a dream or illusion. Unless he had himself died, of sorrow, while tending his little garden of remembrance and he'd spent the last week or so in heaven.

"What did you think of my sonnet? The one in my farewell letter?"

"Rather good." Orlando wouldn't yet reveal the heartache it had occasioned. "All that stuff about infinity. Clever clogs."

"I wrote another one, but didn't use it. Would you like to hear what I might have said?"

Orlando wasn't sure he could cope with any more emotion, happy or sad, but a man had to be brave. "Of course."

Jonty took a deep breath, slipping into his "reciting voice".

"You were perchance misnamed; you leave no note
No declarations on the trees. No songs
Of love. Yet in your company my throat
goes dry, my heart turns fire, my tired self longs
for you beside. Should you read this, then dead
am I, lost maybe in the mud and slime
of wasted flesh. Then you, in too-wide bed
which emphasizes loss, you face the climb
back up to life. For I would have you live
as rich and full a life—your mind as keen
intently sharp and vigorous. Go, thrive
in you our hopes of greater worlds. I mean
in life hereafter to remember you
Orlando mine, for in you rest all things true".

"I kept reciting it in my mind, all the way across France. Like a creed." Jonty's voice shook.

"I still don't know why you called yourself Cesario all that time." Orlando lay, hands clasped behind his head, trying not to look his lover in the eye, in case he made a big, blubbering fool of himself.

"Really? Have you no powers of logic that extend outside mathematics or solving mysteries?" Jonty picked a few stray hairs from Orlando's chest. "I think I should make you go down to the bottom of the garden and stay there in disgrace until the problem's solved."

"Not if you don't want to be spanked. Tell Uncle Orlando all." He turned, snuggling into Jonty's embrace.

"It's from Twelfth Night. Viola thinks her brother has been killed in the shipwreck so she disguises herself and makes a new life. She calls herself Cesario." Jonty's fingers traced the outline of Shakespeare's words on his lover's abdomen. "*She never told her love but let concealment, like a worm i' the bud, feed on her damask cheek.*"

"We saw Twelfth Night, at Stratford." Orlando let the words be scribed—Jonty could write an entire novel there if it meant they could stay together forever. "It all came right in the end. Each thought the other dead and each was proven wrong."

"Aye. Maybe in choosing the name I influenced the outcome." Jonty sighed. "I can't help thinking about Daniel McNeil, though. No rapturous welcome home."

"No. I won't condemn him, though. There but for the grace of God could have gone almost any of us. Except you." He squeezed his lover's arm. "You would never have done what he did."

"Aye. I know that now." Jonty wriggled out of Orlando's grip. "Come on, let's finish this lemonade." He poured them both another drink. "To us."

"To us."

Postscript

Cambridge, 1961

The Morgan was waiting as they left the Arts Cinema, Mrs. Ward's great grandson ensconced in the driver's seat and lovingly caressing the steering wheel. The position of housekeeper at Forsythia Cottage had passed down through the generations and now included the role of chauffeur, each owner of the house alleging that the other was unfit to drive. And while Drs. Coppersmith and Stewart might be pretty sprightly for men in their eighties, their pins weren't up to walking all the way in and out of the city.

"Was the film good?" Adam Ward opened the door, as any good chauffeur should. And, in the best traditions of his job, he had a blanket ready to place over Orlando's slightly arthritic knees and a hot water bottle for Jonty's feet.

"Not bad at all. One of Dirk Bogarde's best roles, I think." Jonty climbed into his place, settling himself comfortably. He missed the fun of driving, although Orlando always said that the good citizens of Cambridge didn't miss having to scoot out of his way.

"I like Sylvia Sims, myself." Adam helped Orlando into the front seat. "She's such a pretty girl."

"And a good actress with it. Not always a pair of commodities to go together." Jonty put away his spectacles and rubbed some condensation from his window.

"What did you think of it, Dr. Coppersmith?" The car swung expertly out into the traffic under Adam's careful guidance.

"Very thought provoking." Orlando studied the streets with unseeing eyes. The film had touched on so many things which he had lived in dread of. Blackmail, public humiliation, the possibility that society would be more sympathetic to the one making extortionate demands rather than the victim. Celebrity or social standing counted for nothing, the prosecutions of John Gielgud and Lord Montagu had proved that. The last decade had been as dangerous as any Orlando could remember; he and Jonty had been fortunate, very fortunate to have avoided scandal. They'd come pretty close to it at times.

"They should change the law." Adam didn't need to say any more. He didn't share their inclination—he had a nice girl, one who could have rivalled Sylvia Sims for icy beauty and a warm personality—but he was as sympathetic as his great grandmother had been.

"Aye, they should. I just hope Dr. Coppersmith and I live to see it."

"I reckon you will. If half the stories I heard when I was growing up are true it'll take all four horsemen of the Apocalypse to finish off you two."

Adam got no reply other than a pair of snores, keeping a gentle harmony together.

About the Author

As Charlie Cochrane couldn't be trusted to do any of her jobs of choice, like managing a rugby team, she writes. Her favourite genre is gay fiction, predominantly historical romances/mysteries, but she's making an increasing number of forays into the modern day. She's even been known to write about gay werewolves, albeit highly respectable ones.

She was named Author of the Year 2009 by the review site Speak Its Name but her family still regard her writing with a fond indulgence, just as she prefers.

To learn more about Charlie Cochrane, please visit her website www.charliecochrane.co.uk. You can send an email to Charlie at cochrane.charlie2@googlemail.com or join in the fun with other readers and writers of gay historical romance at http://groups.yahoo.com/group/SpeakItsName.

*He looks good on a horse,
but it's hard to love a man with a big ego and a small alibi.*

Half Pass
© 2011 Astrid Amara

Paul King's inheritance is named Serenity Stables, but for him it's far from serene. He has one plan for the crumbling facility: unload it as fast as possible. But two months on the market, and he's still mucking stalls and dreaming of his old life back in San Francisco.

It doesn't help that he seems to have misplaced a horse. Not just any horse—Tux, a million-dollar Warmblood who, despite lacking opposable thumbs, has an Olympic medal to its name. So does its Brazilian trainer, Estevan Souza, a man whose darkly sexual, smoldering glances *almost* make Paul forget his horse phobia.

Intriguing as Paul finds Estevan, distractions are piling up. The boarders are picky. The arena roof is leaking. His drunken cousin is wreaking havoc. Tux's owners are threatening to sue. On top of that, a bucket of blood points to possible murder.

Suddenly, Estevan's glances are looking more suspicious than sinful. And, if Paul can't come up with a plan to save Tux, he could lose not only his chance with Estevan, but his life.

Warning: Includes beautiful horses, men in tight breeches, murderers, horse thieves, Olympic champions, cowboy hats, anal sex, broken dreams, and the conquering of traumatic childhood fears.

Available now in ebook and print from Samhain Publishing.

HOT STUFF

Discover Samhain!

THE HOTTEST NEW PUBLISHER ON THE PLANET

Romance, fantasy, mystery, thriller, mainstream and more—Samhain has more selection, hotter authors, and everything's available in ebook.

Pick your favorite, sit back, and enjoy the ride! Hot stuff indeed.

SAMHAIN
PUBLISHING

WWW.SAMHAINPUBLISHING.COM

GREAT CHEAP FUN

Discover eBooks!

THE FASTEST WAY TO GET THE HOTTEST NAMES

Get your favorite authors on your favorite reader, long before they're out in print! Ebooks from Samhain go wherever you go, and work with whatever you carry—Palm, PDF, Mobi, Kindle, nook, and more.

SAMHAIN
PUBLISHING

WWW.SAMHAINPUBLISHING.COM